THE HEARTSTONE CHAMBER

Jim Stein

Magic Trade School

Also by Jim Stein:

Legends Walk Series

Space-Slime Continuum

Digital ISBN: 978-1-7335629-7-3
Print ISBN: 978-1-954788-00-8

First printing, 2021

Jagged Sky Books
P.O. Box #254
Bradford, Pa 16701

Cover art & design by Kris Norris
Edited by Caroline Miller

Visit https://JimSteinBooks.com/subscribe to get a free ebook, join my reader community, and sign up for my infrequent newsletter.

Dedicated to those who keep our homes, industry, and country running smoothly.

1. Invitations

H ERB TWO NEGOTIATED the twisting labyrinth with something less than grace. I cringed as he careened off a rusty pipe in the dim passage, but the little guy quickly caught his balance and felt along the block wall for the doorway into the convenience store. He wobbled as he walked on too-small feet, but steadied himself with stiff, over-long arms.

I squirmed on the polished wood chair, trying to work feeling back into my butt as Herb's progress unfolded on the courtroom screen. The video was crystal clear, a testament to the wireless button cameras that tracked his mission.

The janitor's closet drew Herb's attention, and it looked like he might head for the deep sink. But his blocky head swung in negation as he worked things out and made for the double swinging doors, determined to find his fallen brother.

No matter what anyone said, I was proud of the little guy. He was like a Marine; no man left behind. Then he exploded.

A knife jabbed into my gut and twisted as Herb's right side erupted into a silent fireball, and his arm flew off-screen. Either the flying appendage or the secondary explosion that shattered the poor guy's legs must have taken out the trailing camera because the screen shifted to grayscale security footage. Just my luck that the store's back room was monitored after hours.

I took a deep breath and exhaled through my nose, trying to keep calm and settle the raw wound the phantom knife left. With a shaking hand, I slicked back hair a week past needing a trim, using the faint reflection in the polished table to get the mess under control. Keeping my straw-blond hair cut close at the ears undercut the messy style and played to my narrow face and wideset gray eyes. I cringed at my graphic tee, wishing I'd dressed nicer, then steeled myself and looked up. Losing one of my creations always hurt, and watching the scene made it feel like Herb had died all over again.

It wasn't all that big of an explosion, not that a little autonomous robot made mostly of PVC and gears should have been able to explode in the first place. But my constructs had a flare for drama and always managed to self-destruct in the most inconvenient way at the least opportune time. Herb One had been no exception, having melted down after loading his cargo pouch with roller-dogs from the Quick-Y mart just a few nights earlier. Before he'd had a chance to check out, Herb One had ended up fused to the floor. He left wavy linoleum where Mr. Fulton, the owner, had pried him up after our failed munchie raid.

I'd been counting on Herb Two to get his predecessor's melted remains back so I could do a post-mortem. It was the only way I was going to improve. But the stupid owner had kept him behind the counter like some kind of trophy, or maybe he was waiting for CSI lower Delaware County to show up and do forensics. Either way, no one was getting their hands on either Herb now.

The black and white video told the rest of the story. Although Herb Two left this world in something far less spectacular than, say, a C-4 blast, he'd been standing right beneath the store's gas main and managed to engulf the decrepit regulator bolted to the wall in crimson death. A momentary whoosh of gray flames filled the screen perched on its rolling cart, drawing a sharp intake of breath from the handful of people gathered in the courtroom.

"You see?" Mr. Fulton shook an angry finger at the screen, then at Judge Michelson behind his fancy wood desk, and finally at me. "He blew up my store with one of his killer robots! Jason Walker is a menace and needs to be put down."

"Frank, this isn't a witch hunt." Judge Michelson was a big, soft-spoken man in his late fifties. His salt-and-pepper hair stuck to its neatly parted lines as he tilted his head and held placating palms out to calm the shop owner. I liked how the flecks of gray in his eyes matched, until he turned his glare on me. "But the charge is more than a misdemeanor. And this fact-finding and preliminary hearing will determine how we proceed. Mr. Walker, you may consult with your counsel before answering questions, and of course are presumed innocent unless we proceed to trial and a jury finds otherwise."

"He was caught red-handed watching it all on his computer! That's where the police got this video and…" Fulton fell into sputtering silence at a glare from the judge.

"I wouldn't say someone who comes forward voluntarily has been caught. Jason, why don't you tell us your side of the story." The robes and elevated desk made him seem ten feet tall as he looked down.

Five pairs of eyes turned to me, none of them sympathetic. The judge tried for an air of studied neutrality, while Mr. Fulton's swarthy Italian face flushed red, and dark eyes smoldered from under his bushy scowl. The DA, a round, dark-skinned lady with curly hair pulled back into a tight bun, looked on with glee as if eager to sink her legal teeth into me. Regis Gladstone, a slender fortyish man with premature white hair, stood to the left of the seated judge, green eyes shining as he chewed at his pencil-thin moustache.

Even Phil, the court-appointed lawyer sitting to my left, gave me a good-fricking-luck eyebrow-lift and shrug. The top of the little shit's curly head only came up to my shoulder, and I just brushed five-ten on a good day. His blond mop nearly matched my own in color, but was a wild, unkempt parody of the messy undercut crop I'd sported since high school.

Phil sure seemed to be hanging me out to dry. But he'd already explained that the proceedings were not a trial and to be candid but guarded in what I said so as not to prejudice anyone against me when I went to trial. His use of "when" instead of "if" had not escaped me, and the fact that he sat there like a fat little toad had me thinking I just might be in over my head.

"That gas regulator was a ticking time bomb!" I blurted. "Check my video. Joints were nearly rusted through and the calibration tag had to be from the civil war."

My heartbeat pounded in my ears and air refused to enter my lungs. I wasn't ready to be locked up and had to clamp down on a giddy little laugh when the irrational desire for Mom to be there arose. She had enough irons in the fire, and it wasn't like I was a teenager anymore. Of course she'd probably find out after a few days when my car and sorry butt failed to make an appearance at the apartment over the garage.

All those eyes bored into me. Even the judge disapproved of my outburst, but I knew what I'd seen on my high-definition feed. I'd been tracking Herb's progress from across the street, ready to welcome him and Herb One back, hopefully with a bag of leftover roller-dogs. Not only was the regulator on its last legs, the whole natural gas system had been a train wreck waiting to happen. The line ran way too deep inside before the pressure step-down, and taps along the way sent high-pressure gas off to the fryer and who knew what else.

Given time, I could have fixed it; I was a technomancer. That's how I was able to build the Herbs and tons of other gadgets out of spare parts and bubblegum—almost like magic. Of course, my creations still tended to self-destruct, but I was working on it. I'd done plenty of repairs around the house for Mom and neighbors, and no one's home had blown up yet.

Clearly, role-playing games, science fiction, and fantasy novels had shaped my self-image, but the fact is I was good with machinery and electronics. I had a super soft spot for everything I built. Even walking by what had been a simple repair made my stupid chest swell with pride. So sue me; I was sticking with the technomancer title, and I'd swear on a stack of bibles that the Quick-Y mart was destined to be a smoking hole in the ground even without my help. At least this way, no one was hurt. I'd always scoffed at our little corner of Philadelphia suburbs having the only known 18-hour "convenience" store, but not anymore.

I went on to explain my assessment of the store's faulty utility systems, noting the frayed wiring and other safety issues—none of which impressed those present and only served to raise Mr. Fulton's blood pressure to the point I thought steam would shoot out of his ears.

"Maybe you should stick to why your robot was inside," the DA prompted.

"He's an automaton, not a robot. Core electronics are essential components for…" I trailed off at a glare from the judge. "Okay, well, this is how it went down."

I did my best impression of an extrovert, railing at the injustice of Mr. Fulton keeping Herb One, pointing out that the hot dogs I'd coveted on that fateful night were destined for the trash anyway, and again ticking off the unsafe conditions in the dilapidated little building that had supplied underage kids with cigarettes since its opening.

The judge interrupted my impassioned plea for leniency and my offer to help the owner bring his other properties up to code as recompense—a thought that likely had no grounding in legal precedence.

"So you sent both robots into the Quick-Y mart with no intention of causing damage." The judge selected a pen from the cup on his desk, speaking slowly as if working out a line of logic. "There could be a larger liability issue here. Where'd you buy them from?"

"I didn't." His question caught me off-guard. "I made them myself, mostly from spare parts. I'm handy that way."

His eyebrows and cheeks sagged as he blew out a breath and traded the pen for a pencil. My answer had disappointed him, but Mr. Gladstone quirked an eyebrow and gave a little nod as if impressed. I'd originally though he was a bailiff of some sort, but the black three-piece suit and thin black cane were too businesslike—if a bit antiquated. Maybe a neutral lawyer or consultant given how close he stood to the raised desk, that seat of power that would soon proclaim my fate.

"You live with your parents, correct?" Judge Michelson asked.

"Yeah." I had no idea why that mattered, but his scowl reminded me to be respectful. "Yes, sir, in an apartment above the garage."

"Any pets?"

"No, sir."

"And your job." The judge opened a leather-bound legal pad and scribbled notes. "Do you need to notify your supervisor of a leave of absence?"

Ah, so that's how it's going down.

"I'm between employers, mostly doing the odd repair job. So, no."

A few more questions pulled me toward the inevitable conclusion: I was a criminal and going to trial. *Innocent until proven guilty*, I reminded myself. But this was going to break Mom's heart. Hell, it wasn't doing mine much good either. Freedom had never been a concept I dwelled on, but the prospect of being caged to await trial and then possibly for a very long time afterward had me reeling.

The DA—I never did catch her name whole name, Vivian something—made a few perfunctory remarks about the court's coming case load and her assessment that I wasn't a flight risk. I think Phil even chimed in on some point or another. I just blinked down at the wood grain table, wondering what had happened to my life.

"Jason, I don't see many options here. There's too much linking you to the explosion. Unless the owner is willing to drop the charges?" He dangled the question out to Mr. Fulton and lifted an eyebrow.

"No and no!" The shop owner crossed his arms and glared. "I want him off the streets for a long time."

"It'll be a trial then." The big man nodded in resignation and made another note. "Vivian, check the schedule for—"

"Sir, I may be able to offer an…alternative." Gladstone had an odd accent, a cross between Brit and Scott that was somehow gruff while sounding quite polite as he interrupted. "The Attwater Trade School has programs for gifted individuals. Mr. Walker clearly has mechanical talents. I'm sure their vocational counselors could recommend a trade for him to be trained in, thus making him a more—shall we say— useful member of society and getting him off the streets."

That last was aimed at Mr. Fulton who was having none of it.

"Absolutely not. You break the law; you go to jail."

"Sorry, Regis." The judge shrugged his broad shoulders, and his neck disappeared into those midnight robes. "I think we're beyond something like that."

"Of course. I understand your concern." Gladstone tapped his cane in a light, playful rhythm against the edge of the desk and looked to the store owner. "But won't your insurance pay to build a new store, one that isn't riddled with safety issues, one that has all the equipment you've always wanted?"

"Sure, my premiums are all paid up." The cane tapped faster, and the little gold snake head that served as a grip flashed under the fluorescent lights. "I've been trying to figure out how to unload that dump and start fresh." Fulton shook his head and blinked. "I guess this really is a windfall for me. I could even get a drive-thru for the kitchen. But that doesn't change things."

"Of course." Gladstone rapped the desk and put a hand on the judge's shoulder. "But if charges were to be dropped, you'd have latitude to order something akin to community service. Training at Attwater would fit that bill."

"That's a huge if, but still—" The judge scratched his chin in consideration.

"Now wait a minute!" I shot to my feet. "If I could afford college, I'd already be there" *Probably.* "And I wouldn't just ship off to some place I've never heard of."

"Not to worry. This is a trade school specializing in vocational training matching your skills. You can keep your garage apartment and commute. Attwater just opened a local branch to better serve the community. Your timing's perfect." Gladstone hovered over the seated judge and swayed as he spoke. "Or you could simply send him to the Army. They've got plenty of technical programs and would certainly whip this young man into shape in no time."

That wasn't a real thing, was it? Could the court order someone into the armed forces to avoid jail? Forget about her broken heart, Mom would have a cow. The cane tapped on. The room held its breath, or maybe that was just me being frozen like a deer in headlights. *The army?*

"What do you say, gentlemen?" Something flowed from Gladstone to the others, a palpable earnestness, as if he were impressing sincerity on the two men.

It's difficult to explain, more of a feeling than anything that I saw. But the pressure hanging in the air reminded me of the force I willed into my automata in the pregnant moments before their first test—a kind of superstitious ritual I'd started years ago after an initial success at getting one to work.

"Well…" Fulton wrestled with his conscience, and it was touch and go for a good twenty seconds. "I could let it go if he's off the streets and gets some focus beaten into him."

Nice way of putting it—not!

"Judge, Attwater or Army?" Gladstone winked at me and tapped the snake head in a hypnotic little rhythm until the judge gave a sharp nod.

"Jason Walker, what's your preference?" The judge's pencil hovered over his notes.

Looks like I'm heading to school.

* * *

The damned bike quit again in front of a massive stone building off the city square. The towering columns reminded Owen of the natural history museum, but he didn't recall anything like that downtown. Lettering chiseled into the granite above the entry steps read "Attwater."

Owen swung his leg off the bike, shrugged out of his leather riding jacket, and scratched at the stubble on his chin. His hair was a wild mess thanks to the half-helmet, and he brushed back the few dusty-brown strands plastered to his eyebrows. Summer in D.C. was no time to be standing under a blazing morning sun dressed in black. But he'd planned on heading out into the Virginia countryside to ride the Blue Ridge Parkway for a couple of hours so needed some level of protection.

The big v-twin engine pinged as it cooled, and Owen poked around with calloused, grease-stained hands, checking the oil, spark plug wires, and a couple other things. He blew out an annoyed breath. There just wasn't much to check without a code reader. The fuel injected Harley was damned near bulletproof compared to the old Indian motorcycle he'd been wrenching on for the last month. That beast of a project had painted his fingers and beneath his nails with the indelible skin art of old oil.

Sometimes you had to do things the old fashioned way, the Zen motorcycle maintenance method like the old book claimed. But this wasn't one of those times.

Owen ran a hand over the seat, stilling his mind and "listening" to the bike. He'd picked up the trick years ago, the ability to imagine what the engine felt. More Zen master crap, but for some reason it always worked. He supposed it was more a matter of unleashing his subconscious to point out subtle signs he missed in a hurried inspection.

But sometimes, like now, no insights materialized. The engine seemed fine. So Owen gave one more little push, a kind of prayer to send a spark of life into the bike, and thumbed the starter. The engine roared to life.

"Sweet! Winding blacktop, here I come."

"Bethany, you've got mail!" Darren called from the bottom of the steps. "Looks official."

"Be right down!"

Bethany sighed at the need for code words. Her stepdad was all kinds of cool and supportive of her late decision to apply for college, but Mom was an entirely different story. Mom had issues with her own lack of higher education and for some reason liked to take them out on her daughter. That was why she'd had to apply in secret, and swear Darren to keep his lips zipped as the replies came in. If Bethany could score a decent scholarship, even her mother would have to agree it made sense to pursue graphic design.

So far the only response from her college applications had been a hard no, which was odd given she'd graduated in the top of her class. Slots for fall semester had filled up way before high school graduations kicked into gear, but she'd hoped starting in the summer would improve her chances.

She pinned the last couple locks of tightly coiled hair into the neat black bun she'd been experimenting with. Even though Mom was all about hair extensions—especially because she was—Bethany preferred to work with her thick natural mane. The coils came down past her shoulders, framing an oval face with full lips and wide set dark eyes. She'd always liked the contrast of midnight black plaits against her coffee-colored cheeks, but the bun exposed her elegant neck and delicate shell ears, which made her look sophisticated and sexy—like a college woman.

A peek out her bedroom window showed Darren's old beater of a Chevy parked on the oil-stained cement of the drive. Mom was still at the plant, so it'd be safe to check the mail.

The envelope Darren handed over downstairs looked more than official; it was positively ostentatious, with a gilt seal boasting a stylized A across the flap, and addressed in flowing script.

"Thanks." Bethany scurried back upstairs, unwilling to open another rejection, even in front of her stepdad.

"Good luck, kiddo." The big sweetheart's smile flashed in painfully white contrast to skin several shades darker than her own.

She plopped down on the edge of her bed and worked at the envelope with trembling hands, cursing her short nails when it took three tries to pry up that ornate seal. The paper within was heavy stock that resisted unfolding. She skipped right past the letterhead and salutation to the opening paragraph.

"We are pleased to inform you,"—her heart fluttered—"that you have been accepted to attend summer semester,"—her pulse thundered— "at the Attwater Vocational School."

Attwater? What the hell is an Attwater?

She'd sent out over a dozen last-minute applications, but that name didn't sound familiar. Maybe this was the Arts and Architecture program at one of the big universities she'd targeted.

Bethany compared the return address with the letterhead. No, the reply came from an institution she'd never even heard of, let alone applied to. Which probably meant it was junk mail dressed up fancy like an application reply just to get people to open it. *Slimy trick!*

She scanned on, just to see what sales pitch was at the bottom line, picking out phrases like "report for summer session" and "pleased to have you as a new student." It went on to acknowledge her desire for entrance into a graphics design program, but stipulated her current skill level and talent would be assessed to place her in the appropriate course of study.

Hell, this wasn't even a degreed program, just some adult training course that gave you a certificate of completion an employer would likely laugh off. Of course the back side of the letter—she hadn't even realized there was more info there—promised career guidance and guaranteed job placement. *Like that's possible.*

Hopefully, the real replies would start rolling in soon with at least a partial scholarship—even a work-study program would help. Ten hours a week at the local print shop for the past few years had taught her a lot about the trade and contributed to a growing college fund, but the few thousand she'd managed to save wouldn't make much of a dent without financial help.

Bethany lowered the letter toward the little square trashcan by her nightstand, but paused at a flash of crimson on the page. She scanned the black and white text and shook her head. Nothing printed in red, but how had she missed the big bold typeface along the bottom?

"Attwater School offers Bethany Daniels a full scholarship." The fine print went on to say accepting would cost zero dollars out of pocket for an eighteen-month program spanning three semesters. Although a non-residence course of study wasn't ideal, there were apparently opportunities for students continuing enrollment past the first semester to find on-campus housing—she'd need that to keep sane given Mom's passive-aggressive skills.

Maybe this Attwater place would be a good fit after all.

* * *

The bike purred its way along the twisting grandeur that was the Blue Ridge Parkway. The smooth ribbon of blacktop brought quiet serenity despite the ever-present throbbing of the big v-twin. Owen sighed and settled deeper into the saddle as the forest slid past.

A vibrant patch of purple carpeted a clearing off to the left, tiny flowers dangling in clusters from a forest of stalks rising above leafy green plants. Virginia bluebells flowered late, and he inhaled their delicate sweet fragrance along with the scent of hot asphalt.

Light pressure on the handlebars and gentle leans guided the big cruiser through more hypnotic curves. Traffic remained delightfully light so that he'd only been trapped behind a line of cars once, and they'd been trapped behind an ancient motorhome chugging its way up an incline.

Halfway down the off-ramp into a sleepy little town, the engine cut out for the third time. Owen cursed, kicked into neutral, and rode the hill down into the valley with just enough momentum remaining to turn into a little strip mall. He rolled to a stop and kicked out the jiffy stand in one smooth motion like he'd meant to park in front of the big ironbound doors. The heavy wood doors and stonework didn't match the glass storefronts to either side.

Owen stripped off his helmet and scratched at the neatly trimmed stubble running from sideburns to chin as he glared at his ride. Not only had the bike shut down in the city, it'd crapped out again when he cruised through suburban hell looking for lunch. He'd managed to limp into the entrance to a sprawling estate surrounded by high wrought iron fencing. He again hadn't been able to pinpoint the problem, but got the engine restarted through sheer force of will. Maybe the cam sensor was going; that would cause the pea-brain computer to shutdown ignition to protect components.

He pulled off his gloves and was about to dive into troubleshooting, when the placard at the head of the parking spot caught his eye. Flowing white lettering stood out against a blue background, declaring the spot "Reserved Student Parking."

"Just great." Hoofing a dead eight hundred pound bike over a few spots wasn't the end of the world, but what a pain in the ass.

The spots stretching off to either side of him were empty, but a similar blue sign watched over each. Somebody got more than their fair share of parking, and that would mean pushing the bike too damned far. But hey, it was the middle of the afternoon and the lot was nearly empty.

If the owners of—he squinted at the door looking for a sign, but there were no posted hours or business name. He mentally kicked himself when he finally spotted the massive lettering carved into the stone high above the ridiculous doorway. Well, if the folks at Attwater Academy wanted to complain about a little temporary parking violation, they could come out to chat.

Attwater?

Odd, wasn't that the museum name he'd seen downtown just this morning? For that matter, there'd been a big golden A hung across the gates to the estate he'd broken down in front of at lunch. Sometimes events that seemed related were simple coincidence, but this pushed the bounds of believability.

As on his prior unplanned stops, a quick inspection didn't uncover any problem with the bike. But no amount of coaxing and cajoling could convince the beast to fire up this time.

"Son of a—" Owen bit off the curse, not due to any sense of propriety, but because the sign over the parking space he'd appropriated appeared to have changed. The blue placard with its ornate script now read, "New Student Registration Only."

Owen looked to the double doors that better suited a medieval castle than a strip mall training institute. He shook his head and started to pull off the leather jacket, but a cold wind rose out of nowhere, making him shiver and abandon the motion. When he looked up, the left-hand door stood a few inches ajar, and he just had to shake his head. *Unbelievable.* Someone was already spying on him for illicit parking.

He let out a mighty sigh and strode toward the doors, engineer boots clomping on flagstones set into the cement to form a path to the doors. He hated to call for a tow, hated even more the thought of killing time until some country bumpkin driver finally showed up. There was no way this was going to be quick.

While he waited, maybe someone inside could explain why Attwater was suddenly cropping up everywhere.

2. A New Chapter

"**W**ASN'T THIS THE old Beer Barn?" Billy asked as he climbed out of his jacked up truck and scratched at his camo ball cap.

Shiny black curls fought their way to momentary freedom before he yanked the cap down tight. As the only high-school friend I'd kept in touch with, Billy insisted on seeing me off to what he called the next chapter of my academic life. The fact I'd be commuting and we'd still get together for gaming and pizza didn't matter to the big goon.

I stood about five-ten to Billy's six three. He had the frame of a wrestler, not the muscle-bound federation type, but the old-time pros with thick legs and torso. He raised an eyebrow, his swarthy face more resembling a middle-aged pirate than a twenty-year-old computer geek—I mean engineer.

"Yeah, like a decade ago." I double-checked the address on my court paperwork. "But it's the right place."

The big roller door that once let cars drive through the rectangular brick building only held a few artful tags, and was in the process of being painted dark blue. There would be a matching garage exit around back to let folks drive away with their beverage of choice. A glass door by the window to the left allowed for foot traffic, and a pallet of bricks sat off to the side next to a pile of broken ones. Several patches of bright new bricks stood out against the dingy red walls where repairs had been made.

"Looks like they're fixing the place up," Billy said. "Hope your one-room schoolhouse has air conditioning."

"It ain't *that* small," I said.

Tiny windows ringed what I hoped was an upper floor. Two stories would probably leave room for four classrooms, but I had to wonder who else would be attending. From the look of the empty and cracked parking lot, I wouldn't be surprised to find the place locked up tight. Okay by me. Anxiety darkened my mood so that it matched the gloomy oppressive clouds overhead. Even this early, the Philadelphia summer mugginess threatened to have me sweating, and I found myself seriously considering hopping back in my car and driving off.

"On this auspicious occasion and in the event our paths do not again cross, I'd like to offer a toast." Billy reached through his window, pulled out a paper sack, and produced a pair of foil wrapped breakfast burritos. He handed me one and raised his own high. "To you, valiant wizard, may your quests ever lead to fortune."

Yeah, we definitely spent too much time gaming. And I may have called myself a tech wizard or technomancer on a few late night occasions, especially when showing off new gadgets to my friend. Billy was accepting of my delusions and had even checked over the navigation module code installed in Herb.

I shook my head at his outstretched breakfast, but mimed clinking glasses and proceeded to tear into delicious goodness. As we sat on the hood of my car and chowed down, the knot in my stomach eased. Billy's antics and further declarations of what may lie ahead had me approaching the glass doors with a lighter heart and feeling a bit like Frodo heading off to save the world. Still, my hand grew sweaty against the spiral notebook and paperwork. This was a big deal.

I'd traded the next two years of my life to get out of hot water with the implicit understanding that if I failed out or quit I'd find myself back in front of the judge. There were worse things than training in a trade. Mr. Gladstone had been confident I'd fit right in at Attwater. I wasn't so sure.

The slim packet of material I'd received the week after my preliminary hearing made the place sound fantastic for getting you ready for the workforce, but I hadn't seen any curriculum spelled out that really suited my interests. I liked to build things—interesting things—and fix stuff, but wasn't ready to just be a plumber or welder.

With one last glance back at Billy, who held his cap over his heart in a farewell salute, I reached for the handle. The door swung open smoothly, breathing cool air out into the building mugginess, and I left my troubled past behind.

I'd like to say the entry was amazing, but the long rectangular room was more like the waiting room at a doctor's office. A pretty cool mural decorated the opposing wall with a collection of mechanics, lab assistants, chefs, and others hard at work in their chosen profession. The inspirational montage clearly had been designed to instill a sense of endless possibilities, and I had to admit it worked well.

Padded wooden chairs dotted the carpet in front of an L-shaped desk. Four other people, presumably new students, sat or stood filling out paperwork. I glanced out at the parking lot, but the front glass had a frosted coating that obscured the view and sparkled with bright shifting patterns. The sun must have broken through the cloud layer. I ducked my head back out through the door and waved. Billy gave me a thumbs up, climbed into his truck, and made an over-zealous U-turn as he headed off under the leaden sky. So much for sunshine.

"Can I help you?" The shrill voice of the pinch-faced woman behind the desk had me sighing and turning back.

I approached the desk and held out the application the court provided. "They said to report for new student orientation."

The dark-haired woman—Margaret, according to the black letters on a gold nametag pinned to her purple sweater—took the packet with a sniff of disdain. She scanned the top page where Judge Michelson had stipulated the conditions of my enrollment.

"Don't think a court appointment will get you through the door." Her declaration was unnecessarily loud, and I cringed as those nearest turned with interest. "If anything, trouble with the law counts against new students. You'll have to demonstrate exceptional ability if you want to stay with Attwater."

"Yes, ma'am." Like I'd ever heard of the place before. *Jeesh, lady, get a life.*

She gave me a hawkish glare as if reading my thoughts, adjusted her silver wire-rimmed glasses, and flipped through the rest of the packet. Something in there surprised a huff from Margaret, and she craned her long neck, head tilting like an owl examining a morsel as she read on.

"Handpicked by Mr. Gladstone himself." She stamped and signed the bottom of my papers and handed them back along with a clipboard holding blank forms. "They'll expect big things from you indeed. Fill these out, sign on the highlighted lines, and bring them back up. Orientation starts in fifteen minutes so don't dawdle."

Though still sour, the look she gave me had thawed a few degrees, and she even offered the ghost of a smile at my mumbled thanks.

The paperwork was much like countless other packets I'd filled out over the years for everything from temporary jobs to the school baseball team. Attwater wanted to know my home address, education stats, and the like. A discreetly labeled next-of-kin section gave me pause, but I supposed wasn't too different than the emergency contact fields above.

One at a time, the others worked their way to the desk and turned in their own papers. One round-faced blonde about my age kept looking my way, but I didn't recognize her. The other woman had to be in her late thirties and wore a dark trim business suit that made her look more like an executive than a student. The two guys couldn't have been more different. The younger, a hefty rapper wannabe in torn jeans, black tee, and gaudy gold neck chains wore a perpetual sneer as he turned in his clipboard. Yet, he somehow managed to coax a glowing smile from Margaret.

The other twenty-something dressed like a cowboy, complete with brown leather boots, flared jeans, and a vest over his blue flannel shirt. A white ten-gallon hat perched above a tan face with the weathered look not many in the Northeast ever achieved. The guy would stick out like a sore thumb, though I'd never seen him around. He spared a friendly nod for me as he dropped off his papers and strolled over to examine the mural.

Light from the window danced across the painting, making the figures almost come alive as each toiled to complete its task. In fact, if I didn't know better, I'd say the iron-masked character welding panels to the skin of a ship had managed to complete half the project while I filled out my papers. And hadn't that dental assistant been arranging the tray of implements instead of handing a clamp to the doctor?

"Five minutes," the receptionist announce with a pointed look at me.

Time to stop daydreaming. I flipped through the remaining forms, filling in blanks and applying my John Hancock before hurrying up to the desk.

"What's this mean?" I spun the board around and pointed to a block of text on the last page. "This check box says I agree to accept whatever course of instruction the school assigns."

"That's right." Margaret squinted at the page and nodded. "Instructors can only handle a set number of students, and not everyone is suited for the career they might think. Don't worry. I'm certain Mr. Gladstone already has something special picked out for you."

"Um…okay."

Not exactly the limitless flexibility the brochure implied, but I really didn't have much choice. I checked the box, signed, and handed over my clipboard.

"Excellent!" She beamed, hawk eyes shining with triumph.

But she gave a nod of encouragement and shooed me toward the interior doorway where the others gathered. I took it as a good sign that her attitude toward me had improved a fraction more.

"Hey, robo-boy." The rapper's greeting wasn't friendly and neither was his shark smile. "Heard you got busted."

His nod toward the desk set the gold chains to clinking, but I was busy wracking my brains trying to figure out if I knew this guy. The freckles and dull brown eyes seemed familiar, but it was the sneer on his too-red lips against his pale round face that tipped the scales.

"Larry Ashburn?"

His snide smile broadened. *Just great.* Between his poser clothes and drastic fade turned flattop hairstyle, I hadn't recognized the shaggy brown-haired schoolyard bully.

Larry had been a thorn in my side since sixth grade. Even though he had thirty pounds on me, a quick headlock in the hallway after he'd pushed every last one of my buttons in senior high led to a quiet detente. We'd avoided each other ever since, and I'd happily continue that trend at Attwater.

"I go by Lars now." He tried for a friendly smile and failed miserably. "Don't let whatever crap you're into mess this up for the rest of us."

There was no mistaking the challenge in his eyes. I looked down at the hand he offered, but wasn't falling for it. He'd pulled too many dirty tricks over the years.

"No worries, Laaaars." I drew out the vowel in his name way too long and lifted my chin in acknowledgement. "I'm just here to learn." *And to stay out of jail.*

He looked about to jump on the way I butchered his cool little nickname, but the door flew open, drawing everyone's attention.

3. Orientation

I ALMOST DIDN'T recognize Mr. Gladstone. He'd traded in his dapper three-piece suit for an ensemble heavy on brown tones with pants and a jacket of light leather. His white hair was slicked back, and a pair of goggles perched on top of his head. Even his sleek black walking stick had transformed into a twisted wrought-iron cane, the gold snake handle replaced by a primitive iron serpent with fangs bared. The theme for his outfit seemed to be a mix between welder and train conductor.

A rotund matron to Mr. Gladstone's right with slate-gray hair caught up in a net wore stylish off-white slacks and a tunic with big flat buttons running down the center. She looked about forty, with stormy eyes that glinted like steel. By contrast, the young woman to his left would be in her early twenties, tall and attractive without flaunting the fact. She stood only a hair shorter than the man, with vibrant blue eyes beneath wavy copper-colored hair. Her long face fit her friendly smile; she looked like a good listener.

"Good morning. For those I haven't met, my name is Regis Gladstone, your dean of student studies." He gave the group a shallow bow and flashed me a smile. "Welcome to the Attwater School. I am so very pleased to have you all here today and look forward to getting to know each of you over the coming months.

"We'll start the morning off with an orientation talk in the main lecture hall. Hilda and Miranda"—he waved a hand at the women flanking him, and I bit down a laugh because the matron really did look like a Hilda— "will help answer your questions and ensure everyone gets a new student package once we get to the room. So without further delay, please follow close and keep the noise to a minimum. We have a few more students to pick up along the way."

He rapped the floor with the cane, turned briskly on his heel, and led us inside. What lay beyond the door made no sense. We stepped out onto an atrium balcony overlooking a massive indoor park. Sunshine streamed through domed skylights high overhead, impossible given the exterior dimensions of the little brick building.

As I gaped down at the handful of people strolling along gravel paths or talking at benches, our group headed off to the right where the walk changed to a hallway with doors to either side.

"It's important to remember that you came in through doorway U32 on the third floor," Gladstone called over his shoulder. "That is the correct door to get back at the end of the day."

The number was set in brass above our doorway, and we walked on past several others, stopping twice more for Mr. Gladstone to repeat his welcome to a new group. Our numbers grew to twenty by the time we left the open atrium and plunged down corridors more reminiscent of a traditional university. But where piping and electrical conduits would normally be hidden above a false ceiling, Attwater liked to keep its infrastructure in plain sight. I smiled in appreciation as we walked on under junction boxes, valve manifolds, and open girders.

"What do you make of this?" the cowboy asked with a wave that encompassed the hallway in general. He and I brought up the rear, both gawking at the scenery, though I suspected for different reasons. "Name's Chad, by the way."

"Jason. Nice to meet you." I gave the friendly hand he shot out a quick shake. "Yeah, I don't know. I mean, there can't possibly be this much room in here."

"Exactly!" Chad shook his head and continued in what sounded like a light Midwestern drawl. "I've seen some beautifully restored outbuildings, but you just can't do this with an old barn."

I puzzled over his words for a second before catching on. "Oh, as in beer barn. I get it. I agree. It just isn't possible."

Chad scratched under his hat and gave me a quizzical look. "No, not a beer barn. I'm talking horse barn. Putting a school like this on an abandoned ranch outside town didn't make a lot of sense to start with. I'm surprised this many people found the place."

"I hate to tell you, but it's weirder than you think." I stumbled over the words because they didn't make sense. "I came in this morning through a little brick building that sits on the edge of a parking lot outside Philadelphia. I get the distinct feeling that isn't the place *you're* talking about."

"No…no, it isn't."

Before we had the chance to get further down the rabbit hole, our group filed into the back of an auditorium much like the one in every high school ever built. Being the last ones in, Chad and I were unfairly ushered down to the front and put in the empty end seats of the first two rows. Some manufacturer of squeaky cushioned seats must have enjoyed a corner on the market.

Other groups had arrived before ours so that maybe two hundred people filled the front half of the auditorium. Ages ran the gambit from blackjack winners like me to mid-fifties if my estimates were correct. Judging by skin tones and clothes, the room was socioeconomically diverse as well.

"Can you believe this place?" the cute girl I'd been seated next to asked in an eager whisper.

"Morning." Yep, I was a social genius.

Her smooth brown skin didn't quite give her high cheeks a baby face, but it was close. Those hazel-brown eyes twinkled with barely contained excitement, and I adjusted the room's age bracket to include teens.

"I'm Bethany Daniels and shooting for graphic arts. You?"

"Jason." I pointed to myself like a complete idiot. "Computers and stuff. I build machines, but who knows if there're any jobs like that in the burbs. I'd rather not commute into south Philly."

I made a mental note to research the job market better. Doing that before enrolling probably would have been a good idea, but with little choice in the matter of attending, I'd felt the time was better spent goofing off with Billy.

"Philadelphia?" Bethany looked surprised. "You sure came a long way."

Thump, thump, thump!

Matron Hilda—I really needed to stop thinking that— slapped the microphone on the podium with three fingers, demanding silence. The wave of chattering voices crested, dropped to a murmur, and died.

"That is better." Hilda gave a curt nod. Damn, she actually had a slight German accent. "Under each of your seats is a welcome package. Do not read during Mr. Gladstone's remarks. We will walk through that packet at the end of the presentation."

She yielded the floor to Mr. Gladstone, who offered a gracious nod, adjusted his steampunk attire, and placed a hand on either side of the podium.

"Welcome to the Attwater Trade School. Unlike full universities, our core offerings focus on vocational training. Our principle goals are to put skills in your hands and you in a job with true career potential."

A spattering of polite applause rose from around the room, and Gladstone went on about the benefits of their certification programs. I should have been listening. The people around me paid better attention. Bethany's eyes were glued to the stage, but she gripped a pencil in her left hand, scribbling furiously in her open notebook.

At first I assumed she was taking notes, but her hand blurred across the white paper adding curves, lines, and shading to an image that took up the top half of the page. The sketch was of a squat bat-like creature with fangs, wings and a long ropy tail—a gargoyle or demon. Despite never once looking down, she drew well, and I couldn't pull my eyes away from the hypnotic rhythm as her hand worked on autopilot.

"And you want plenty of money, don't you?" The dean asked. "How about twice the national average for an annual income? That's what our alumni earn."

Oh-ho, now he's talking my language.

I pulled my attention from Bethany's doodle and leaned forward, eager to hear more. Renting my parent's garage apartment saved serious coin, but there was something oppressive about living that close. Even if I wasn't under the same roof, guilt had been a constant companion since graduation. Not just when I had to pay the rent late because another temp job fell through, but every time I came home after midnight, or had friends over for gaming. Okay, that was usually just Billy, but it was time for me to get on with my own life. Money—the great equalizer—was required for that.

"Every one of you has special talents. We will put your gifts through their paces to figure out the vocation for which you are best suited. In just a few minutes, you'll meet our staff." He waved to the line of people sitting in chairs across the back of the stage. "Excellent tradespeople one and all. But our placement office is just as important to your success. Setting your feet on the right career path is paramount."

This time the applause echoed from the high domed ceiling, accompanied by a few whistles and shouts. My gaze drifted back to where Bethany now drew something roughly the shape of a butterfly below the other sketch. Maybe they were characters from a game like Pokémon.

"Work hard, earn your certification, and let us place you in the very best positions. Now, there *is* a catch." Mr. Gladstone leaned in, cupped the microphone with one hand, and continued in a conspiratorial whisper that of course rang from the speakers across our hushed group. "Some would wade into sensitive topics slowly like a swimmer testing the water temperature with a toe, while their friends dove into the lake embracing the shock of cold. Such shocks are invigorating. They wake the body and mind. That jolting contrast, the excruciating moment of discovery and acceptance, is what makes us alive." His voice rose with his passion, then dropped back down to a quiet question. "So I ask you, my new friends, do you want to tiptoe into your short time here with us, or do you want to dive in headfirst and learn?"

"Dive in…dive in…dive in."

The chant rose from the corners of the room, surely seeded by administration lackeys. But I surged to my feet and joined in anyway, blowing off steam and the nervousness of being in new environs with so many strangers. Stupid, but it helped.

Bethany and I grinned at each other, and Chad slapped me on the back, nearly driving me to my knees—stupid cowboy. But we all were smiling by the time Gladstone motioned everyone to sit back down.

"I guess I had better dive right in then." His comment brought chuckles of agreement. "So the catch is—" he looked left and right as if for prying eyes. "In order to be successful and make the kind of money you've dreamed of—" again with the sideways glances and pregnant pause. "You'll have to learn magic."

Another wave of quiet laughter punctuated by a few high-pitched giggles crested quickly and petered out at the look of sincerity on the dean's face. Bethany gripped her notebook tight, positively quivering with nervous energy, or maybe anticipation.

"Magic is real, my friends. Each and every one of you have the gift."

"Yes!" Bethany hissed out the word and leaned forward, eyes shining.

"Yeah right." Chad's derisive exhale blew wetly across the back of my head.

"Think back to your childhood," Gladstone said. "They called you special. If not your parents, then a relative, friend, or even an enemy." He smiled to himself, the action warming his clear blue eyes. "Admittedly, some of us more…mature folks may have to think harder than others." That brought a tentative laugh from several older students. "But the memories are there. Even if you never thought much of such praise, look to your inner monologue, at how you defined yourself.

"You've felt the power, even used it. The feeling was magnificent, like you could accomplish anything. Take a moment to reflect on those times. Your subconscious holds the truth. Many of you have thought of yourself as wizards at one time or another. Others daydream of more specific abilities such as speaking to animals." He looked at a hefty girl with wild black hair off to his right, then those pale eyes turned on me. "Or perhaps you've joked with friends about your skills as a technomancer."

Wait, what? Had the school been spying on us, on me? I'd clung to the technomancer fantasy ever since running across the concept in a cross-over sci-fi novel where the main character used mystical forces to power his tech. But it wasn't like I honestly believed in magic. Sure, I kidded around with Billy all the time. He was an easy target, especially when he played along and insisted the electronics I used couldn't possibly get my creations to do what they did.

Sure, back in school we'd kicked around how cool it would be to fly, turn invisible, or be bullet-proof—normal teenage daydreams. None of that made us superheroes. And the occasional rush I got from fixing something beyond repair or getting a new automaton up and running didn't mean I was ready to go all Harry Potter. Yet I shivered under the dean's lingering gaze and huffed out a sigh when he released me to look out over the crowd.

"Your formative classes are structured to help recapture those accomplishments and bring that feeling of wonder you once enjoyed to the surface. A word of caution." He looked to me briefly, then captured Bethany with his gaze, and took a few moments to pointedly skewer others in the room before continuing. "What you imagine yourself to be, this thing you feel you were born to do, may be different from what lies ahead. Training will hone your innate ability, and I ask you to keep an open mind about where that may lead."

As Gladstone spoke, he raised his right hand and a ball of fire appeared, drawing a collective gasp from the students. The flames danced and floated in lazy circles a few inches above his open palm.

"You all will master simple magic taught in common core classes before delving into study of your particular talents. First and foremost we will drive you toward a lucrative vocation that leverages your skills to earn money and benefit society. Your trade will be the conduit for your powers. Wizard or conjuror, beastmaster or empath, do not trip over labels. We will help make the best *you* possible."

The dean threw the fireball up into the tangle of piping where it exploded in a shower of multi-colored sparks, indoor fireworks. I found myself on my feet, clapping and cheering along with the others. Damn, this guy could stir up a crowd. He knew how to get under your skin. Despite my prior reservations and the impossibilities laid before us, I actually looked forward to more.

Smiles, grins, and laughter spilled from nearly everyone. There was the occasional doubtful or dazed expression, but as the fireworks continued, even those individuals seemed to realize the opportunity being offered. One by one, the holdouts joined in the revelry.

A massive blue starburst blossomed overhead, followed by an icy cold deluge of rain. The water hit hard. Bethany yelped and tucked her sketchbook under her shirt trying to keep it dry.

"Don't worry, Dean Gladstone, I've got it!" a lanky man near the front called over the din of voices.

The fellow wore khaki pants and a button-up blue shirt. He materialized near the door to my right and hurried past heading for the back of the room. His dark hair was trimmed close in a buzz cut, and his friendly, open smile reminded me of Dad.

"I do apologize," Dean Gladstone said over the speaker system. "My display sometimes confuses the sprinkler system. Mike Gonzales, our maintenance manager, will sort things out momentarily."

"It's already stopped," I said to Bethany when I realized we weren't getting dowsed anymore.

Water still sprayed with a high pressure hiss from the piping, but a translucent blue bubble arched over the seating area like a force field out of a comic book. Rivulets streamed down over the umbrella and splashed noisily into the aisles. One of the teachers, a slim, elderly woman in a white lab coat, stood in front of her seat with arm raised toward the ceiling. The gushing water overhead slowed to a trickle and stopped.

"All clear," the maintenance guy called from the back.

Lab-coat lady dropped her arm and the shield disappeared with an audible pop like a burst soap bubble.

"My thanks once again, Mike." Mr. Gladstone had managed to stay dry. "Please take your seats everyone so that we may continue with the program. That's it. Thank you." He let the commotion settle down. "Now look left and right. Say hello to that bedraggled woman squeezing water from her hair or the grinning fool who enjoyed the surprise soaking."

"Hi, nice to meet you again," I said to Bethany as she inspected her notebook, which was safe from the water that did indeed still drip off the back of her thick ponytail. After the ups and down of the last few minutes it was easier to talk. We were no longer strangers, having survived the great flood of orientation. "Hello, Chad," I called in falsetto and wiggled my fingers over my shoulder. I ignored the friendly slap to the back of my head and spun right to greet the man sitting across from me. "Hey, name's Jason Walker."

"Owen Jones." He gave a nod and derisive smile.

Besides the faded jeans, plain white tee, and week-old facial scruff, Owen's general demeanor screamed "too cool for school." His shaggy haircut completed the unkempt look as he lounged back with feet on the seat in front of him, somehow making the position look comfortable. The smile touched dark eyes with crow's feet radiating from the corners—though I couldn't say if those were frown or laugh lines. Jaded was the best descriptor I could come up with even though he looked to be in his mid-twenties.

"Now that you've all met your neighbors, consider this," Gladstone said. "One of them will soon be gone."

Smiles slid off faces all around because, quite frankly, the statement sounded ominous. Between comparing notes and magical demonstrations, I suspected most had figured out that the Attwater School wasn't exactly around the corner for any of us regardless of where we'd entered. We were effectively at the mercy of the staff just to get back home tonight, and if some nefarious plan was afoot to knock off a portion of the students, there was nothing much we could do about it.

"No need to fret," the dean continued. "Just a cold reality that I want you all to bear in mind. Trade schools in general do not offer easy courses of study, doubly so for Attwater. Some of you will not want to stay, others will fall short during the evaluations. There is no shame in this, but you must work hard to secure your seat here. Statistically, due to weak trade aptitude or issues with your innate talent, about one third will not sign the student contract required before progressing into your first semester."

"Ain't going to be me," Bethany whispered. "I *need* this!"

"But statistics are simply a predictor, and I'd be more than happy to see every last person in this room sign on for a full course of instruction. So I challenge you all. Prove me wrong."

He stepped back from the podium and Hilda took his place.

"Time now to review those packets under your seats, assuming they aren't too soggy." She shot a glare at poor Mr. Gonzales, who stood dripping by the side exit. Instead of protecting him, the magical umbrella had dumped a literal waterfall on the man.

The paperwork was dry enough and included a school calendar of events, curriculum information, and even personalized schedules. How they'd managed to match the latter up to the random seating was a mystery.

With Miranda's help, the two women explained the basic course structure. Where other schools might foist a bunch of theory and philosophical courses on students, Attwater believed in cutting to the chase. Common core courses would start immediately and focus on tapping everyone's magical potential. Although rare, it was possible that one or two generalists would crop up. Those individuals would master all the basic spell work, but might struggle to home in on a talent suiting a particular profession.

Students had been accepted—and in cases such as my own, recruited—precisely because they tended toward a specific talent. The vast majority could expect limited proficiency in the core course work. It honestly sounded like little was expected, but the process of trying to get things to work helped the staff confirm each student's core talent. From that point an evaluation board determined suitable professions for everyone. Hilda assured us that the board took student preferences into account, but were by no means constrained by them.

After everyone got to try their hand at core disciplines like manipulating fire, water, and the like, we'd move on to more obscure sub-fields to isolate each student's dominant ability. Once the teachers and board assigned a talent and profession, we'd each have to sign a contract to continue into trade training. Those that didn't were shown the door and sworn to secrecy, promising never to reveal what they'd seen within Attwater's walls.

Those of us who signed on the dotted line would begin a two-pronged curriculum. On one hand we'd receive traditional vocational training. Learning to weld, be a veterinary assistant, or work on engines would lead to eventual job placement. But it was the other coursework the room grew increasingly excited about. I had no idea how each of our magical talents would be honed. We'd be broken into more manageable class sizes for core classes. Given the dozen instructors still waiting patiently to be introduced, both vocational and talent training would also have to be in groups. Otherwise, they'd need a staff nearly the size of the student body.

Staff introductions proved an anti-climactic blur. There was no way I was going to remember who was who. I'd hoped for a demonstration of their unique abilities, but instead got an earful of personal info. I supposed that with student of all ages, they wanted to be relatable, but I honestly couldn't care less if a teacher enjoyed hiking, cross-word puzzles, or raising labradoodles for fun and profit. Tell me about raising griffons or dragons, and we'll talk!

Vanilla biographies in the student orientation package mirrored the lame presentations, but at least had pictures to help keep the names straight. In a way it made sense. The school wouldn't want to send home paperwork that spelled out how your physical therapy instructor specialized in shamanic healing. We didn't even learn what magical talent each staff member possessed. Maybe they didn't want students lobbying for a profession just to get friendly instructors.

That might have been the whole point of those introductions, to put us at ease with the staff so we wouldn't care who we got assigned to. From that perspective the last portion of the orientation lecture worked like a charm. I'd have no problem with anyone from the trim woman who'd cast the magical umbrella and happened to be the avid dog breeder to the burly Viking-of-a-man who enjoyed kayak fishing and took gourmet cooking classes in his spare time. The only instructor that would drive me crazy was the tall Nordic blond with her ponytail dangling from a leather wrap. Rather than share hobbies and pleasantries, she took the opportunity to berate prior students as lazy sacks of crap that often didn't deserve the education Attwater provided. She never called anyone out by name, just voiced her disappointment in how poorly many did in applying their talents to their professions in the execution of their duties after graduation.

Bethany, Chad, and I exchanged confused glances as the woman ranted, blaming everything from inattentive parents to loose morals and weak minds for what she saw as typically poor student performance. Some of her allusions made it clear she didn't even hold much regard for her fellow instructors.

All of a sudden Hilda looked positively warm and nurturing by comparison.

"You will do better," the woman said with a scowl and curt nod, thankfully putting an end to her time at the mic.

I suspected that last statement was meant as an encouraging endorsement of how our class would do so much better than those that went before. What a delightful individual—not! I knew who I *didn't* want for core instruction.

"What was her name again?" I asked Bethany as the woman strode off the stage.

"Can't you remember anyone?" the girl shot back, but softened the rebuke with a dazzling smile. Her enthusiasm for this whole thing was contagious. "Anette Schlaza, that's who you don't want..." Her smile faded for the first time as she consulted her course schedule. "Oh."

"Sorry." I looked at the page she turned toward me, grimaced at the name by her finger, and quickly rifled through my own packet.

My pages had managed to get out of order already. I flipped past the calendars, bios, student questionnaire and finally found my class schedule. Two morning sessions before lunch and two more after. Each day started with Mary Eisner—I sighed in relief—and Anette Schlaza.

Son of a—

4. Lessons

"AGAIN!" MS. SCHLAZA'S icy gaze matched the ice water I figured ran in her veins as she walked the line of students, demanding completion of the task at hand.

Her cold demeanor should have helped me with the ice ball I willed into existence above my outstretched right hand. So far, all I had gotten in return was frosty rime coating my fingers and pain lancing through each knuckle. Pressing on was a contest of determination, like the time Billy and I had the bright idea of seeing who could keep their hand submerged in ice water longest—but at least back then I'd had a shot at winning a free cheeseburger.

After a disastrous attempt at creating fireballs, the cold had initially felt wonderful on my singed fingers. But now the ache far outstripped the light charring I'd endured in our prior exercise.

Ten of us, about a third of our common core class, stood in a line under Edison bulbs dangling from the ceiling on long silver cords. Each student had a hand out and concentrated on their inner energy flow. The goal was to move heat away from a point just above the palm in order to form the desired sphere of frozen water.

We'd been at this particular task for about an hour. As with prior exercises, at least our drill-sergeant instructor had demonstrated the technique to prove it could be done. But after that, it was simply rinse and repeat for those of us who couldn't manage the simple spell in our first few attempts.

Mary Eisner scurried up and down our line adjusting a stance here, giving words of encouragement there, and basically trying to mitigate Schlaza's morale-crushing blunt-trauma approach to "learning." The dark-haired woman read auras with her hands, sensing each student's inner reserve of power, or chi, or whatever, while delightful Ms. Schlaza bellowed out orders in what I could only assume was some extremely ineffective attempt at reverse psychology. For crying out loud, it was only our first day.

Mary should have led the class instead of being relegated to the roll of assistant instructor, but Schlaza made it very clear that she alone was in charge. Before jumping into the drills, Mary had just enough time to hit us with the basics of spell casting and assure the class that the power indeed resided within each of us. A set of slim texts that under no circumstances were to leave the premises were also provided to each of us, though we'd not had time to crack them open. Each volume supposedly contained basic theory of a particular category of spells, a cross between "the idiot's guide to magic" and a child's "so this is your body" book set.

We were not going to dwell upon silly things like theory and fundamentals because our beloved instructor believed doing was the only way to learn. I'd hate to see Ms. Schlaza in charge of a skydiving school.

"From the diaphragm, dear." Mary Eisner materialized beside me and placed a reassuring hand on my stomach just under the ribs. "Breathe from here." Pressure from her palm

41

radiated with tingling warmth. "Like you're playing a wind instrument. Proper breathing keeps you centered and balanced to help the energy flow."

I exhaled with an audible sigh, contracting the muscle beneath my ribcage under the gentle guidance of the assistant instructor's hand.

Mary was warm summer sun to Schlaza's winter ice, short to the other woman's tall, and dark-complexioned to her light. Above all, Mary proved patient and understanding as students crumpled and failed in their attempts.

I sucked in another deep breath and pushed the air out as a smooth, calming exhalation. It helped. Tingling energy gathered in my core. Just like that, the warm hand was gone along with the teacher who'd moved on to help a gray-bearded man who had accidentally encased his hand in ice.

The energy faltered, but I pushed it on toward my palm, focusing the power on an imaginary point between my curled fingers. I envisioned a pinprick of heat expanding outward, leaving cold in its wake. I dearly wanted to shove that warmth at our ice queen instructor—she could certainly use some— but we'd been warned to dissipate the heat evenly to avoid catching anything on fire.

Tiny heat waves shimmered up toward the hanging lights. They were more than simply bare-wire replicas of early bulbs. I'd gazed into matching bulbs lighting our lockers along the back wall and found the glowing filaments crawled around inside the glass.

I pushed more heat off to the right toward the jumble of desks that we'd moved out of the way. Though configured along the lines of a traditional lab classroom, the desks were antique wood on metal casters that made them easy to reposition. The high-backed chair stacked atop each reminded me of the butt-numbing torture devices found around fancy dining room tables.

The room itself was heavy on dark wood trim. Instead of drywall or plaster, stacked stone lined the walls, giving the place a dungeon vibe. Ms. Schlaza had pleasantly explained that early classes were held where buffoons using magic for the first time could do little damage.

The other odd fixture in the room was a roughly round wheel of stone, maybe granite, the size of a small car tire with a fist-sized hole worn through its center. In addition to the ultra-brief instructions on how to channel our internal energies, we'd each laid hands upon the stone. In these early stages, the magical relic helped bypass internal mental blocks that would eventually be overcome through progressive training.

The weathered Celtic symbols chiseled along the stone's rim glowed when touched. I'd felt the power resonate under my palms, a cool energy like crisp springtime when new growth struggled to break through the icy crust. I'd imagined standing on a windy bluff in late spring with the surf crashing far below. Snowmelt trickled down rocks at the edge of a greening pasture. Grasses and scrub made their first push during the scant daylight hours. But cold evening winds scoured the rocky shoreline bringing late snows and shoving the greenery back down into fitful slumber to await the morning—

"Mr. Walker, stop it this instant!" Ms. Schlaza's voice cracked like a whip, shattering my daydream and the energy flow I'd been feeding the spell.

I staggered as the spell broke. My fingers, white with frost, stung like a son of a bitch. I shook them out, spraying glittering shards across the flagstone floor. No ball, but at least I'd achieved ice. I worked feeling back into my fingers with the other hand, then realized the class had fallen silent. Everyone gaped at me.

"What's going on?" I side-whispered to Bethany, who stood off to my right—having gotten her spell perfect on the second try.

Mary pulled Ms. Schlaza into a huddled conversation at the front of the room, clearly trying to calm our irate teacher who sputtered and glared at me over the shorter woman's head. Then she looked to the Celtic stone. An irregular lump of ice clung to the side of the wheel as if it were a cookie dipped in crystal clear chocolate.

"Geez, I didn't mean to…" I had no idea how to finish the statement.

"Of course you didn't, dear." Mary hurried over to pat my arm and examine my aching hand. "You just got distracted. It's ever so important to stay focused on the desired results. But you definitely created ice, so that's a good thing."

"It certainly is *not* a good thing." Schlaza stalked over, eyes flaring, to tower over the other woman and me too—easy to do since in that moment I felt three feet tall. "It is decidedly not okay, even in training, to do something that irresponsible. What if that had been another student instead of a sacred relic? You could have turned poor Mr. Merkel over there into a popsicle." She jabbed a finger at a nervous little guy maybe a year younger than me who held a dripping frosty marble in his right hand and looked as though he might bolt from the room.

"I was just remembering how the stone felt." I cleared my throat, seeing that excuses weren't going to cut it. "I'll be more careful. Promise."

"See that you are." Schlaza spun away and headed to the front to inspect the stone, which freely dribbled water onto the slate floor. She huffed, turned to the class, and held her hand out like a director calling her choir to attention.

"Don't worry," Mary whispered. "It's still very early."

Yeah, like I hadn't even known magic existed this morning. But instead of grousing, I had a better idea.

"Hey, shouldn't we have wands or something? You know, to help focus the magic like in movies."

Mary opened her mouth to reply, but didn't get the chance.

"Wands, Mr. Walker? You're suggesting we hand out wands?" Ms. Schlaza's narrow face went crimson. "An Attwood certified plumber can't be seen whipping out a gnarled bit of wood to beat back some nastiness crawling from the sewers. Our medical assistants wouldn't be caught dead wielding a baton trailing pixie dust to subdue rampant patients. And can you imagine an information technology specialist needing to grab her rowan wood branch before banishing a dark web attack back to whatever hell had spawned it? Can you?"

"Um…" I stammered grasping for a good response.

She'd used really odd examples to make her point. I hated to tell her, but magical abilities or not, computer nerds like Billy probably already had a reproduction phoenix feather or elder wand tucked away in their toolkit. If not that, then a sonic screwdriver. It just came with the territory for us geeky types. Those kinds of toys were the present day equivalent of pocket protectors.

I bit my tongue, clamping down on making a sassy reply. Her technique sucked, but teaching adults had to be a nightmare. Kids were conditioned to at least pretend to listen and follow instructions. Plus, it had been a long day, and I didn't want to say something I'd regret, especially given I teetered between a free ride to a well-paying profession and a swift trial followed by incarceration. Yep, I needed to keep the peace.

"No, I guess that wouldn't make sense." I did look her in the eye to let her know I wasn't a total pushover.

"Indeed it would not." Ms. Schlaza gave a curt nod and swept back to the front. "Blending in will be paramount for you to succeed. Each of you all will use this power to advance your profession and do things others cannot. Magic makes your work easier, faster, and in some cases cheaper. You will carry the tools of your given trade, and only those tools. Your powers must remain hidden. But when you need it, the magic will be there to help and protect you."

She raised her hand, bringing us back to the drill, and more than a few disappointed sighs rose from the class. With a sigh of her own, Ms. Schlaza dropped her arm.

"There will be much more on this subject after you sign your contracts." She fixed me with an imperious glare. "*If* you sign your contract. But enough for one day. All books go in your lockers. Leave all notes dealing with magic behind. You may use the common areas and park, but do not venture deeper into the school. The inner rings are off limits until core assessments are complete. New students must be clear of the building by eight o'clock sharp.

"As Mr. Gladstone pointed out, be certain to use the doorway through which you entered if you want to spend the night in your own bed. Step out through the wrong portal, and you will find yourself unable to reenter until morning. I want everyone in their seats well before eight a.m. Remember, to be early is to be on time; to be on time is to be late."

* * *

"Well isn't she a little slice of heaven?" I asked as cold water ran over my hand, slowly bringing my fingers back from their near-frostbitten state.

Bethany poked through the cabinets of the kitchenette that ran along the back wall. Most of the class gathered in the main commons area to talk through the craziness of our first day while nursing our various scrapes and bruises. We needed time to process and get up the nerve to walk back out into the "normal" world where friends and family would want to hear about our first day. There would be a lot of hemming, hawing, and flat out lying tonight.

"Yeah, her methods are a little harsh." Bethany threw me a towel she'd dug out of a lower cabinet, and I dried my stiff fingers. "But they have less than two weeks to get us working on basic spells and assess our abilities before the board assigns career paths and hands out those contracts."

"Whoa dogie, don't you all look like something the cat dragged in." Chad strode between the tables as another batch of students spilled into the commons.

"Oh you know, hard day at the office and all." I couldn't help noticing how fresh and excited the other class looked compared to our bedraggled group.

Mary said magic was fundamentally based on five elemental forces: fire, water, air, earth, and spirit. We'd been dragged through exercises in the first three, leaving the other two so we'd have something to do tomorrow. Of course there were numerous spells of varying levels of difficulty associated with each element. We'd only scratched the surface, trying our hand at the most basic casting. But even those from my class that hadn't singed, frozen, or otherwise harmed themselves had often taken the brunt of another's errant magic.

My spell had not been the only one to go astray. I just happened to be the guy Schlaza decided to turn into an example. Of us all, Bethany looked the least disheveled in her bright blue peasant top and slate gray pants.

"I guess." Chad looked around the room, perhaps also noting the sharp distinction between his class and mine. "But exciting. Trying to learn this stuff is like riding a wild bronco. Hope I don't get bucked off before getting into the rhythm. This is only day one."

"Yeah, I'm hoping to survive day two," I kidded, but the funny way Chad looked at me got me wondering. "What are you guys starting out with? Fire spells, earth magic, what do they have you throwing around?"

"Tossing around ideas mostly, getting into spell hierarchy, a little history. We did an hour-long round table on the distinctions between druids, clerics, wizards, and witches. That was interesting. The really ancient history gets pretty dry, but I guess it's all about laying the groundwork."

"You're not casting any spells?" Bethany asked.

"Hell no! They don't want us to incinerate each other." Chad chuckled then sobered as he looked down at my white fingers and maybe caught the charred odor wafting from my shirt. "Crap, you've actually been playing with magic already?"

"Yeah well, our teacher is a masochistic ice queen." Unkind, but I softened the sentiment by poking fun with feigned haughtiness. "Of course, we *are* also *so* much more advanced than your class. So it's sink or swim for us, deep end only."

"Jeez, be careful. We aren't scheduled to get to spells until the end of the week. They outlined a pretty structured laydown to run us through for evaluations. But it's baby steps as far as we're concerned."

"Giant leaps for mankind down this end of the hall," I assured him.

"Chad, my man, come grab some chow. It's all free." Lars and his chains jangled up. He slapped Chad on the back and lowered his voice to a stage whisper. "I hate to interrupt, but if you hang with the losers here, you'll get a reputation, so…"

"Dick," I mumbled, not quietly enough.

"What's that, Jay Walkie?" Lars asked, his inner bully rising to the surface now that he'd found a new crowd.

It was a stupid nickname from years back that for some reason the idiot found funny. Geez, it wasn't even insulting, and sticking with it said a lot about Larry's intelligence—or at least his maturity.

I counted to ten.

"You know, it's a new school. We're going to be cooped up together for almost two years. Nobody here's a loser." I was proud of taking the high road.

"I'll be here for the duration." Lars gave Chad another slap and an over-friendly neck pinch. "Cowboy will too. You dweebs? Guess we'll see." He laughed at his own wit and headed over to a packed table near the snacks.

"Chad, I barely know you, but Larry and I go way back. He's usually trouble." I wrote a capital T in the air with one finger.

"Definitely not the most mature guy, but apparently we're in the same public speaking class. I'm stuck with him for the time being." He must have seen me cringe. "You don't have to tell me it's gonna suck. But hey, like you said, new school and all."

5. Coffee and Crackers

I GRINNED AT the fact Chad stayed with us to grab snacks and find a table while pointedly ignoring Lars's head bobs and some weird gesture he kept making with his elbow raised and fingers splayed wide like a frog with a broken arm.

An array of packaged goodies had been laid out as a kind of welcome feast. In addition to cold drinks, tea or coffee could be dialed up from a machine standing near the doorway. We grabbed some beef jerky, cheese crackers, and soda and scouted out an empty table.

Chad called his drink a pop, which had me raising an eyebrow. "Where exactly are you from?"

"Grew up on the wide open plains of southern Montana," he replied with an exaggerated drawl and tip of his hat, which made me think it was a well-worn line.

"And now?" I made a beeline for an open table in the corner and plopped down on the bench.

Like the antiquated desks, the commons furniture looked to have come out of a museum. Overhead, exposed utility conduits and pipes dropped down to panels and gauges nestled into alcoves around the room. The glow from more crawling bulbs dangling above bathed the commons in warm yellow light. Between the exposed wiring and dancing shadows cast by the peculiar illumination, I felt like we sat in the nexus of some vast engine room. It reminded me of my lab in our unfinished garage, but on a much grander scale. I liked it.

"Still out west," Chad said. "Though I live a few miles over in a small town called Canyonville. The portal system into this place sounds wild. We talked about it a little in class, which helped put things in perspective. I thought you were tripping this morning when you claimed to come in from somewhere other than the converted ranch."

"Yeah, outside Philadelphia," I said. "Bethany?"

"Mid-Tennessee up toward Nashville," she said. "Not close enough for the tourist traffic to be a problem."

Whoa! I took a minute to process the idea of magic twisting the physical world on such a massive scale. There'd been a lot of indicators during the day, so the news didn't come as a huge shock. A clear explanation would have been nice though. Once again, the other instructors were being a bit more thorough with their indoctrination day.

"So how is it that you and I came in through the same door?" Judging by the empty parking lot, I doubted anyone in the waiting room this morning had been from my town, except maybe Larry.

"The system's set up to avoid crowding and slots us to different rooms. I guess it encourages mingling too, maybe so we don't come to school in existing cliques. Gotta trust the system to spit us out to the right town when we head home tonight. If it doesn't, I might have to crash on your couch."

"Magic." I blew out a big breath. "This is getting hard on the brain. But if push comes to shove, I've got an air mattress."

"Cool." Chad looked from me to Bethany. "So what are you two gonna train for if the board approves?"

"You first," Bethany said.

"Shoot, I don't even know if they have a program for what I want to do. But the weather out west sucks. One minute the skies are clear blue, the next we've got hail like golf balls. It's hard on the farmers, but I've got a sense for it and can tell when storms are brewing. I want to be the guy who makes accurate predictions that help people prepare."

"A meteorologist," I said.

"Or however close a trade school can get me. I've gotta see what they offer. How about you, Jason?"

"I like building little robots and piecing machines together." I didn't really know what profession that would fit into either. Despite my gaming persona and dreams of superpowers getting a nod today, I'd never seen a technomancer help wanted ad. "I just have a knack for it, but everything I build usually breaks pretty dramatically. I don't want to get into the details, but that's part of why I landed here." I turned to Bethany to change the topic. "This girl draws like a pro and wants to be an artist, right?"

"Graphic artist," she amended with a smile, still clutching her sketch pad tight. "I'm good at cartoons and things, but really want to graduate to computer designs. I've played around with animation packages and image rendering, but just at the layman level. I need training. I'd love to work on commercials or advertising like this."

Bethany flipped her pad open, paging past the gargoyle, butterfly, and other drawings to stop near the back of the book. A lanky striped kitten sat holding a bottle with Japanese writing down the side. The colored pencil drawing had a Hello Kitty meets Chester Cheetos vibe and wonderful detail. She'd painstakingly drawn individual hairs along the cat's sleek form.

"That's excellent." Chad nodded in appreciation. "You've got it made. I *know* they have a graphic design program."

"I'm hopeful." Bethany beamed and closed the pad, the bending page making the tiger kitten seem to lift the bottle and take a drink.

"What about magic?" I asked. "That's what it's all about now. I've always felt foolish for thinking this, but I give something extra to the things I build, make them stronger or better than they should be."

"My designs?" Bethany fanned the edges of her pages, refusing to meet my gaze. "I'm good with cartoons. You know, stringing drawings together so they make little movies."

"Chad?" I caught the cowboy squinting at the stone column across from him.

"I feel those weather changes coming in my bones. Training will help me land a decent job. Just saying you're good at something isn't enough."

"No, it isn't," came a reply from the next table over.

Owen, the guy who'd sat across from me in the auditorium this morning, sprawled on the bench, still looking like he owned the place. For all his swagger, he'd kept a surprisingly low profile in class. I'd half expected him to get up in Ms. Schlaza's face over her draconian teaching style. But then again, he'd managed most of the tasks almost as easily as Bethany had. His unkempt hair and stylishly sloppy clothing made it hard to tell if he'd been hit by fallout from any errant spells.

"Is that your deal too?" I was a little surprised he'd jumped in on our discussion. "Need that formal training?"

"Hardly. Cars, trucks, if it's got an engine, I can get it running." Owen gave a shrug of concession. "But it's all self-taught so a cert can't hurt."

"You have skills like mine." Maybe we could compare notes.

"No, slick." Owen gave me a cocky smile. "My work doesn't self-destruct, never has."

My jaw clenched so hard that my teeth ached. The inability to keep my creations going was apparently a sore spot. I'd put together dozens of automata designed to perform specific functions over the last few years. They'd graduated in complexity from early throw-the-ball types up through my current Herb series of Humanoid Emergent Recovery Bots. I'd be knee-deep in the little buggers if not for the fatal flaw I accidentally built into each. That shortcoming was the whole reason I was here, and I didn't need to be reminded by some arrogant jerk.

"If you're so perfect, why are you here at all?" Bethany's eyes flashed as she laid a protective hand over mine, which turned out to be clenched into a fist. "I'm surprised you can afford time away from such a thriving business."

"First off, I don't owe you any explanations." Owen's anger rose to meet the challenge in the girl's eyes. He seemed about to say more, but then snorted and the mocking smile returned. "I get it. Shift the attention so no one pokes at why you're so keen to get away from home."

Her hand tightened over mine. "I'm not—"

"It's okay, I'll bite." Composure regained, Owen sprawled out across the bench again, the picture of cool detachment. "My talent only extends to the engines. I can get anything running, no problem. Not so much with the other systems: coolant, brakes, electronics, and the rest. Plus I've always wanted to work on motorcycles. Even if I don't open a shop for them, I could use pointers to finish up the project that's in pieces in my garage. So there you have it. Just a guy from Chicago trying to make good in a *normal* blue collar job. I guess we'll just have to see if Attwater has programs for weather psychics and suicidal robot production."

Owen was really full of himself. My constructs didn't self-destruct on purpose. Something just wasn't aligned right, and I was going to learn how to fix that. If nothing else, today's exercises drove home the fact that I'd been unconsciously using magic all along to will a spark of life into my machines. That bit of information along with gaining a feel for how the power flowed in tingling waves up from the well in my core had me thinking of ways to improve the build process.

Bethany tensed, her grip on my hand painful. Owen's attitude set her off. For me, the sting of his words already had faded. He wasn't a jerk like Larry, just thoughtless, a kind of playful scoundrel. Or Owen got his kicks by stirring the pot to see what surfaced. The way his dark eyes twinkled from within their crescent slits made me think the latter more likely. Either way, I tried to think of a safer topic, but Chad beat me to it.

"Two weeks and we'll have our contracts locked in. That takes us just about to the end of July." Chad flipped through his packet. "I've got the schedule here somewhere. Just wondering if we get any time off to enjoy the summer."

When he failed to find the calendar, Bethany let my hand go, opened her own binder, and pulled out the school schedule. After a brief examination, she nodded and pointed out several dates.

"We just missed getting the fourth off. It fell on the two week break between semesters." She turned the page. "Nothing else until September, but it looks like most of the big holidays are here. We get a nice long break for Christmas and Hanukkah."

"Why's this week after the winter holidays blocked off?" I asked looking over her shoulder. "Says O.E."

"Objective Evaluation." Chad leaned across the table. "I guess it depends on your curriculum, but Mr. Marshall says we'll all have practical evaluations or exams to assess progress before the semester officially ends in mid-January. OEs are Attwater's equivalent to finals."

We'd signed on for three semesters and would have OEs roughly every six months. Focusing on the calendar got us looking forward and kicking around ideas for collaborative study before those evaluations. Even if we all ended up in different specialty tracks, common core classes continued, and we'd help each other prepare for those OEs. Chad promised to share what he learned of magic theory and history if Ms. Schlaza continued to keep us in the dark. That should give those of us who didn't exhibit a natural talent for core spells—namely me—a better shot at developing passable skills.

We found ourselves laughing, spinning outlandish tales of our future magical deeds, and throwing crackers at each other. Owen watched with detached amusement until a peanut butter Ritz landed in his hair. We soon learned he'd snagged a box of gummy bears and knew how to use them. Those things hit like rubber bullets, but it was all in fun. When a sullen Lars tried to join in by launching cold coffee into our midst, Owen shared his ammo and the two of us beat back the jerk under a hail of flying chewables.

As the clock marched toward eight, the room thinned out until just a few pockets of students remained. We all knew the inevitable was upon us if we were to stick to the rules on our first day.

"Hey, Mr. Fix-it!" Lars yelled as Mr. Gonzales headed past the commons from the entrance to the inner-ring classrooms. "Need you to get this crappy beverage dispenser working so my buds and I can get some java for the road. Your POS equipment is going to make us late."

Lars stood by the coffee machines, a grande-sized cup clutched in his hand. He whispered to the Asian man and woman behind him, laughed, and turned to watch the maintenance manager change course and head over. Too-red lips formed a familiar sneer on the round, pasty face that had mocked me all too often in school.

Maybe the lack of coffee was going to make Lars late, but the other two were definitely not his "buds." The pair exchanged a few words, put their cups back, and drifted away, clearly wanting nothing to do with his condescending attitude. I'd been on the receiving end of too much of his bullying growing up.

"Excuse me," I said and pushed up from my seat.

I had no intention of picking a fight on my first day, but the school staff didn't deserve that kind of crap. I strode across the commons with a vague notion of reminding him that the staff didn't work for him and to take it easy. But bullies never responded well to reason.

So I "accidentally" plowed into Larry from behind. Dregs of brown liquid splashed over the lip of his cup and across the back of his hand. The cup fell, loose grounds swirling in the bit of coffee he'd managed to coax from the machine.

"Hey, watch it!"

"Sorry, Lars. I didn't see you there." I picked up the cup, handed it back, and pointed toward the kitchenette. "There're towels and napkins over there." Without waiting for a response, I turned to intercept the approaching man. "Hey,

Mr. Gonzales, awesome job this morning getting the sprinklers under control."

"Why thank you." A smile blossomed beneath the man's bushy moustache. "I just wish the dean would take it a little easy."

Larry sputtered and tried to catch my eye, but I kept my back to him. After a few seconds, he huffed and slunk off to get cleaned up.

"It was quite the display though." I stuck out my hand. "Jason Walker, new student."

"Mike Gonzales." He gave my hand a timid shake and shot a look past me to where Lars dabbed at his jeans and grumbled to himself.

"Does every class have one of those?"

"Oh, there's at least one of everything in each group that rolls through Attwater. You get used to it." He offered a wry smile, set down his black canvas tool bag, and opened an access panel on the side of the coffee maker.

"Lars has always been a jerk," I said. "Some of us know how hard it is to keep everything behind the scenes running."

"Thank you. That means a lot." White teeth flashed as he fished in his bag for an odd long-shafted screwdriver with two facing crescents for the blade. "I get the sense that you have a way with machinery yourself."

"I'm pretty handy." The memory of Herb blowing apart rose unbidden. "But I've got a lot to learn. Sometimes things go south no matter what I try."

"Such is life." Mr. Gonzales tapped the screwdriver against his chin in thought for a few seconds, then got to work on the innards of the machine. "It's getting harder and harder to keep up around here. Dispensers and sprinklers are nothing compared to maintaining the antiquated infrastructure of the inner rings. Did you know we have a steam system? Anyway, the last few weeks have been particularly bad."

"Time for an overhaul?" I'd seen it before in aging buildings—like the one I'd blown up—obsolete equipment, faulty wiring, and metal fatigue crept in over time.

"I'm not saying the building is too old." He pulled his head out of the access and looked to the conduits and pipes high overhead before turning back to his adjustments. "The school wouldn't like that, but something's gotten into her."

So the maintenance manager thought of the school as a she. Luckily, he couldn't see my grin. "Does that mean—"

"Que!" A string of Spanish curses followed as Mr. Gonzales pushed away from the machine, the back of his head cracking on the edge of the opening.

Something long and black slithered from the coffee machine and dropped to the floor.

6. Harder than it Looks

T HE SINUOUS THING that dropped from the coffee machine was three feet long and as thick around as my wrist, but it wasn't a normal snake. In fact, it wasn't an animal at all. The round head was the size of a fist with one glowing red dot for an eye. The thing was midnight black, but where a snake would be all shiny scales, the lines of its tapered body were indistinct as if blurred or made of smoke. It curled in front of us testing the air with a wispy yellow tongue, fire to the smoky body.

"It's okay, Jason." Mr. Gonzales drew a copper cylinder that looked like an oversized battery from his bag.

The creature whirled and struck out as Mr. G. carefully set the object next to it. A tongue of flame zapped the inside of his forearm, and he jerked his hand back with a curse. The snake continued to hiss in warning, but the sound consisted of high-pitched vibrations rather than escaping air.

"What is it?" I stepped back a pace, but froze when the head whipped around to follow.

"Stand still and give me a minute," the maintenance man said. "A gremlin like this shouldn't be here."

Another vibrating hiss rose. The red laser-dot eye expanded, taking over half the face as it bored into me.

"Mr. G., I don't think it likes me." My voice cracked, and I cleared my throat.

Energy built in the gremlin snake, a dark imitation of the power we'd been playing with all day. It contracted, coils compressing into a tight s-shape as it prepared to strike.

"Keep very still." Mr. Gonzales touched the side of the cylinder.

Even though he was moving and I didn't so much as breathe, the stupid thing's attention stayed riveted on me. The crimson dot shrank to a pinpoint, and the snake shot forward. I pulled back, but too slowly. That bulbous head jerked to a stop inches from my right knee. The body stretched long and straight as an arrow.

The very tip of its tail thrashed and twisted, caught on the top of the copper device. The snake hissed and writhed as it drew back—not retreating, just shrinking. Mr. Gonzales's cylinder reeled in the struggling snake, seeming to consume the gremlin. From tail to mid body, it quickly disappeared. The rate slowed as the thicker coils strained, trying to pull free right up until a few inches and the head remained. The red eye pulsed, gathering energy. With a snap the rest of the gremlin vanished into the cylinder.

Two contacts on top of the device glowed orange for a moment before fading back to shiny silver and releasing a curl of smoke.

"What's going on?" Bethany called from the table.

Feet shuffled up behind me. I turned to find the others bearing down fast.

"Just a little trouble with the coffee machine," Mr. Gonzales answered for me as he stuffed the copper device back into his bag. "I'll show this to Dean Gladstone. But critical repairs come first." He went back to work on the machine and called over his shoulder. "Watch your time, kids. Don't miss curfew."

"What curfew?" Owen asked as he and I walked back to the table.

"The out by eight o'clock rule, I'm guessing."

We had about twenty minutes left. Mr. Gonzales wasted little time with the coffee machine and slipped the access panel back in place by the time we sat down. Apparently the gremlin had been the main issue. He spared a friendly wave on his way out of the commons. I'd expected him to head left toward the administrative wing to show the dean what he'd caught. Instead, he headed back the way he'd come from, entered an access code into the keypad by the metal security door at the far end of the hall, and disappeared into the inner ring of classrooms.

Having missed his opportunity for mischief, Lars finished cleaning up and headed back to the exit along with the last few students who'd stayed to socialize.

"Did you two have a nice chat?" Owen watched the door close behind Mr. Gonzales, then gave me a nod of approval. "By the way, good job hamstringing poser boy. That guy is a royal pain."

Maybe he wasn't an aloof douche after all.

"Thanks. Keeping the drama around here to a minimum is in all our best interest. Plus, I want to stay on Mr. Gonzales's good side. I get the feeling he keeps the gears oiled around here. Could be helpful in a pinch." I waved the others in close. "You guys missed something pretty weird."

I described our encounter with the gremlin and how the maintenance manager had trapped it in a magical storage device.

"This place is an ancient relic," Owen said when I'd finished. "Bet it's full of all kinds of vermin and falling apart at the seams."

We all jumped as a water hammer boomed through the steam piping overhead. The phenomena was a largely harmless byproduct of excess condensation in the lines, but noisy— literally like a sledgehammer beating on the metal steam pipes.

"Nah." Chad studied the stony alcove above, then ran his hand down the stacked stone pillar behind our table. "The old girl has good bones. She'll be around long after we're all gone, gremlins or not."

The thumping subsided and the water slug worked its way out with a sigh of escaping pressure as if the system was pleased. I shook my head and grinned at the image. Machines were people too. I mean, you had to think of them that way when you're trying to give life to a bunch of components.

"What's with the gender assignments?" I found it funny that Mr. Gonzales and now Chad referred to the building as she.

"Place just has a certain feel." Chad looked for support from the others, but shrugged at their blank stares. "Well, it does to me." He patted the stone again just as another relief valve sighed overhead.

As we finished snacking, over a dozen people shuffled in wearing overalls, smocks, and the various uniforms of different trades. Most headed straight for the coffee dispenser, and I realized Mr. G. wasn't kidding about it being critical equipment.

When I commented on the fact everyone had a laminated green badge dangling from somewhere on their person, our resident cowboy had a ready answer.

"Access badges for different wings and rings." Chad tapped his information packet, which had been more thoroughly briefed than our own. *Damn, wish I was in his class.* "We'll get them after we sign on the dotted line. First semester gets yellow. Green means these are all second year students about to graduate and enter the job pipeline. Doors are equipped with proximity sensors, and each badge is keyed to access certain areas. That's how you get to your vocational classes held in the inner rings."

"I've got my eye on green," Bethany said.

"Just have to hang in long enough." I fingered my own packet of information, vowing to give it a thorough perusal tonight.

"If you four aren't in night school, you better get back to your assigned doorway." A freckled-faced young woman with goggles nestled in curly auburn hair bordering on frizzy approached.

The thick brown gloves folded into her belt matched her heavy leather apron. She tapped her watch and waved the steaming cup in her other hand at the wall clock. It was seven fifty.

"Ten minutes!" Bethany yipped.

"Yep, we better get going. Thanks." I looked to our self-appointed time-keeper.

She was pretty in a kind of rugged way, but that could have just been the welding outfit and the fact she was nearly as tall as me. Hell, she could have the body of a goddess or a linebacker under that outfit. A button nose fit her round face nicely, but those twinkling brown eyes were what caught my attention as one side of her mouth quirked up in a half smile.

"Regina, but you can call me Reggie or Gina. It doesn't really matter. What's in a name, as they say? Of course, it's a good way to identify everyone." Her brow knitted tight in thought. "Without names we'd probably just call each other 'hey you.' So, yeah, names are important. I can see that."

"Well, so you have names with faces, I'm Jason." I quickly listed the others as we cleaned up the table and gathered our things. "And…we gotta run."

I got the feeling Reggie-Gina-Regina might be even more socially challenged than me.

"Literally!" she nodded, and the goggles slipped down to her forehead. "Take the stairs by the atrium. The others will be clogged with incoming night school students. You don't want to get trapped with us upperclassmen." She screwed up her face, closed one eye, and growled out the rest like a movie pirate—or angry kitten given the way she raised her free hand and clawed the air. "Argh, we're a nasty lot."

"Um…okay. We're gone then." Yeah, I think she was trying for pirate.

The number of people drifting in for night classes surprised me. Then again, who knew what time zone they all came from? I didn't hear much in the way of interesting languages, but the magic doorways made anything possible.

Maybe there was a special project going on or these folks all had day jobs. Either way, taking the central stairs saved our bacon. Chad and I made U32 with two minutes to spare, and I assumed the others had made it to their respective doors in time.

It would have been interesting for us to walk out at the same time, just to try for a glimpse of how the magic door sorting worked. But Chad waved me ahead, so I stepped through the glass door into the humid evening heat of my hometown.

Even though Chad was close on my heels, the door remained firmly closed, so the magic must have whisked him away to Montana. A couple of minutes ticked by, and the lights behind those opaque windows flicked off. Our friendly Attwater branch was closed for the night.

My beater car sat exactly where I had parked it. I fished out the keys and strolled over to find white foam on my windshield.

"Wonderful."

Someone had written "loser" across my windshield with shaving cream. It wasn't the worst trick Larry had ever pulled, but I did check behind my tires for nasty surprises. Windshield wipers and many squirts of fluid got me on the road, but left a smeared mess down my paint that I'd have to rinse off before it dried. On the bright side, my ride smelled menthol fresh.

The week progressed in similar fashion to that first day, except without the big welcome assembly. We started each morning in our respective classrooms, and threw ourselves into the core studies that would determine our future. After two days of banging our heads against new spells, our training fell into a familiar routine. At first I found myself looking forward to the challenge despite the good-cop bad-cop routine between Mary and Ms. Schlaza. But after days of questionable accomplishments, my enthusiasm waned.

Bethany pointed out that each new day gave us another opportunity to excel. She even took to tutoring me and a few other struggling students, trying to help us harness the magic in the same easy, confident way she did.

Owen quickly became one of the more accomplished casters and only struggled with spells involving water in those early rounds. Given how he tended to talk down to Bethany, I was surprised to see him accepting tips and getting his issues sorted out.

Water was the most difficult element for me too—well, next to fire, and air…and earth. That isn't to say I had zero success.

I was able to produce decent wind gusts, finally get that ice ball formed, and even zap a few sparks from my fingertips. But those were tiny successes, applauded by Mary Eisner and looked down upon by Ice Queen Schlaza, who scribbled copious notes in her ledger every time I attempted a spell. Honestly, I couldn't see the school offering me a contract.

"Slick, you need a tutor," Owen said as we grabbed lunch that first Friday.

"Bethany tried, but apparently I'm unteachable." I grabbed half of a BLT and dropped it on my paper plate. "But since we can't even take notes home and Lars is the only other person near me enrolled in Attwater, I'm sort of stuck."

We'd graduated from pre-packaged snacks to sandwich and veggie trays. I breezed past the latter, snagged a bag of chips, and threaded through the crowd to our little corner of the commons area.

Chad tore into a small mountain of food while flipping through a thin blue textbook describing the various water spells. Bethany sat on the far side of the table with another girl in her late teens. At least, that was my guess. It was hard to tell under the black lipstick, dark eyeshadow, and heavy makeup. I'd seen Mon around a few times. Though quiet and small, the Japanese girl stood out in those dark outfits heavy on lace and chains. I hadn't realized she and Bethany were friends.

"Lars wouldn't be much help anyway. He's even worse with spells than you. Bitches all the time about how you must cheat." Chad said around a mouthful of corn chips, having heard our conversation even over his crunching. "Oh, sorry, dude."

I waved away the apology and sat next to Bethany, sparing a nod for Mon. I wasn't at the bottom of the class, just pretty darn close. The standing didn't bother me all that much. But with so many failures, my motivation grew increasingly thin. I honestly didn't know what would happen if I bombed out of common core classes and wasn't offered a contract. Would Judge Michelson really pull me back into court?

"I'm not worried," Bethany said. "You're making progress, which is all that counts. You sense the magic fine and understand the elements. It's just a matter of practice. Next week will be better." She gave my knee a squeeze, but let go quickly and clasped her hands on the table. "Sorry, but you'll see." She looked around the table, avoiding eye contact with yours truly. "So, who has plans for the weekend?"

"I've got a trail ride scheduled," Chad said. "Parents run a dude ranch, so I get to play tour guide for city slickers who want that authentic cowboy experience."

"That sounds fun." Bethany bounced in her seat.

"Yeah, we do the whole nine yards: the ride, pit barbeque, stories around the campfire, and sometimes a dance."

"Ooh, I bet plenty of hot city girls would kill for some time with a hunky cowboy like you." Bethany didn't usually go down that path, probably because we were all several years older than she. I had to wonder what she and Mon had been talking about.

"Well…some…" Chad stammered. "Some of them aren't too hard on the eyes."

"I'm sleeping in till noon and taking a six-pack down to the races." Owen liked throwing outlandish statements around, but the four of us still meshed surprisingly well.

"Hopefully not driving," I said with eyebrow raised.

"Just a spectator. I've got friends running in the sidecar races."

He went on to explain the concept of racing motorcycles with sidecars. One of his friends was the "monkey," who climbed around on the open platform to counterbalance the bike so her husband, the driver, could take the turns as fast as possible. It sounded ridiculously dangerous, and apparently crashes and flip-overs were not uncommon. But the community was tightly knit, and he wanted to support his friends.

"How about you?" I asked Bethany.

"I have a few projects to finish." She clutched her ever-present notebook tight.

"Don't be the lonely artist in your fortress of solitude." I didn't catch the irony of my statement until later. "Your friends will think you're ghosting them."

"Not many of those." She looked down and tucked a strand of hair behind her ear.

"And back at you about hot guys." Chad was clearly going for supportive, but Bethany sucked in a breath and shook her head.

"Nothing like *that* either," she mumbled. "Dad probably has a picnic or something planned. I know they want to squeeze out more info on how school's going. More time to get the third degree."

"It's weird that we can't say much outside." I'd talked to Billy a couple of times during the week, but of course couldn't spout off about magic and spells.

"This time next week will certainly be interesting." Chad gaped at our blank expressions. "Oh come on, parents night?" Nothing. "They've sent letters home announcing the school open house between six and eight. See the school, learn about the curricula. Event's being held after contract signing, so it's just for the parents of those staying on."

"We don't all live at home with Mommy and Daddy." Owen threw up his hands in disgust. "Hell, some of these people are pushing fifty. They certainly aren't bringing old Dad down with his walker to hear some B.S. about how little Johnny's training to be a carpenter."

"Parent's night is sort of my term." Chad backpedaled in the face of sarcasm. "I think it's technically family night. People can bring spouses, parents, kids, whatever. Magic will be on tight lock down, so I think it's more of a tour in the outer ring, light hors d'oeuvres in the atrium, and a lecture on how job placement works."

I'd better talk to Mom and Dad to see if they'd gotten an invitation and planned to attend. If so, how the heck was I going to explain why we were the only ones in the parking lot?

7. Fingerprints

OUR SECOND WEEK flew by, and despite Ms. Schlaza's brutal teaching methods, no one ended up in the morgue. I certainly would have fared better under Chad's instructor, but luck of the draw and all. Tense silence stretched over the class as we waited for the next student to be called away. We'd pushed the desks into three neat rows so it was easy to tell that a third of us had already left for their one-on-one contract meeting.

Owen had been first to strut out the door and meet with the advisor that came for him. He was one of the most accomplished spell casters, so we'd assumed they took the best students first. But Ms. Schlaza manned the clipboard of destiny and assured us we'd be called in random order having nothing to do with the likelihood of being offered a contract. Her statement was borne out when Theodore, a pasty-faced thirty-something with curly red hair, got called second. The guy had never managed to master a single spell with fire or air.

After two weeks of constant practice and the occasional dribble of theory, quietly awaiting our fate had me ready to scream. My fingers flexed, eager to do something, anything. Thanks to the flickering lights a headache pounded behind my temples. Digging into the panel by the lockers for the problem would give me something to do besides worry, but would cost me whatever small rapport I'd built up with our instructor.

Mr. G. would be on the issue shortly. Several more gremlins had cropped up during the past week if the smoking traps the man discretely carried off were any indication. The problem kept the maintenance manager hopping, but he always managed to clear up the resulting issues in short order. So I folded my hands over the evaluation report on my desk.

The colorful graph on the cover sheet stapled to each personalized report summarized our aptitude for magic. Intersecting axes—five representing the magical elements and a sixth mystery axis—formed the framework of the graph. An unlabeled scale ticked off ten increments along each from the central point. The plot of relative strengths along each axis was joined along the perimeter of the graph to form a colorful amoeba, our magical fingerprint.

Graph points along the perimeter both on and between axes had been based on how well an individual handled the varying levels and combinations of spells we'd practiced. The resulting starburst pattern was uniformly distributed around the center for students who could handle any type of spell with the same level of competence. For those of us with weaknesses or strengths, the defining points along the graph's perimeter would dip toward the center or stretch toward the edge of the paper leaving a lopsided spatter of color. In addition to the magnitude scale, fill colors of red, yellow, and green formed spokes every few degrees around the center to indicate more subtle characteristics like control, flexibility, and endurance.

I looked to my left and peeked at Bethany's summary. Her graph formed a big, bold, nearly perfect circle that stretched to the edges, a bright green apple with a few yellow sections and tiny spots of red. Clearly, she'd proved well-rounded in accomplishing the bulk of Schlaza's exercises. Owen's graphic had cut a similarly large swatch, but not quite as balanced. Though nearly as strong as Bethany in most directions, his had notably dipped along the axis representing water, an element that always gave him trouble. His colors tended more toward yellow with a good bit of red.

Compared to those two reports, my little amoeba was an embarrassing splash that liked to hang out at a magnitude of two or three. The red and yellow color gradients helpfully emphasized my anemic abilities. One notable exception laid along the spirit axis. I'd shocked Mary and Schlaza by crushing most of those exercises on my first attempt. That should have lifted me out of the doldrums. But it's hard to take pride in catching a glimpse of a person's aura or finding a hidden object when the lady next to you is busy throwing fireballs that could take out a charging rhino.

"Jason Walker," Ms. Schlaza called from the front of the room, her face pinched as though she'd just bitten into a lemon dipped in dead ants.

This is it. My hands trembled as I scooped up my evaluation sheets.

"You got this." Bethany flashed a supportive smile.

While Schlaza scowled, Ms. Eisner waved me forward and opened the door. I'd expected one of the unfamiliar assessment officers that had been cycling through to take the others out. Instead, Dean Gladstone stood outside, dressed in his button-heavy brown leather outfit and leaning on the metal cane.

My heart sank as I glanced down at my abysmal results. I was about to be booted. The dean would probably walk me straight over to Judge Michelson to ensure I didn't run for it.

Schlaza glared in annoyance at my hesitation, while Mary nodded encouragement as she tried again to shoo me out the door. I took one last look around the room, taking in the quirky dungeon atmosphere, my fellow students patiently awaiting their own decision, and Bethany's hopeful nod.

I'm going to miss this stupid place.

They'd taken a page from corporate playbooks, gathering us at the end of the day for our debriefing. After our private session, each of us would head straight home to celebrate the start of a year and a half years of magical education or curse being dismissed from Attwater's hallowed halls. There would be no gathering in the commons to compare notes, complain about our evaluations, or lament being sent away. Businesses handed out evaluations and layoffs at the end of day, usually on a Friday, so that managers didn't have to deal with disgruntled workers—at least not right away. The tactic kept the masses from talking and stirring up trouble.

With students scattered across the country, we wouldn't even know who had been offered a contract until tomorrow morning when those who did showed up for class. Those of us who didn't? Well…

"Jason?" Mr. Gladstone beckoned with his iron cane.

I steeled my resolve and strode through the door to my fate. Gladstone walked me down to his office in the administrative wing, which was conveniently close to the exit that I'd be using one last time after the meeting.

Dean Gladstone's office had the comfortable feel of a well-used workshop. Even with its rich wood paneling and plush rug, the place reminded me of the corner of the garage I'd closed off for my projects. Shelves and bins covered most of the mahogany, offering tidy organization for sprockets, gears, and a wide variety of other mechanical components. Tools stood in neat rows along the back wall of a long desk covered in green felt to provide a work surface. Tiny jeweler's tools got their own little nook at the end of the bench, where a magnifying glass on an articulating metal arm stood guard over a pocket watch undergoing repairs.

The dean crossed in front of a stone fireplace set off to the right and motioned for me to take the chair opposite a wide desk of dark wood that sat under the high-arched window. The mantle clock above the cold firebox was an artful wave of walnut with a brass face that read ten till eight. I checked my phone to verify it was approaching four.

A variety of clocks ranging from a stately grandfather clock in the corner to pendulum wall clocks and an intricately carved cuckoo adorned his office. Each showed a different hour, like the array of clocks tracking different time zones in a newsroom or command center.

The warm, eclectic atmosphere dredged up a pang of longing. This was the kind of shop I desperately wanted, a fortress of solitude to perfect my projects, a location to horde the servos, circuit boards, and other hard-to-come-by parts I'd so often had to work without. Eighteen months at Attwater would have set me on the path to that dream.

I looked down at my stupid evaluation report as the dean sat down and pulled out a tall leather ledger, so similar to the one Judge Michelson had used for notes at my preliminary hearing just a few weeks earlier. He rifled through the thin stack of legal-size papers, checking if everything was in order for my reintroduction to the judicial system.

A lump formed in my throat. The biggest kicker of failing out was not just missing out on my dream, but the fact I was likely to land in jail. I wouldn't even get the chance to say goodbye to my new friends.

"So, Jason, I think you know why you're here." Gladstone flipped open the binder and pulled out a copy of my evaluation. The abysmal results stared up from the polished wood surface, a mocking crimson-yellow eye.

"Yes, sir. I do."

Mouth dry, I fought to swallow my disappointment. The thought of court proceedings and jail pulled my chest tight. It grew hard to breath. I needed to head this off. There had to be another way to let me out of the program without turning me over. I had to say something before it was too late.

The dean leaned in, both elbows on the desk and fingers steepled in front of his face.

"Just let me disappear," I blurted out. "Don't tell the judge."

"We need to settle on your career path." The dean spoke overtop my plea.

"I know, but I can't go to jail. Just let me—" wait, what had he just said? "Career path?"

"Yes, your core class evaluation helps us pinpoint your magical talent and match you up to the best possible vocation."

"So you're not kicking me out for those terrible results?" I waved my copy of the cover sheet with its red and yellow starburst graph. "Look at this. Just about everyone else in the class is better than me."

Mr. Gladstone sat back in his chair, crossed his arms, and brought a hand up to stroke his thin white moustache. "Jason, do you know why we call these fingerprint graphs?"

"Sure, because each one ends up different."

"Correct. We run you through all the core spells and exercises to assess your abilities across the board."

"Ms. Schlaza explained that to us." *Eventually.* "But I don't seem to have an aptitude for anything."

"Jason, you can't have a wrong or a bad fingerprint, just a unique one. The goal isn't to be strong in all the elements and their various nuances—although some students are—it's to build this pattern of interdependencies and relationships that determine how your powers fit into the arcane world. Think of your psyche and affinities represented by this graph as the cuts along a key. That key fits perfectly to unlock the exact talent you possess. We use some very sophisticated algorithms to help us understand that lock and project where your magical abilities lie. Of course, we then match that up to the more mundane marketplace demands to guide students into a career that compliments their powers. A solid match up lets us place graduates where they can do the most good. After all, lucrative and rewarding employment leads to high student satisfaction.

"But if one in three don't get a contract, it just doesn't seem like I could fit in the top percentile."

His sparkling green eyes grew hard and his voice dropped to an earnest demand. "Jason, do you want to leave Attwater?"

"No." I blinked at his intensity. "I want training and a good start. But—"

"Then stop arguing." He nodded sharply in satisfaction. "I'm offering you a contract for a fully paid training program. You are not going back to stand trial. You will complete your obligation to us, three full semesters over the next eighteen months. The guidance department will then place you in an appropriate entry position. Is that acceptable?"

"Yes, that would be great."

"Excellent." His face brightened and he flipped open my evaluation papers. "Let's get to the task at hand and assign you a course of study. Once we agree on that, you can sign your contract to make things all official."

"But hasn't the school already picked that for me?" I glanced at the papers on the other side of his folio. Now that he'd made it clear I wasn't getting shipped off to Judge Michelson, I saw that rather than court seals, the papers held the Attwater letterhead, so would be the contract I was expected to sign.

"We do take your desires into account," he said. "You show an affinity for a very specific and narrow set of capabilities that underpin each element."

"That's putting it mildly." The wry smile froze on my lips at his sharp glare.

"Son, this is no time for self-deprecation. We need you in the right career and to ensure you know where your magical talents lie. You used these skills before coming here; it's how I found you. So tell me what power you think you bring to the table?"

"I like building…things, useful automata and machines. But programming them doesn't always work out. I push my energy into those machines to help them do more than should be possible, blending science and magic." I looked around at all the parts and pieces arrayed around his shop-office. "Maybe sort of like you do? Books and movies call that technomancy."

"I do live for crafting fine machinery." The dean had been nodding as I spoke and now waved at the office walls. "These are my creations."

"You make clocks?"

"And more. From timepieces to metronomes, anything and everything that measures off the rhythm of existence on its journey through the three dimensions of physical space. But technomancy is not a discipline we here at Attwater recognize. I don't believe any of the schools do. I've seen fingerprints similar to yours only a couple of times before, and both of those individuals had the same talent."

"Really?" It sucked that I'd lose the cool title I'd built my imaginary persona around, but excitement overrode the disappointment.

Deep down I'd known technomancers were comic book and roleplaying game fabrications. But I sat in a mysterious academy that could tell me about my skills. Hunger flashed in the dean's emerald eyes. This was something big, really big. My crappy scores didn't matter. Destiny awaited.

"You, Mr. Walker"—he gave me a broad smile, and I leaned in close, eager to hear what form of mystic wizard or arcane magic user I was destined to become— "are a tinker."

Say what?

"Ah…tinker?"

So much for conquering the universe with my awesome skills. I was pretty sure he'd just called me a janitor.

"Come now, don't look so glum. Yes, a tinker." He beamed as if proclaiming me king of the world. "At the core of it, you fix things. I'm sure you've noticed the ability to put materials together that typically do not work well or stay joined. When you use adhesives or joining techniques the results exceed logical expectations. You can diagnose problems in a wide variety of systems and get them operational and running at peak performance with little effort."

"All true, but there's big problems. My projects keep melting down. You remember Herb."

"I suspect that's because you apply your skills in an unnatural way. You've likely been trying to fix your creations into existence instead of building them. That's something we can help with, but as for building golems and magical constructs?" He consulted my chart and shook his head.

"That's not fully within your magical capabilities, not a good match for your talent. Tinkers have been a crucial element in the magical community throughout the centuries. Traditionally, they were one of the few ambassadors of magic that could freely travel and be welcomed by all. People of all ilk needed household objects mended and their places of business to run smoothly.

"Not only have tinkers spread acceptance and use of magic, they were an important communication backplane, helping bridge the gap between common people and those of ability."

"So what vocation does a tinker train in?" I asked.

"Well, there are a number of options typically dealing with the repair aspects of your talent. We don't get many tinkers through Attwater. I would recommend something in fabrication, perhaps welding. Alternatively plumbing—"

"Not a plumber," I interjected. "I couldn't stand that."

"Well, let's roll up our sleeves, and select something that resonates. Shall we?"

He pulled a course catalog from the desk drawer, and we dove into the search for options matching my awesome…tinkermancy.

8. Classes

T HE NEXT MORNING found me sitting alone at our table in the commons. Four steaming cups awaited my friends. A fitful night's sleep had left me sweating and puzzling over fragmented dreams in which I traveled the medieval countryside in my horse-drawn wagon. So I'd gotten an early start and was the first to arrive.

We'd agreed to meet Friday before class to discuss our contracts meetings. Gathering beforehand also gave us the opportunity to ensure we'd all signed on the dotted line. Others drifted in, meeting with their own newfound friends. Relieved laughter and hearty congratulations greeted each new addition.

Chad was first to show. He scooped up the cup of ultra-bold, took a big swig, and slipped into his seat by the pillar.

"Late night?" I couldn't help but notice the dark circles ringing his eyes, but judging by his satisfied smile he wasn't too broken up about it.

"Understatement of the century." He nodded and grinned at the yellow badge hanging from my shirt pocket. "Congrats by the way. I knew you were worried for nothing. Anyone else here yet?"

"Thanks. We're the first." I resisted asking about his meeting because we'd agreed to share only after everyone arrived—if everyone arrived.

As for my own meeting, Dean Gladstone and I had spent nearly an hour debating the merits of different careers. All the trades we discussed fell under the manufacturing and repairs umbrella. I certainly appreciated the fact that he took my desires and concerns into consideration. But for some reason, he always circled back to job location, favoring industrial settings over shop work and in-home services.

"There's my men!" Bethany called from the doorway and hurried over with an excited squeal that hurt my ears.

She wrapped me in a big hug, did the same to Chad, and slapped her things down on the table. Although she acted all bubbly and pleased, her bloodshot eyes told a different story.

"You okay?" I asked as she lifted her paper cup and inhaled the rich aroma of dark Sumatra coffee—not quite the genetically engineered paint stripper Chad preferred, but a close second.

"Nothing I can't handle." Bethany was sharp enough to realize she wasn't completely fooling anyone. "Mom's being a royal pain again, but I just told her to deal with it. Her issues, not mine. Being mad about free education makes no sense." She gasped at the slip. "Sorry, still need Owen, so I'll hold that thought. No need to wait on Mon by the way. I ran into her near the atrium. Her new advisor called for an early meeting so she can't join us."

"Sure, no problem." I hadn't realized Mon was part of our inner circle. "Owen's nearly as good as you; he *had* to make the cut."

Didn't he?

I'd grown to like Owen. Sometimes it was good to have another guy in core classes that I could talk to. Bethany was great, but still a little star struck about the school and bright future she'd planned out in great detail. Though arrogant and self-centered, Owen's dry humor helped the group to not take things too seriously. His jaded outlook balanced Bethany's rosy one. Even though we'd be pulled into our respective job training, our tyrannical core classes and hanging after hours would continue. As the clock approached eight, I started to worry.

"So where's your badge?" Chad's laminated yellow rectangle dangled from a clip off his sleeve.

"Um…in my purse." Bethany cast a worried glance at the slim blue bag perched on top of her books. "It doesn't exactly match my outfit."

Now that she mentioned it, I noted how nicely Bethany had dressed. Her over-the-shoulder pouch matched a trim-fitting blue suit jacket and pleated skirt. The high-heeled pumps wrapped her feet in silver coils, very fashionable. My jeans and tee-shirt suddenly felt overly casual. Even Chad wore a nice short-sleeved button down with his stone-washed denims.

"You look great today." Maybe the horse was out of the barn, but my compliment still earned a smile.

"And the gang's all here!" Owen's sardonic smile and well-rested appearance had relief and annoyance warring in my skull as he strolled over and plunked himself down.

"At least one of us got to sleep in," Chad said, echoing my thoughts. "Well, crew, we've got like five minutes. Looks like everyone signed on for all three semesters. I'm gonna train as an operational forecaster. Not quite a meteorologist, but I'll get to analyze weather conditions and issue forecasts. So I'm happy. What about you all?"

"Welder." I looked at the clock and figured I had ten seconds to expound. "Specializing in industrial techniques for work on pressure vessels and submarines."

"Our boy Jason's going to be a Navy man," Owen said.

"No way!" That hit too close to the threat of shipping me off to the military. "Plenty of civilian applications like power plants and oil refineries. You?"

"Bike mechanic through and through. Too easy."

All eyes turned to Bethany, who seemed oddly subdued.

"Graphic design, just what I always wanted." Her lack of enthusiasm had me wanting to ask questions, but that would have to wait. "Oh, and Mon is studying cosmetology."

"Really?" I thought back to the girl's heavy-handed makeup and shrugged. "Good for her."

The last minute warning bell sounded—really more of a steam whistle note that screamed factory worker. We gathered our things, promised to meet at lunch, and headed to class.

Ms. Schlaza didn't waste time on pleasantries like congratulating her returning students. Instead, she showed her appreciation in other ways.

"Now that you've all signed on,"—she started off nice enough— "the time for coddling is at an end."

Say what?

As crazy as it sounded, she wasn't kidding. We soon found ourselves knee-deep in spell work. The things we'd tried before were simple tests to gauge each person's aptitude—we'd known that going in—but her new quest was to make casting second nature. It wasn't that the new spells were harder, just that quitting and moving on was never an option. Even Ms. Eisner looked relieved when the ten o'clock whistle signaled it was time for all first semester students to rotate into vocational classes.

I left with Owen and Bethany and made a beeline for the metal door leading to the inner-ring classrooms. Although Mr. Gonzales used a code for the keypad set in the wall, our yellow badges afforded us access coming and going. I waved mine over the reader. The LED set in the pad flipped from red to green and a metallic snick sounded near the handle.

"Ladies first." I stepped aside to let Bethany go, but Owen held out his hand to block her.

"No drafting in behind someone else," he said, reminding us of Ms. Schlaza's stern warning. Everything the woman said came out like she was the harbinger of doom, which made it hard to keep track sometimes. "Everybody has to use their own badge or the system will go nuts when you try to leave."

"Oh, sure." Bethany dug in the little purse slung over her shoulder, palmed her badge in front of the reader, and stuffed it away again.

"What kind of badge is that?" I'd caught a glimpse of crimson as she tucked it away.

"Just what they gave me." She didn't meet my eyes and hurried through the door. "Have to run. My class is way around the other side. See you two later."

Bethany hugged her books tight, headed off to the right, and disappeared around the corner.

"That wasn't all kinds of weird at all." Owen swiped his badge and we both stepped through.

The first thing that struck me was the charred odor, a cross between burnt insulation and wood smoke. Subtle undertones of oil and gas, sawdust, and baking bread flooded the halls along with students heading to their next class. Our schedules were broken into two-hour blocks. For the foreseeable future, we'd start in common core magic class together. Mechanical Systems class came before lunch, then on to Industrial Design.

I wouldn't get to any welding instruction until my last block in the afternoon.

Tuesdays and Fridays were the exception. Tuesday morning classes were shortened to accommodate a special lecture, and my Friday afternoon was a solid four-hour block of Basic Welding

"Looks like I'm down this way." I spun my map around to get oriented and pointed in the opposite direction of where Bethany had headed.

"Me too." Owen compared his schedule to mine. "We're both starting in Mechanical Systems. After that, you're on your own."

He managed to make it sound as if he was doing me a favor. Sometimes I just had to marvel at how self-absorbed Owen could be. Still, there was odd comfort in knowing someone in my first inner-ring class.

We walked on under the piping and glow bulb runs as people ducked through doorways and the crowd thinned. I certainly hadn't memorized everyone from our class in the first two weeks, but figured most of the people disappearing into the doors set at oddly uneven intervals had to be a semester ahead of us. Most everyone wore yellow badges, but two greens and an unusual blue one flashed past as we rushed down the hall.

Classes turned out to be smaller and more structured than Ms. Schlaza's boot camp. Including Owen and me, a dozen students gathered in the small classroom and took up half of the desks facing the two big smart boards at the front of the room. Unlike our morning dungeon, the room's off-white walls and speckled linoleum floor gave no hint to Attwater's unique nature. It was easy to imagine myself in class at a normal, run-of-the-mill university. The only real giveaway were those creepy glow lights.

We each received electronic copies of a big fat textbook and specifications for everything from internal combustion engines to hydroelectric power-plants. Without constant badgering to correct our spell work or better apply elemental power, I soon found myself settling in to enjoy the block of instruction.

At lunch, the atmosphere was markedly subdued. An undertone of determination had settled over us, and quiet discussions and debates replaced the typical raucous exchanges. Everyone ate with purpose, as if unwilling to waste the scant thirty minute break. Moving beyond the initial excitement and wonder of being exposed to magic, we'd launched toward our careers. Things suddenly felt very real.

"Your folks coming tonight?" I asked Chad as the time to head to class drew close.

I didn't bother asking Owen, who'd already made his thoughts on the subject clear. Neither Bethany nor Mon had shown up, so it was just the three of us pounding down lasagna and garlic bread. With no sign of a kitchen, I had to wonder where the food was made. Maybe the culinary students had a wing and used the student body as their guinea pigs—not that I was complaining. So far, the food was top notch.

"You bet they are. Mama's gotta see where her baby boy spends his days." Chad crossed to the bussing station and sorted out his dishes. "The big problem is going to be keeping all the visitors from talking about where they live. I mean, how's that going to work? We've got students from California to Maine."

"This isn't their first rodeo." I thought he'd appreciate that term, but Chad just rolled his eyes at my self-satisfied grin. "I'm sure the school has a plan."

"That's another thing," Owen said as the three of us headed out of the commons. "How long's this place been in business? A decade? A century? Most schools boast about their age. You'd think there'd be a big stone monument in the atrium saying, 'founded by Percival Needs-a-Job-Quick Attwater in year such-and-such to help his fellow man.'"

"Do you think Attwater is a family name?" I asked.

"No idea." Owen shrugged and stepped up to the access door to swipe his badge. Rivets the size of eggs outlined raised panels on the burnished metal that looked to be a cross between stainless steel and bronze. "I'm just saying that a little history on the place would be nice."

"Feels like it's *always* been here." There was a quiet presence to even the contemporary classrooms that gave me the bizarre notion that Attwater might be really old, or even timeless. I snorted at the thought. "Wherever *here* is. How's it possible that a place this big doesn't have windows?"

The only window I'd run across so far had been in the dean's office. Or, more precisely, there had been a set of heavy curtains behind his desk that I assumed hid a window. Aside from giving a hint as to where we spent our days, being able to look outside would definitely make the place cheerier.

"Actually, next Tuesday's lecture is supposed to cover the school's history and mission. Ought to get an answer then." Chad swiped and hustled through the door. "Gotta run. I'll see you gents tonight."

Industrial Design class went fine and was similarly attended by just over a dozen students. The only bad thing was my growing suspicion that both classes would require a ton of study, memorization, and testing, things I had hoped to avoid in a trade school. On the other hand, it made sense. I wasn't really here just to become a certified welder. Learning specifics about a variety of systems and equipment might be necessary for me to apply my magical talent to best effect. I just didn't yet understand how the curriculum would shape my overall training.

My last class of the day, Welding Basics, was fun and kept me from obsessing over the academic challenges ahead. We got to play with stick electrodes, spot welding, and cutting torches. All just small exercises to give us a feel for the gear, but it was nice to roll up my sleeves and get down and dirty.

There were only eight people in my class, which gave Mr. Martin, our wild-haired instructor, time to work with each of us individually. Between his seven-foot frame, pointy black beard, and fly-away hair-don't, the man struck a cross between Einstein and Abe Lincoln. Another pleasant surprise was Gina. The cute curly-haired woman who'd chased us out of the commons that first night filled in as a teacher's aide and second pair of eyes to walk us through each technique we got to try.

All in all it proved a satisfying first day. As I headed for the iron-bound door amidst a small herd of people with badges in hand, it struck me that the odors from earlier in the day might come from the students themselves. Even after removing my leather smock and gloves, no one could miss the acrid reek of smoke and hot metal wafting off me. No wonder trade classes were held at day's end. I took a mental note to shower before returning with the folks.

9. Parents' Day

O DDLY, EXCEPT FOR Dad pointing out that we were only the second car in the parking lot, neither of my parents seemed surprised or questioned how the waiting area could be packed with so many people. The other car would have been Larry's. I spotted him tucked in a corner behind a tall trim couple in matching business suits who I assumed were his parents.

The three bigger-than-life people wearing cowboy hats were impossible to miss. Chad gave me a friendly wave and pulled the other two over.

"This is Jason Walker," Chad said by way of introduction. "He's the welder-to-be I told you about. We should have him out to the ranch sometime."

Mr. and Mrs. Stillman both had a hearty, calloused grip. After a short handshaking bonanza and exchange of names, my mother went straight for what I'd worried about.

"Not many farmsteads around here." Mom tapped her chin as if trying to work out the puzzle. "The old du Pont farm on the edge of town has been converted to housing so…" she trailed off as a subtle trace of magical energy shimmered around our small group. Then Mom's face brightened. "Oh, I just love your hat. It's always hard for me to pull off headwear. May I?"

Mom held her hands out, and Mrs. Stillman handed over her Stetson with a laugh. The next thing I knew, the two women were over by the plate glass window checking out their reflections and swapping accessories. Meanwhile, our fathers launched into a pointed discussion on how it was long overdue for trade schools to come back into fashion given the critical shortage of skilled labor.

"That was weird," Chad whispered.

"I'm guessing there won't be a problem with families comparing where they live."

Whatever spells the school used to keep curiosity at bay unfortunately didn't extend to civility or good manners. The Ashburns, Larry's lovely parents, were in a shouting match about why they never got a free ride to college. The pair seemed to be mad at their son and wanted to know what kind of scam he'd pulled "this time." A no-man's zone formed around the trio, despite Mrs. Ashburn trying to bait those closest into the conversation with pointed questions about their view of unearned handouts.

Everyone soon headed into the building proper to mingle. Hors d'oeuvres and drinks flowed from discreet wait staff who filtered through the crowd refilling glasses and offering heavy snacks. Mr. Gladstone welcomed the group from atop a boulder along the atrium path, thanking everyone for taking time from their busy schedule and giving a thumbnail outline of how the evening would progress.

Following an hour presentation in the auditorium, families would be led through the school in small groups by second year students and finish the night in vocational classrooms. To encourage wandering and exploration, many doors had been left open for the evening, but the dean cautioned visitors not to try to enter closed areas. These remained off limits due to the sensitive nature of certain advanced studies.

The big gathering reminded me of our first day's orientation, although the information focused much more on the school's training objectives and did not conclude with magical fireworks that set off the sprinklers. Instead, the question and answer session opened the floodgates to a deluge of pedantic concerns about how to make up sick days, handle family vacations, and other mind-numbing scenarios that just wasted time.

Financial questions were notably absent since we'd all received full scholarships. Bethany's question about second year housing seeded a lively discussion and earned her a sharp glare from her primly dressed mother.

Owen showed up alone dressed in his best jeans and a Seether graphic tee showing a bizarre scene from one of the band's music videos. He wasn't tethered to any particular tour by family members and tended to drift between groups. After the large assembly split up, he'd tagged along with Chad, apparently curious about the cowboy's path to weather forecasting. But later, another loud altercation where Lars's parents bemoaned their own lack of opportunity while simultaneously insisting their son be given some sort of special accommodations drove him toward the welding lab.

"No wonder that poser Lars is so messed up." Owen slid into the back of the classroom while Mr. Martin and Gina discussed the certification process. "My ears would be bleeding if I had to live with that crap twenty-four seven."

"Who knew?" I actually felt sorry for the bully. "Have you run into Bethany since the groups split off? It looked like her mom was ready to drag her home after the housing discussion."

"Yeah, not sure I'd want to live here, but to each his own." He jerked a thumb down the hall. "Last I saw, Schlaza was reading their group the riot act back in the dungeon, going on about discipline and putting in extra effort to make something of themselves. Honestly, I think some of those parents were scared. Bethany's mom kind of looked fanatical though, piled on like she'd been trying to get her daughter to pick up the slack since birth. Her dad seems cool though and threw out a couple mild comments about teacher responsibilities that actually set the ice queen back on her heels."

I knew our friend had issues with her mom, but was glad she had someone in her corner back home. "Can't wait for this circus to be over."

"At least your parents are normal," was the last thing Owen ever said.

Okay, well, the last independent thought he voiced for at least the next twenty minutes because my folks descended like vultures as the formal presentation finished.

"What a handsome friend," Mom gushed as she closed on us with Dad in tow.

From there, she peppered poor Owen with questions and compliments, almost like she was crushing on him, which of course wasn't the case since my Dad was right there chiming in too. What the heck was in those drinks?

I'd managed to break in on Mom's monopoly when the lights flashed and sent everyone into a tizzy, but the teacher assured us that it was probably just a warning that the open house was about to end. By the time we broke away and got clear for a few minutes, Owen's cocky veneer was thoroughly cracked. To be frank, I wasn't sure why he hadn't just excused himself after the first salvo.

"Sorry," I said as we headed for the commons under the pretext of grabbing more food before they kicked everyone out. "That was brutal."

"Exhausting." But Owen wore a kind of faraway smile.

"I get that it's kinda silly at your age, but if your mom was here she would have run interference with my mom to give you some breathing room." I thought back to my mom swapping accessories with Chad's. "They come in handy that way."

The smile slid from Owens face and he shook his head, suddenly sobered. "Dude, I'd give anything for that. Mom died in a car wreck a few years back."

"Aw geez, I didn't know." I felt like a real jerk for dropping not-too-subtle hints all week that he should bring his folks.

"Old news." He snagged a plate by the entry and headed for a platter of sliders one of the wait staff had put on the kitchenette counter. "Before you ask, Dad was never the same after the accident. I'm not exactly welcome in his life."

Ground beef goodness replaced the awkward thread of discussion, but standing by the fridge felt odd. Especially when the lights dimmed, another not-too-subtle signal for everyone to go the hell home.

We hoofed our laden plates over to our usual table out of habit only to find Bethany had slipped in behind us. She sat with head down, drawing furiously in her sketchbook.

"Hey, little girl, what's up?" Owen looked happy to have a new subject.

I couldn't tell if his greeting was condescending or just flippant. That deceptively charming smile often made it hard to tell. Owen tended to skirt the line with Bethany. Chad and I had called him out on it a couple of times, but Bethany herself made it clear she could handle Owen if he went too far. Maybe he just thought he was being funny. Either way, she ignored us both, selected a thicker stick of graphite from her mobile supplies, and added shading to the figure taking shape on the page.

The lights flashed frantically for a good thirty seconds this time. Last call for burgers for sure. Herds of visitors already hustled past the commons, talking excitedly as they headed for the gateways home. Banging sounded above us like another water hammer that couldn't quite make up its mind which way to go. It finally rattled along the pipes heading out into the corridor, but instead of dissipating, if anything, it grew louder.

People in the departing crowd scanned the ceiling in alarm, and the flow toward the exit sped up considerably as the damned lights sputtered again. Bethany sucked in a sharp breath, and her hand flew even faster across the page.

"Do they *want* to cause a panic?" Whoever manned that dimmer switch had issues, but at the moment I was more worried about our friend. "Bethany?"

She lifted her head as if noticing us for the first time, and the crushed look in those shining hazel eyes broke my heart. Black streaks stained her cheeks where she'd wiped away tears with a graphite covered hand as she worked.

"Jason, I—" She sobbed and tried again. "I screwed up big time."

All I could figure was that she'd had a fight with her mother. I'd already bungled a discussion about parents with Owen and didn't want to make her feel even worse.

"Do you want to talk about it?" I chose my words carefully and shot a warning look at Owen, who raised his hands in surrender to show he'd be good. "Or maybe we could go find Mon for you?"

I was an only child, but plenty of my friends growing up had sisters. The mother-daughter relationship could be a precarious beast, and advice from guys probably wouldn't be helpful. I just hoped she hadn't burned her bridges too badly because Attwater seemed pretty strict about not offering residency to first year students. Given the sour look on her mother's face during the Q&A session, I was pretty sure that's what this was all about.

"One of my drawings escaped!" she wailed as the floor lurched sideways and dumped me onto the bench.

10. Bad Lines

I TOOK A minute to process Bethany's statement. Being thrown off my feet didn't help the neurons fire, nor did the fact that the floor still shook like we were in the middle of an earthquake. Dust cascaded from overhead, and the swaying lights flicked off for a full three seconds, came back on at half strength, and then proceeded to flicker and buzz. The electric hum grew louder, and several bulbs over our heads exploded in a shower of sparks. We clearly had bigger problems than missing art, but Bethany looked miserable.

"You lost a picture?" I asked carefully.

"Jesus, *that's* what this is all about?" Owen threw up his hands. "Maybe we should focus on getting our butts out of here before the building shakes apart and worry about your lost masterpiece later."

"I didn't *lose* anything." Bethany's face hardened, and she thumped her sketchpad with a fist. "I had to get away from all the judgmental bull and slipped off to a little equipment room where I could be alone. I only put my pad down for a second, but something crawled out and slipped into one of those big upright power panels. That's never happened before."

"What slipped into the panel?" I asked. "This doesn't make sense."

"I had to search for who was missing."

She flipped through her drawings and laid the pad out flat to show a winged insect rendered in pencil along the bottom of the page. I recognized it as the butterfly creature she'd made the day we'd met. The upper half of the page was blank. *Impossible!* I pulled the book close, but the space above the butterfly was smooth and pristine. Not so much as a smudge remained of the squat gargoyle that had shared the page. It was as if it never existed.

"No eraser works that well." I jabbed a finger at the blank section, then turned to Owen. "There used to be a monster there."

"I told you that I make pictures come to life," she said with a huff.

"Yeah, but like cartoons." I should have realized she'd meant magic cartoons.

"They've never left the page before." She looked down at the paper and stroked the blank spot. "But I saw something slide onto the metal panel, slip through the seam, and disappear. It happened so fast that I thought it was my imagination. I was flipping through my drawings to double-check when the lights started going wonky."

"But why?" I asked.

"I think maybe my drawing sensed how that gremlin snake was messing around with things." Her eyes went round with the thought. "Oh, no! Mr. Gonzales is already poking around the inner ring trying to fix things. If he catches Mortimer I'll get expelled!"

Of course she'd named the gargoyle.

"So how do we track it down?" Owen shrugged at my raised eyebrow. "A two-dimensional living sketch that's slipped into the electrical system could be anywhere by now. Hell, it must be jumping between systems judging by the shaking and angry plumbing up there." He jerked his head at the ceiling.

"That's why I made this." She pulled the book around and flipped to the page she'd just been working on. "Sheila can find Mortimer."

This new creature resembled an anteater with a long prehensile snout, except that big bat ears rose from either side of the narrow head and a wide flat tail dragged the ground. A collar circled its neck, and the connecting leash trailed off the edge of the page. Bethany had drawn a matching loop around her left wrist, a magical tether connecting her to her drawing.

"We can follow her and get my other drawing back before someone finds him."

"Good plan. What could possibly go wrong?" Owen's words dripped sarcasm, but the thought of a covert operation must have had a certain appeal because he clapped his hands and pushed away from his plate. "Where do we start?"

"I just need you two to keep watch and run interference. Buy me enough time in the equipment room to track him down. I'm pretty sure I can coax Mortimer back."

Heading to the inner ring was like swimming upstream, but the departing crowd quickly thinned. Luckily, we didn't run into our parents, and I texted Dad to let him know we were helping hunt down the problem as a form of on the job training. There was a bit of truth to that.

"Okay, so where's this equipment room?" I asked as we circled around to the far side of the inner ring.

We'd already passed several alcoves with access panels I thought might be our destination, scurried out of the way of teachers hunting up stray visitors, and pretended we were heading out instead of in. We headed down one flight of stairs to a fresh hallway of rooms. I didn't think any of us had classes on the atrium level.

"The next ring in." Bethany's reply didn't make sense.

I was about to point out that we were already skirting around the inner ring of classrooms, when she headed down a short hallway that ended at a distressed metal door like the one leading in from the commons. But this door faced the wrong direction. Instead of leading back to whatever was under the commons in the outer ring, it pointed inward so must have guarded some high-security classroom.

Bethany slid her badge from its hiding place in her books and swiped us through. I got a good look at it this time, yellow with a bold red border.

"You two don't have access, so we have to leave together. Okay?"

"What kind of room…" The question died on my lips as we stepped through into another hallway.

This new hallway was lined with iron-banded wood plank doors set at intervals similar to how our classrooms were set up. The corridor turned off at right angles in the distance to either side, a second inner ring.

"Hurry." Bethany jogged off to the right, and we followed. "There's more to Attwater than you think. This isn't even the last set of rooms. I don't know how many nested hallways there are, or really how many levels. Here it is."

Not all the doors required badge access. We stopped in front of one of the occasional maintenance alcoves. Fortunately there were no teachers in sight at the moment, but I didn't know how we'd explain ourselves if one came along. I voiced my concerns to Bethany, urging her to hurry.

"I'll be as quick as I can," she said. "Hide your badges so you don't stand out and just be cool."

She ducked inside and eased the door closed behind her.

"As I said before." Owen stuffed his bright yellow badge into his pocket, and I did the same. "What could possibly go wrong?"

The building rumbled again as if in answer. We stayed glued to either side of the alcove, presumably ready to shoo away any prying eyes. A pair of students popped into the hallway a few doors down and headed toward us. I braced myself for a confrontation, casting about for an excuse as to why we were lurking in the shadows, while simultaneously trying to melt into them. But there was no way the two girls wouldn't see us. For once, Owen's gregarious smile and age worked in our favor.

"Hey there, ladies." He stepped right out and greeted the girls. "Can you believe these lights?"

"I know, right?" The redhead shared a look with her blond friend before smiling down at the floor. "It's a little scary."

"I wouldn't worry." Owen turned up the wattage on his smile and it actually…worked. "We've got a super staff here at Attwater. Just keep to the center of the hallways on your way out and you'll be just fine. Everything will be sorted out shortly."

"That's good to hear." The girl looked like she wanted to say more, but her friend tugged her arm. "Well, have to get going. Maybe we'll see you around?"

"I certainly hope so." He winked, and the girls laughed as they linked arms and continued on.

"That was fascinating, yet disturbing." And I wasn't jealous at all.

A muffled series of thumps followed by a curse sounded from within the equipment room, and the door flew open.

Bethany rushed past, but her feet weren't moving fast enough to keep up with her body. Her left arm was pulled high in the air, and the leash inked around her wrist stretched away to disappear into the electrical conduit secured near the top of the wall. It was like the doodle encircling her wrist had been sketched out into the air.

"Sheila's on the trail!" was all she managed as she held on for dear life.

We hurried to follow as the leash jerked Bethany left and right on its way down the hall and disappeared into the next alcove. She caught up enough to throw the door open before plowing into it.

"You okay?" I grabbed the door before it slammed shut.

"Mortimer's really spooked." She pulled out her sketchbook. "Give me a minute to calm him down."

I nodded and eased the door closed just as Owen cleared his throat.

"What are you two doing down here?" Mr. Gonzales strode up the hall carrying his tool bag and a jangling handful of chains.

"Oh hey, Mr. G." I kept my back to the door, but he waved me aside and peaked inside—no reaction. "We just…um…wanted to help."

"Yeah, help." Owen piled on with a nod for me to continue.

"You know with all this," I waved at the flickering lights and rumbling pipes, "I'm thinking it's a condensation issue, and probably a bad junction box with a partial ground."

"I *wish* it was something that simple." He actually laughed as he separated out a short length of chain and proceeded to thread it first through the door handle and then around the conduit penetrating the wall. "But someone's been monkeying around with the building's systems. Equipment rooms are off limits until I get this under control."

"But wait, we—"

"I get it Jason; I was young once. You want to prove yourself." He snapped a brass padlock onto the chain, but his tone softened as he misinterpreted my expression. "Don't worry. I promise that Attwater will give you plenty of opportunities to use your talent. Let me handle this one. Maybe you can help out after you've had more training." He clapped me on the back. "Heck, I could use an apprentice around here. It's a big place."

"Sure, okay, Mr. G. I can help lock up if you want." I reached for the chains and locks, thinking maybe I could sneak the key to Owen, who just stood there gaping.

"Next time, my friend, next time. You two finish up and go help make sure the visitors all get out without trampling each other. Mr. Gladstone would appreciate that."

I nodded numbly as he continued down the hall and ducked into another alcove further on. We heard the chain rattling as he secured the next equipment room door, then watched him move on and disappear around the corner. Once he was out of sight, I tapped on the door.

"Bethany?"

"Still working," came her muffled and strained reply.

A string of curses followed. The words were indistinct so she must have moved back from the door again, but her tone could have blistered paint. I tugged on the padlock, which of course accomplished nothing.

"Let the master handle this." Owen cracked his knuckles, cradled the lock in his palm, and gathered power.

I might not be the best at handling magic yet, but could feel the distinct "flavor" of earth energy trickle from his fingers and flow with steadfast resolve into the lock. Since metals were of the ground, it was an appropriate element to manipulate the lock or simply melt the shank.

"Shit!" The brass flared with power and Owen snatched his hand back. "Stupid thing is warded."

We hadn't learned diddly about wards yet, only that they offered magic protection to objects or locations. An accomplished practitioner could set wards to simply deter meddling or amp them all the way up to lethal. The other problem with wards was that they could trip an alarm, so we might not have much time before the maintenance manager or someone else on staff came to investigate.

Owen shook his hand out, but didn't look any the worse for wear as we studied the lock. A knock on the door made us both jump.

"Okay, I've got him." Bethany sounded out of breath as she tried to open the door, but of course it didn't budge. "You can let me out now."

"So, funny thing." I kept my voice light as I whispered through the seam. "Mr. G. locked you in with a magic padlock. But we're working on it." I added that last at her squawk of protest.

"Maybe the chain…" Owen reached out a tentative hand, but pulled back before touching the links. "Damn!"

"The conduit can't be protected." I felt the thick plastic sheathing that insulated the electrical run that the chain looped around. "But we'd have to cut the power to keep from getting fried. Maybe a shunt—"

Something poked my left arm, and I looked down to see a sheet of paper sticking through the seam around the door. I blinked at the dancing page. Was Bethany passing the gargoyle out to us?

"Touch it to the lock," Bethany said, wiggling the sheet so that it jumped faster.

I grabbed the edge. A little tug of war ensued, but she didn't release her end.

"I need to keep hold. Just push it against the damned lock—please!"

The sheet just reached the padlock, and I pressed the back of the paper against brass, keeping my fingers clear of the metal surface. A pencil sketch of a key stood out against the page under the dim lights. Jagged black teeth formed an irregular pattern along the blade extending from the leering skull that would be used to turn the key.

As soon as the paper made contact, the drawing billowed and shimmered. The key crawled toward the lock, shrinking so that it could enter the hole, and disappeared. I cringed, waiting for a flash of warding energy like the one that had repelled Owen's attempt. With a quiet click, the lock fell open.

Owen stripped the chain away and opened the door. Bethany smiled in triumph, but looked terrible. Her hair appeared to be trying to escape in all directions, and she leaned on me as she limped through the door.

"Better lock it up again," I told Owen, who did so after a moment's hesitation. "Bethany, that was awesome."

I gaped at the blank page I still held and offered it to her.

"Not now." She shook her head. "Let's just get out of here."

She stumbled again, but not because of fatigue. Wisps of smoke rose from the sketchpad clutched in the crook of her free arm, and she held tight as it bucked and tried to pull from her grasp. That was one ornery drawing.

On the way out, we only had to take cover once. Luckily, we heard Ms. Schlaza berating some poor soul from a good distance off and were able to hide in the stairwell. When she finished her tirade, Mr. Gonzales skulked past our hiding spot, still carrying his beloved tool kit and with his proverbial tail between his legs. That woman was as bad as Lars.

Owen pulled me back when I took a step forward, intent on giving the ice queen a piece of my mind. Crisis averted, we made our way back to the commons as the catering staff finished cleaning up. A handful of hardy visitors still roamed the hallways around the atrium now that the building no longer seemed in danger of collapse. From start to finish, we'd probably only been gone twenty minutes.

"You guys are the best, thanks." Bethany looked a lot less frazzled than she had after picking the lock.

She gave us each a quick hug before plopping down at the table and cautiously setting down her sketchpad. The book no longer fought her, but she bit her lip before reaching out with a shaking hand.

"Happy to help," I said with a glance at my phone. "But our parents might have a cow."

"I know mine will," Bethany said. "Let me just check on Mortimer."

Really? After all that drawing had put us through? But part of me understood. If those sketches were anything like my own creations, she'd have an emotional connection with them. It always tore my heart out when my automata self-destructed. Having her pet cartoon run amuck couldn't feel much better.

"Any idea why he went crazy?" I asked softly.

"None at all." Bethany shook her head as she found the page she was looking for and flipped the book open. "And I don't know what took a bite out of him either."

The gargoyle Mortimer was back on the page, cowering under a wing of the giant butterfly creature. His right arm ended in a jagged line just below the elbow and a big sickle of flesh—well, pencil—had been chomped out of his side, like the rogue drawing had been hit by a great white shark. Graphite dribbled from the wound, forming a pile at the bottom of the page, and Bethany grabbed her pencils.

"Give me a minute to patch Mortimer up. Then we can find our folks."

11. School Mission

M OM AND DAD were the last ones in the waiting area, and the receptionist was doing her best to get them out the door.

"There you are!" Mom cried when she spotted me.

I'd been hoping the Stillmans were still around to entertain them and keep my folks from obsessing over the "earthquake" that the administration blamed for the lights and rumbling.

Bethany needed to figure out what her drawings were up to so she could keep that from happening again. As it was, I figured the school's experts still had a chance to ferret out what went wrong and maybe trace her drawing's magical signature or something. We needed to dodge that bullet. But first I'd have to confront the parental worry engines and try to assure them that continuing at Attwater was safe.

"Sorry we got separated," I said, crossing into the room. "A few of us went down to make sure our projects were safe."

That was a lie, but one with the ring of plausibility.

"Let's get you home before this death trap building comes down around our ears." Dad put a protective arm around Mom, pushed me toward the door, and called back over his shoulder. "Thanks for letting us wait."

Lars and his parents were still in their car in the parking lot, so must have not left too long ago themselves. I didn't want to think about what they might have discussed with Mom and Dad. As it was, judging by the muffled shouting, the trio was deep in a heated argument. Thankfully their windows were up. I ducked into the backseat of Dad's car, but not before Lars caught me with a pitiful look that quickly turned to a sneer before more shouting drew his attention.

The ride home started off quiet, too quiet. I felt the storm brewing, and braced for the onslaught of questions about unsafe conditions in Attwater. But when the tsunami broke it wasn't at all what I'd expected.

"That Bethany is a cute girl," Dad said as we turned out onto the main road.

"Well sure, just a friend." What an odd thing to focus on. "She's barely eighteen."

"Sometimes a younger woman keeps you spry." He reached over and squeezed Mom's leg.

"You're terrible." Mom swatted his hand away. "Eyes on the road, mister. I think you missed the obvious."

Here it comes. I readied my Attwater defense. The school was decades if not hundreds of years old. The heating system was undergoing an upgrade. The stone foundation had withstood an unexpected quake better than any contemporary building. I was even prepared to spill the beans about the Quick-Y mart and Judge Michelson's deal, which would land me in jail if I withdrew from school.

"That Regina girl was the one making eyes at your son all night."

"Gina, the teaching aide?" I squawked. "I barely know her."

Thinking back, she *had* glanced in our direction several times, wearing that cute smile that crinkled her nose. But Gina had been helping describe the certification process. She'd looked at everyone that way. Hadn't she?

"A mother knows the look. Be careful not to break her heart if you're not interested. You'll have plenty of time to make friends, and, of course, schoolwork comes first."

They launched into a discussion about friends of theirs in college who'd been ogling each other for years before admitting their feelings and how that had almost kept them from getting together. The names of other people I'd never met flew about the car on the short drive home as my parents shifted into reminiscing mode.

They never once brought up the failing lights and shuddering building. It was as if they'd forgotten all about their emergency exodus from Attwater—as if by magic.

* * *

Everyone threw themselves into their studies, and the days flowed by. Although our individual schedules differed, the gang still got together in the commons to compare notes on common core classes and to complain about various instructors or exercises. Even with Attwater's focus on job certification and training, there was still plenty to harp on when it came to the supporting coursework.

"Common Core is actually fun now that Mary is in charge." I told Chad at lunch on Tuesday.

Owen nodded his agreement, but Bethany just kept her head down and worked in her sketch book. She probably hadn't even heard. The class had always been a breeze for her anyway, but she still cringed whenever the ice queen tried to beat expertise into less advanced students like yours truly.

As if in answer to our prayers, Mary Eisner now ran our morning class. None of us were certain what the deal was with

Ms. Schlaza, but the rumor mill claimed she had taken a sabbatical to handle a special school project. She hadn't been seen since the open house, which suited most of us just fine. Under Ms. Eisner's gentle guidance, I'd actually managed a few small successes with spells that I'm sure would have been impossible before.

The floor rumbled.

Out of reflex, we all steadied our trays as the table vibrated. I hunched over my burger, shielding it and the fries from whatever debris might fall from the ceiling. Most of the gunk up there had already shaken loose, but I hated crunchy surprises in my food.

"Easy, old girl." Chad patted the stone column he leaned against as the tremor subsided.

"Man's got a way with more than just horses and hogs," Owen said.

The rumblings never lasted long, but the building still shivered occasionally, like a dog trying to shake off fleas, aftershocks from the damage done during the open house. Whatever mischief Mortimer had gotten into left lingering effects. Mr. Gonzales had a team looking into what had happened so we weren't entirely off the hook. But with each passing day, our confidence grew that we wouldn't be found out.

"Any diagnosis on Mortimer?" I asked when Bethany finally looked up.

"Nothing definite." She closed her sketchbook. "Whatever security measures the school has in the electrical system really did a number on him. I had to redraw his missing bits three times before the repairs stopped crumbling away. His arm is still touch and go. Other than that, he's recovering. I've examined my bond with him every which way I can think of, but nothing's out of whack. Of course, Mort's still pretty agitated. All of them are on edge, but that's not too surprising, considering."

She stroked the book in thought, but didn't elaborate. In her spare time, Bethany had been working non-stop to figure out why her drawing had run amuck. I assumed he'd gotten a whiff of something tasty in the power lines, but had no idea what a magically animated gargoyle drawing might eat. Apparently, neither did Bethany.

The whistle blew and we all scrambled to our feet.

"Sit together at the lecture?" Chad asked as he slung his bag over one shoulder.

"Sounds good." I got a confirming nod from Owen, and Bethany mumbled what sounded like agreement.

Thanks to the Tuesday lecture series, a particularly dry discussion on gear ratios in Mechanical Systems class got cut short. Owen and I found Bethany working on her gargoyle again in the back row of the auditorium, and we whistled Chad over when his wide-brimmed hat floated in on a sea of late students.

The lecture started with the usual announcements, but I sat up straighter when the dean invited Mr. Gonzales to take the microphone.

"I'm sure everyone is wondering about the odd events on the night of our open house." The dean frowned down at his hands before continuing. "Regretfully, we had to ensure word did not spread. Your instructors have no doubt explained that all visitors were nudged away from remembering the emergency, but rest assured that your safety is of the utmost importance to Attwater. Maintenance and security continue to investigate the matter further. Please give Mr. Gonzales your attention."

The maintenance engineer nodded graciously and stepped up to the podium. "An unknown magical force breeched the school's defenses and attacked several key systems. Although we cannot pinpoint the specific spell used, we are in the process of repairing the damage left in its wake. You can expect a few more days of tremors and lighting issues. Please contact myself or an instructor if you see anything out of the ordinary. Under no circumstances should anyone attempt to directly approach suspicious activity or use the elevators until they are declared safe."

We have elevators?

"Bet they figure it's more gremlins." Chad gave Bethany a nudge. "I think your sketches are in the clear."

"Ixnay on the etchskay, okayay." I sucked at pig Latin, but they got the point. Talking about our involvement in a crowded room could be risky.

"Thank you, Mike." The dean again took the podium as Mr. Gonzales departed. "In light of recent events, I'd like to focus today's lecture on our school's mission. This discussion would normally come after the holiday break, but I feel you all need to be aware of certain…truths about your education here and the terms of your contracts."

A collective groan rose from the audience. Even the more mature folks in the crowd didn't relish the idea of talking through the pages of legalese underpinning our signatures. Over the years, I'd registered for too many online games that required agreeing to indecipherable terms of service to have been bothered by the fine print on our contracts. I had of course skimmed the document, but hadn't noted anything egregious.

"They better not be talking about student loans," Bethany said. "That scholarship is the only reason Mom hasn't yanked my butt out of here."

"I promise, this will not be dry material." Gladstone gave a rueful smile and tapped a button on the podium.

The big screen behind him lit up with a high-def image of the Earth, the vibrant "blue marble" view as seen from space. A yellow triangle popped up over North America accompanied by the stylized A we'd come to associate with Attwater. Finally, a clue as to where the heck we teleported to each morning. Somewhere in the Midwest—no, the west coast. Wait. The damned icon drifted over the continent, never settling in one spot.

"The Attwater Academy is one of three trade schools in our system." The Earth rotated, and another triangle labeled B showed up over Africa. "Bashar and Chingyow, our sister schools, have the same mission, to train and prepare students for vital work in key areas around the globe." A third symbol inscribing a C drifted over Asia. "You will each become a master of your trade as well as your magical talent. As stated in our literature, the placement office will carefully weigh your abilities and match you up to appropriate jobs. While keeping vital infrastructure and industries manned is important, your main purpose will be to counter this."

He pressed another button and the image lit up with red starbursts, as if someone were bombing the surface of the planet. Lines spread from each impact, shooting the globe with a network of crimson—thick lightning bolts in some areas, thin tendrils in others.

The spots where the spider webs originated also varied in size, ranging from simple pinpricks of red to larger patches that could cover a small state. The larger areas throbbed, giving the impression of living tumors that clung to the surface with pulsing roots or arteries. Of the dozen patches, most sat along a seaboard or river, metropolitan areas.

A gasp rose around the room, followed by shocked silence.

"What the hell *is* that?" I hadn't meant to speak out loud, but Gladstone heard thanks to everyone else suddenly going mute.

"That, Mr. Walker, is the network of evil that Attwater students have fought since the beginning. There are entities in our world that do not belong here. Their sole purpose is to disrupt the course of human civilization. They accomplish this by attacking infrastructure and industry, destroying what they can and weakening what remains. Our goal is to place you in the most advantageous position to counter this threat to our way of life."

Mr. Gladstone went on to explain how all three schools protected their respective sections of the globe, occasionally coming together to share information and strategize over new threats. As technology evolved, so did our opponent, so that placing students in facilities on the cutting edge grew increasingly important. Virtually no segment of society was safe. Every discipline from healthcare to Wall Street was under siege.

"I don't want to leave you with the impression that our graduates are in constant danger. Other systems are in place to shield the world, but things do slip through. There will be good days and bad as the threat does tend to wax and wane over the seasons and years. We can usually predict high activity far enough in advance to give warning and even hire in additional help when warranted. That being said, something changed ten years ago. Activity has inexplicably ramped up over the past decade.

"We've had to scramble to identify and train more workers. Thousands have gone before you to build out our network of graduates. You will be placed in a position where your talents are best suited to stem the threat. I'm sure you have many questions, all of which will be answered in the coming months, but you deserved to know. Do you want to see the face of your enemy?"

Cautious nods were followed by spurious calls for more info that rose to a chorus of agreement. The dean nodded and pulled up a montage of images. Ugly brutes with squat bodies and tusks stood alongside dapper businessmen and -women. Blurry outlines suggested four legged creatures, insects, and legless abominations made of dark shadows. I thought back to the snake gremlin in the coffee machine, which had the same look.

"The enemy has many faces," Gladstone said. "We will train you to sense their presence, but—as with all magic—you each will have different levels of ability. Regardless of their outward appearance, these creatures have thrived for millennia in their own domain and can take many forms. They evolve like insects, breeding new capabilities even as we move to counter them. They have been recorded as far back as aboriginal cave drawings, and religious texts more accurately depict them as demons.

"You'll learn details about their hierarchy later in the year. Suffice to say that most are lower level urchins focused on simple mischief and spreading chaos." He pointed to one of the shadowy figures. "Often when you run across inexplicably broken equipment, sick animals, or failed crops, one of these shadow demons will be nearby. More direct opposition comes from these ugly ones. They should be easy to spot, but you'd be surprised at how well some can hide in plain sight. They're called lurkers due to that ability. You and your fellow workers are at risk when this demon is around, so you'll want to act fast to avoid casualties." The dean slid his laser pointer over to linger on a woman in a dark business suit. "Last and most dangerous are the mimics. These creatures assume human form and insinuate themselves in key positions. Fortunately, they are rather rare and there are a few telltale signs that can be used to identify their nature. The vast majority of you will never deal with a mimic. For those that do, the school will ensure you have plenty of backup and intel. Effectively taking down a mimic requires months of preparation.

"So, there you have it. Magic is real. Banishing demons is our objective. And along the way, you each receive top-notch training and lucrative careers. Any questions?"

The room exploded into bedlam, which for some reason made Mr. Gladstone smile. He finally threw one of his pyrotechnic spells into the rafters. The echoing report shocked those flinging out questions into silence, and the dean had teachers call on one student at a time.

Maybe ten questions got addressed, but really didn't bring that much more information to light. Yes, the demons seemed to be bent on destroying mankind, perhaps weakening us for some major assault. No, they didn't necessarily come from a Christian version of hell, just another plane of existence. Those sorts of things. Everyone wanted to know how and why. I was more interested in who sent them. Maybe the mimics were the ones in charge, but it stood to reason there would be someone or something higher in the chain of command. The other bit of info on the more practical side was salary. The school kept touting high pay, so someone was footing the bill for expertise beyond simple trade labor. I also wondered if there'd be bonuses for taking down a demon. But the session ended before I could ask.

"It's gotta be a conspiracy," Owen said as we gathered after school. "Placing demon operatives high up, taking over industry."

"Yeah, but who's pushing it and why?" I asked.

"Does there have to be a reason?" Bethany asked from across the table. Mon sat by her side nodding in solemn agreement. "Sometimes things are just dark."

"Knowledge is power." I took a swig of coffee to stave off the sugar crash that would come on the heels of the junk food I'd called lunch. "There has to be an end game beyond 'taking over' or disrupting life."

"And what are these other mysterious outfits that have failed to protect the world?" Owen answered his own question and expanded the conspiracy to both sides. "Other schools I'm guessing, but seems like we ought to learn more about how these demons slipped past them before taking on any ourselves."

The discussion became a kind of brainstorming session. We threw out ideas about how best to defeat the demon scourge, never mind the fact that we'd just learned of it and had almost no training. In a way, we were psyching each other up for whatever lay ahead. I think it helped us all overcome the shock of being informed we were to be demon hunters. Plus, it was a fun mental exercise.

"Not something that's going to get solved at a lunch table, I figure," Chad finally said when the recommendations had grown truly outlandish. "But how about this one, who do you think is footing the bill to put us in jobs with inflated wages?"

"If the schools have been around for centuries, they probably have a big old investment portfolio," I ventured. "Demon hunters deserve bonuses."

"Just wonderful." Bethany had grown quiet and dejected as we kicked thoughts around.

"Cheer up." Chad shifted gears. "From the sound of things, I'd say you and Mortimer are off the hook. They don't seem to know what got into the system."

"Isn't that a little weird?" I asked. "All these magical experts and they can't even track something like that down." I got an offended glare from Bethany. "Not that I want them to. It's just... hell, even the gremlin in the coffee machine didn't come up."

"Maybe they don't want to panic the students or look weak," Owen said.

"I for one am looking forward to demon hunting classes!" It was the first time Mon had actually joined one of our discussions, and the hard glint in her dark eyes made me wish she hadn't.

From there the conversation spiraled around the various television series that showcased teenagers hunting supernatural creatures. But I had the feeling we would be coming up against something very different.

12. The Other Half

DESPITE THE ADMINISTRATION'S assurances, the building's disturbances never truly stopped, but over the next several months did stabilize into an oddly familiar routine.

Like clockwork, there'd be a violent lurch just before mid-morning break, cascading light failures come late afternoon, and often a peaceful minute of total blackout in the evening. The eight o'clock curfew remained in effect for the entire first semester, but I liked to stay right up to the last minute. The others usually bailed before then, which gave me time to study and catch up on reading.

Then there was Gina. She always hurried off after welding class, but seemed genuinely happy to see me in the evenings. I'd grown used to sitting and chatting for the fifteen or twenty minutes before she headed for the inner-ring and night classes.

Many things at Attwater had become familiar, including Friday morning rounds with Mr. Gonzales, who'd agreed to let me tag along to learn the job better. Maintenance wouldn't be exactly what I would do for a career, but the constant string of repairs the poor guy got called to deal with made for good experience. Plus, hanging with Mr. G. helped me catch wind of any breaking info that might incriminate Bethany.

After a few weeks, Mr. Gonzales had largely dropped the internal investigation into the continuing power and structural fluctuations, opting for a theory that forces outside the school caused our continued issues. Still, on three separate occasions I'd spotted him hurrying through the halls with a capture device sizzling and smoking in his bag. So he was apparently still finding gremlins gumming up the works.

We never encountered gremlins on our Friday rounds, and whenever I tried to ask if the things still lurked in the school's machinery, the topic always twisted around until I grew worried something about Mortimer would surface. Whenever that happened, I dropped my line of questioning like a hot potato rather than put Bethany at risk. I came to suspect that he'd discovered Bethany's meddling early on and was maybe trying to protect us by steering eyes away from what had happened. That would certainly explain why neither of us much liked talking about the elephant in the building.

Things rolled along smoothly as we all prepared for holiday break, but a surprise invitation had me stopping by the dean's office early one Wednesday for morning coffee. I knocked on the heavy door and entered at a muffled "come" from within.

Dean Gladstone was dressed head to toe in his brown leather button-up steampunk outfit when I arrived. He hunched over his workbench gazing through a magnifying glass on an articulating arm, the object of his attention a granite cube a little larger than a toaster.

"Coffee's by the window," he called over his shoulder. "Carafes are labeled, Colombian, morning blend, and—" he shuddered theatrically "—a horrendous decaf of dubious pedigree."

"Colombian for me." I crossed the room to pour the rich-smelling black liquid into a mug sculpted to look like a stack of gears.

"Good man."

A sip of the scalding goodness slid down my throat, chasing away the last bit of morning chill as the dean worked. I couldn't resist slipping a finger between the heavy curtains. This was still the only window any of us had run across after months in Attwater. Morning sun reflected from snowy mountain peaks in the distance. Closer to the building lay a sun-filled courtyard. A cobblestone drive curved through the manicured lawn along the building and looped back out to a gravel road that wound off across gently rolling hills. Another wing stretched off to my right. Constructed of cut stone and pillars, the architecture looked more like an ornate estate or castle, which better matched the interior than the defunct beer barn I entered through each day. Interesting, but not enough clues to solve the mystery of Attwater's location.

"Take a look at this, Jason," the dean called.

I started at the intrusion on my musings, self-conscious of having sneaked a look, but the man didn't seem to mind and simply waved me over to the clock he worked on. At least, I was pretty sure it was a clock. The square stone box had a circular face, but instead of a pair of hands, two gemstones, one red and the other green, moved on a track around the face.

"Keep your eyes open for issues." He slid both gems to the twelve o'clock position and stepped back, beaming.

The clock rang out with a high, clear chime, and a slot opened above the dial. Figures crawled from within with each successive chime. Rather than little German dancers that might decorate an elaborate cuckoo clock, lizards crawled out with each stroke. With no visible tracks nor wires, they moved quite naturally, climbing to perch on the flat stone top, a Jackson Chameleon, Tokay Gecko, each a different species.

The lizards skittered gracefully up the clock to form a pyramid with heads swaying in time with the chime. Little flashes of magic accompanied their steps. As the twelfth hour approached, the clock face melted away. Power flared inside the fist-sized opening, and a pair of red eyes gleamed from the dark cavity. I jumped back as a black snake lunged from its lair, my mind flashing back to the striking snake gremlin.

But this was no shadowy figure. This was an actual snake, an extremely lifelike replica. Unlike the lizards, the snake moved jerkily, like one of those tourist trap toys made of interlocked blocks of wood that swayed when held by the tail. Rather than striking out, it turned back to the pile of lizards, opened its jaws, and froze.

The dean threw up his hands in disgust, pivoted to the window, and poured himself a cup.

"That's where it fails! There's something about the snake that I can't get right." He took a gulp and sighed. "And I thought two heads are better than one. Not on the snake of course. That would be a bit too much of a cliché."

"Um…I can see it's off, but…why?" I couldn't imagine anybody wanting to buy something like this, so it wasn't a production prototype. Aside from the fact it was clearly powered by magic, or at least the hourly shows were, it wouldn't be something that could be mass produced anyway.

"It's for a friend who has a rather unique reptile house. But Lin's a herpetologist at heart. Snakes are his true passion. This is a gift for his birthday, something he can display alongside his animals."

"Okay." I guess that made sense.

"The snake is supposed to come out and eat the lizards. My friend will like that. But the mechanism keeps getting cross-threaded. It's too jerky, then seizes up."

"*You* want *my* help?"

I was nothing if not good at spotting flaws. My own creations still had plenty of them, although I'd been working independently on a few baseline improvements.

"Yes, exactly. We could set it up as an independent study project. You'd receive a couple of extra credits that would contribute to the general discipline hours needed to graduate. I get relief from being stretched too thin. Spend an hour or two a week working with me. Once we get the clock ironed out, I have plenty of other projects in the works."

"I'd like that a lot." I poked at the snake, skin and scales stretching over what felt like metal framework and gearing. "We ought to construct a mechanism using nylon bushings and a pliable substrate. That would go a long way toward more natural movements."

* * *

Bethany hunched over her sketch, trying to shield it from the prying eyes of Hilda Baxter, her instructor. She cringed at the sound of the woman's riding crop smacking flesh, but at least it wasn't her own this time.

Nathan, the man off to her left, whimpered. Bethany risked a glance at his work. The bearded giant had been brash and confident early on—too confident—as he molded his clay golems with loving care.

"Thicken the torso, or his opponents will tear him to ribbons!" Baxter barked.

Stern as her voice, Ms. Baxter was stout and wide, with iron-gray hair pulled back into a severe bun. She stalked around the circle of six students like an angry badger. As far as Bethany knew, Jason and her other friends were not yet training with their specific magical talents, but in the darkened halls of the inner ring they'd jumped right in.

"It was supposed to be elegant," Nathan mumbled, but not softly enough.

"Think you know better?" Hilda was at his side in an instant, but did something much worse than raise the crop. "Then your golem must be ready for the simulator. Come!"

She marched to an oval metal door set into the side wall. Most of the school's doors would fit in a medieval castle, but this one looked more suited for a ship or submarine. The central wheel screeched as the teacher turned it counter-clockwise and six aluminum blocks—each inscribed with an archaic symbol—slid back to unlatch the door from its matching frame. The entire doorway was set about eight inches off the floor so that people had to step over the threshold. A single round window of thick glass was bolted at eye level as an observation port.

Nathan hung his head, gathered up the clay golem he'd been working on, and shuffled to the door. He looked around the room hopefully, as if for support. Finding none, his shoulders slumped. Bethany hung her head, keeping her eyes on the page before her as it blurred in and out of focus with unshed tears.

Her heart ached for the big man. The way Ms. Baxter changed their work felt like a violation, as if the woman perverted what they created. As Nathan stepped into the test chamber, Bethany studied the dragon she'd been working on. Her picture hadn't started life with razor sharp blades along tail and back, nor had she envisioned it having two heads—one that spewed acid and the other poison mist. Those and other modifications had come from the instructor's helpful…suggestions. The old battle-axe challenged them—hell, required them—to make their creations nastier, ever more deadly to the demon foes they would one day encounter.

Those modifications twisted a knife in her artistic soul. But as promised, each suggestion, each change, became easier, hurt less. All six of them were artisans. Nathan made beautiful statues that had at first reminded Bethany of elegant Lladro figurines that danced and played. One of the other men brought his wood carvings to life and an older woman made art from colored sand. But Ms. Baxter sought to strip the beauty from their work, leaving only raw functionality—fascinating in its deadly intricacies, but grotesque. Worse yet, that ugliness grew inside each of them. Every weaponized detail of Bethany's drawings were mirrored through the bond she shared with her creatures. It was hard to describe, but each mandated stroke left a smudge on her soul.

"Very lifelike, dear." Hilda stood behind her, cooing in appreciation. *Stick and carrot…stick and carrot.* "But make the teeth curved like a moray eel. That way its victim can't pull free."

Bethany imagined herself refusing, of throwing down the sketch pad and screaming at the old bat to let her work in peace. Her hand tightened on the spiral binding. She could throw the book in Hilda's face, tell her Landrake wasn't the kind of evil creature the woman tried to force him to be.

Something heavy thudded against the simulation chamber door, rattling the frame and making everyone jump. After what seemed like an eternity, three weak knocks sounded from within. Bethany blew out the breath she'd been holding. Nathan was okay. Ms. Baxter didn't appear pleased to hear the all-clear knock. She scowled at the door, then down at Bethany with a raised eyebrow, clearly done with carrots.

"Curved teeth, right." Bethany nodded, hating herself as she reached for the eraser.

When the whistle released them for the day, Bethany made her way to the end of the hall, avoiding her classmates. Not that any of the six ever felt like talking after hours of bludgeoning. She hurried on past the big circular doorway with its massive gears and lever that led even deeper into Attwater. What went on in her own wing was horrid enough, and she shivered at the thought of what darker things might lie further inside the school. Several more turns brought her to a little-used spur of corridor.

Opening the narrow access door hidden in an alcove brought a wave of relief, and Bethany sighed as the door closed behind her. She stood in the cool darkness for a moment, reveling in the quiet and breathing in the smooth aroma of charcoal, graphite, and pastels.

Throwing the switch by the door flooded the small room with light. The old storage closet was lined with largely empty shelves to which Bethany had taped her favorite drawings. Empty sketch pads sat in a neat pile near the back alongside a pile of blankets and a pillow. A smaller stack of full art pads were organized by date on a different shelf.

Bethany snuggled down into her nest, selected a thin stick of charcoal, and opened her book to a blank page. This was her sanctuary, a place she could decompress and forget about the world. Without this quiet time, she'd go insane.

Her friends wondered why she didn't meet them in the commons after classes every day. But they didn't have to put up with what she and the others endured.

Only a handful of new students got privileged access to the inner ring like she and Mon had. Bethany assumed everyone with red-bordered badges received advanced training in their magic talent like her little group of artists. But the notion wasn't easily confirmed, and talking about her training just wasn't possible outside the confines of Ms. Baxter's classroom. Even Mon skirted the issue or changed the subject whenever Bethany managed to spin their discussions around to the other girl's cosmetology coursework. Bethany did the same when Mon asked about art.

A small part of her clung to the belief this was all necessary. Her other classes certainly weren't this bad, not even common core studies with Ms. Schlaza. Hopefully, things would improve next semester. After the holidays, her graphic arts course would start up. For now she just needed to keep her head down. Every school had a few crappy teachers. Why should magical Attwater be any different?

Bethany hummed as she worked, selecting various pencils and sticks to flush out a happy octopus. As she feathered in blue shading over its pebbly hide, the drawing bobbed and swayed on the canvas page, nuzzling up to her fingers at the edge of the over-sized sketchpad.

"Now stop that." Bethany giggled at the feathery touch. "Let me finish or you'll have holes."

Her drawing tried to keep still, but just couldn't manage and kept bumping up against her hand so that filling in the rest of the outline took much longer than necessary. Bethany didn't mind. A clean feeling like fresh laundry hanging out on a sunny day washed through the bond she cemented in place with the last pencil stoke. The happy creature wrapped tentacles around her fingers, making soft pops as she shifted position. So tenacious.

"I'll call you tenacious Tina," Bethany proclaimed as she gently pried her hand away and tugged the page free of its binding. "You keep guard over the others and make sure no one gets into anymore mischief."

She shot a pointed glare at Mortimer, who was taped to the bottom shelf where she could keep an eye on the gargoyle. He had the good grace to blush, charcoal smudges rising to his bulbous cheeks.

Tina went on the top shelf near the front, where she could keep an eye on the others. Bethany grinned at the octopus' simple lines and soft curves. There wasn't a tooth, claw, or offensive weapon to be seen, just a friendly drawing scooting from side to side on the page. Her wavy pupils scanned the room, lighting on a sketch then moving to another. She took her task seriously, making Bethany's chest swell with pride. She'd have to take time to draw in a background with fish for Tina to munch on, but it was already getting late, and–

The door rattled as if someone was trying to open it. No, the sound came from the bottom edge of the door where a dog or cat might scratch to be let inside. The sound grew insistent, then stopped abruptly with a muffled pop. Bethany grabbed a short metal cross-piece that had once been attached to the shelves and crept forward. When she pulled the door back, no one was there.

Light gouges ran across the bottom door panel, but she had no way of knowing if they were new or had been there all along. Adjacent to the marks, she found a blackened section of insulation on the cable running up the wall.

What the hell?

13. Time Marches

T HE SNAKE SLID gracefully from its lair. Thick black coils encircled the clock body as the serpent made its way to the pile of lizards, snatched the fat chameleon, and gulped it down.

"Nice work, Jason," Dean Gladstone said as our animatronic construct selected and swallowed a second victim.

All I'd done was change the mechanics to use a coiled polymer, similar to PVC, for the snake's skeleton. That allowed it to stretch and move while keeping its girth. More importantly, the design left the serpent hollow so its meal could be funneled back into the clock housing and reset for the next show. The dean had tied off the supporting spells that simulated the lifelike motion. He also programmed a variety of scripts for the snake to follow, which made each performance a little different.

I'd watched closely and even learned a thing or two about ensuring the magic worked smoothly with mobile and fixed points of the underlying mechanism. His magic felt different than my own, but with enough similarities that I'd been able to spot several rookie mistakes I typically built into my own designs. Mistakes that forced things in vaguely unnatural ways.

The dean assured me that small nuances stressed the overall system, which would be why the more instructions I layered into my creations the more likely they were to quit, meltdown, or otherwise self-destruct.

"Thanks, Dean. Can I try that spare lizard now?" I looked to the drawer under the clock.

The gift included a pile of spare parts, additional lizard species, and even two alternate snake skins to change the black mamba to a diamond back or python. I'd been applying the lessons from our last three work sessions to a sleek blue-tongued skink. I itched to power the little guy up and see what happened.

"I don't see why not." The dean laughed, pulled out the side project, and placed the skink on his workbench. "Please don't take offense, but precautions may be in order."

He ran his hands over our clock. Magic flared as his fingers worked a simple pattern in front of the face, almost like he was tying off a bow. We'd heard about magical shields, but I'd never seen one set. To be honest there wasn't anything to actually see now either, just a sense of quiet power surrounding the clock.

I stepped up to the lifeless skink, suddenly nervous as the dean slipped on his special goggles and picked through the four sets of lenses that poked up on delicate metal arms. We'd worked on the design together, but the lizards were very different from what I usually constructed. These were built on frames with pivoting front and rear legs under a molded elastic exterior. Two simple air and earth spells animated each lizard.

I pushed a trace of power into the small figure, layering simple instructions into the node behind its eyes that I imagined to be its brain. Strings of power connected to the legs and would trigger the spells to guide the skink like a marionette.

I told it to crawl through Mr. Gladstone's big ring of keys, climb the hammer leaning against the pegboard of hanging tools, and scurry back along the shelf that ran the length of the bench.

I cupped my hands around the lizard, breathed the command to initiate the sequence, and gently set him down. The skink shot across the surface and zipped through the ring, the keys jangling in response to his slapping tail. He circled the hammer, ran along the shaft, and jumped to the shelf. I grinned and nodded encouragement as it streaked back and…burst like an overinflated tire. Bit of smoking debris pelted my shirt and ticked across the table, carried by momentum.

"At least there was no fireball this time." The dean slapped me on the back, going for encouragement.

"Yeah, I guess that's progress. You make it look so easy."

"It's the damnedest thing." Gladstone sounded perplexed as he flipped up the left yellow lens of his overcomplicated goggles, spectrum goggles as he called them. He left the red lens over his right eye and examined the remains before flipping that back and turning. The underlying clear lenses made his piercing green eyes comically huge. "As I've said, we haven't seen many tinkers. I know you really enjoy building constructs, but I'm starting to wonder if your power is simply not attuned for this type of application. You may find that repairs are where you need to keep your focus." He waved away my squawk of protest. "Don't get me wrong. Keep pursuing your passion. I'm just saying that there may be limits to how far you can push. It's just something to consider."

"Sure thing, dean." I swept up the bits and pieces, all that remained of the hapless skink.

"Don't look so glum. Now that the clock is finished, we'll find something even more interesting to collaborate on. I'm not giving up on you just yet, Mr. Walker. Learning from mistakes can be highly instructive. But be careful." He handed me the spectrum goggles and pointed to the lizard clock. "This particular issue packs quite a wallop."

It was a good thing the dean had thought to protect the birthday present, or he would have been going to the party empty handed. The shield showed up in the goggles as an azure blue nimbus tied off with a knot of silvery energy where Dean Gladstone had mimicked tying a bow. But the silver threads were torn and frayed, the bow near unraveling. Even though the clock sat a good six feet away from the test track, cracks ran though the face of the shield spell. A gold spider web of fractures radiated out in a blast pattern from the point nearest where my lizard had popped. It really hadn't even been an explosion this time.

"Sorry, I didn't mean to—"

"Of course you didn't." The dean cut off my apology. "Your talent simply released unexpected energy that happened to interact with my shielding spell. Remarkable to watch through the mage glass. Most magic cannot interact with a shield. But no harm done. Lin will still get his gift."

"So when is this birthday party?" I asked, desperate for a new topic.

"I head out Friday. The party and social visit will be this weekend, but I'm staying through the holiday break. It's a slow time here and a wonderful opportunity for me to tour a sister school and compare notes. Patty Robles will be acting dean of students while I'm away."

Oh, that's a new name.

I spent a bit longer gathering up the pieces of my unlucky lizard. Dean Gladstone gave me a crash course in using his special goggles and the array of lenses to detect magical signatures. I traced the residue of errant forces that had torn the creature apart and compared notes with what the dean had observed. My tinker abilities went haywire between the third and fourth micro-instruction, diverting energy from the kinetic triggers and flowing power into the molecular structure of the simple frame, which in turn blew apart.

If the sheer number of layered commands caused the issue, I could use fewer, more complex instructions. Conversely, if complexity was the root cause, then a combination of simpler instructions might solve the underlying problem with my automata. Either way, I had a theory to test on the small-scale versions of Herb I'd assembled back in the garage.

* * *

"Watch this." I grinned at Billy as I launched the next Wart down the ramp.

A half dozen of the small-scale Herb replicas sat to my right as I kneeled by the ramp. Billy stood over the obstacle course he'd helped build. Weekends were a great time to catch up on my projects.

Wart stood for Wrong Attribute Resilience Test. I'd constructed each wheeled automaton with varying instruction sets from simple to complex in order to pinpoint exactly where my powers threw things off. Once I found my natural limit, I could finish programming Herb version three. Not that I had any designs on roller dog heists, but the challenge drove me.

I'd constructed each Wart from similar materials and components to those in my Herb series, but wheels replaced legs to simplify the design. The jointed arms remained, each ending in a simple pincher for a hand. There was no point in putting a ton of effort into these because I fully expected my magic to overload half of them.

The foot-tall Wart trundled to the bottom of the ramp, made an about face, and raised its right arm. *Victory, not even a small explosion!* That had been my simplest set of instructions, just three discreet commands with one positional condition, reach the bottom of the ramp. We'd determined the lower bracket for safe operations, and I couldn't help grinning like an idiot.

"Wow," Billy said. "That was really…underwhelming."

"What? This is huge, basic commands executed flawlessly."

"I guess." Billy scratched at a long sideburn, and I sensed his computer-geek brain kicking in. "Using simple sets of instructions like those, you could piece together more complex behaviors. It'd be like using a high-level language or pre-coded app building blocks."

"Exactly." Except my magic might still be the limiting factor that made things go kaboom at a certain complexity, but that was what this test was designed to determine. "Make sure your safety goggles are on for this one."

Hopefully Dean Gladstone's goggles were impact resistant because I needed them to trace the magic during each trial. I selected the Wart with a big number six painted on its back, and looked past the ramp to the maze of obstacles and challenges strewn across the cement floor. We'd set up everything well away from the walls and had a fire extinguisher handy.

Number six contained a stacked series of complex instructions that were very likely to trigger a nasty reaction. I'd done my best to smoothly layer in the supporting spells and magical directives like I'd seen the dean do for his own constructs. But Dean Gladstone wasn't a tinker. As with the skink, there was no guarantee my precautions would work.

"That's your high-end model?" Billy asked as he took an involuntary step backward.

"Have a little faith, and yes." I couldn't blame him. He'd been witness to more than one of my past spectacular flops.

As soon as the wheels touched down, I trickled a bit of power into Wart Six to activate his program. He set off smoothly, and the bond between us hummed, perhaps echoing with my own nervous excitement. Wart hit the bottom of the ramp, spun in place three times, and headed off to the colorful stack of building blocks. Its right arm reached out and grabbed the clasp to open the gate to the maze.

"Doing great," Billy said, but still kept well back as the little guy deftly negotiated the maze.

"This gets tricky."

Beyond the blocks, a pan of water with shallow ramps up either side blocked the path. I'd left it up to Wart on how best to handle crossing. He hesitated, likely checking power levels and assessing the path around, which was riddled with chunks of rock and patches of oil. He wobbled and backed away from the dead end. The bond vibrated with agitation, a familiar sensation that usually meant problems.

"Maybe we should stop—"

A high-pitched whine cut me off. Wart zipped forward at full speed, shot up the ramp, and flew over the water to land safely on the far side. The move should have drained his battery, but Wart plowed on, lifting the progressively heavy lead weights out of the way as he headed for the finish. Just one more gate to unlatch and we were home free.

Wart Six reached for the latch, but his pincher kept clanking against the aluminum frame of the screen we'd used for the gate. After three attempts, he held the pincher up to the mono camera set in his forehead. Wart backed up as he had when at the water. *What's he up to?*

The high-pitched whine came again, but instead of shooting forward, Wart simply sat there, the sound building to a painful screech. Wart disappeared with a bang and puff of smoke as if he'd been sitting on a powder keg. My ringing ears barely registered a loud clang from above. Wart's head bounced off the garage door opener, leaving a dent like someone had driven a golf ball straight into the metal housing.

Scorch marks fanned out across the cement marking Wart's final position, and the sharp bitter scent of burnt insulation had my eyes watering. I took a minute to catch my breath. A hollow ache below my ribs replaced the buzzing bond that had been torn away with the explosion.

"I think you've established the upper bracket." Billy picked bits of plastic out of his jacket; we should have set up blast shields too. "That needs to go on the spreadsheet as too many instructions."

Disappointing, but not surprising. I'd gotten my hopes up there at the end. The good news was that Wart Six had gotten further than I'd expected, so some of the dean's precautions had worked.

In the end, only Warts One and Two escaped destruction. Version three didn't blow up, just half crumpled, half melted. The more complex the instruction set, the larger the energy release at the point of failure. I didn't have the equipment for accurate measurements, but the dean's goggles showed the destructive release clearly scaled faster than the logic complexity, maybe not exponential, but certainly more than a linear relationship.

Wart Two's set of five instructions was the last safe combination. Three had tried Billy's idea of stacking sets of simple commands that had guided the first success, but whatever effect my magic was having proved cumulative, so that combination hadn't worked either.

"You clearly have a talent," Billy said as we shared a Saturday afternoon pizza in my apartment after cleaning up.

"What?" I furiously thought back through the day's discussion, but didn't recall slipping up and mentioning magic or anything close.

"Only guy I know that can blow shit up without explosives," he said around a mouthful. "I've said for years it shouldn't be possible, but you still manage. You're like the kid in science class whose projects always end with a boom."

We shared a laugh, but Billy gave me a weird look. Despite downplaying it, the guy was sharp and knew circuitry. I had no idea what he'd come up with to explain the unexplainable, but we were good enough friends that he didn't press the point.

14. The Walls

"AND THEN NUMBER six's head shot straight up, bounced off the garage door opener, and damn near killed us." I waved my arm to illustrate the arc of Wart's head, playing up the drama of the scene as I concluded my story.

"So basically, you failed big time." Owen was nothing if not succinct.

"And spilled the magical beans to mere mortals." Chad smiled to show he was joking, but I heard the question in his voice.

The gang had gathered at the lunch table per our Monday routine to recap the weekend and discuss what the week might bring. Chad had his usual seat by the pillar with Owen to his right. Bethany and Mon joined us for a change and sat quietly on the far end.

"Did you even hear the part about getting in two successful trials?" I huffed out an indignant breath. "And no, Chad, the m-word never came up. Billy's helped with my work since we were kids. He thinks the interesting problems associated with my projects are hysterical, not magical.

"But thanks to that experiment, I've got a much clearer idea of the tipping point where my magic goes haywire. Working with the tinker talent is awesome, especially since classes won't start on that until after the holidays."

"Well, I'm super jealous." Chad heaved a sigh as he leaned back against his favorite column, and the ventilation system overhead let out a gusty groan as if in agreement. "Next semester can't come soon enough. I don't mind the introductory meteorology class, but I'm itching to unleash my skills and roll my sleeves up on forecasting."

"Well, I'm getting tons of practice down in the garages." Owen, of course, had to be different.

"Sure," I said. "But wrenching on bikes and not actually using your talent yet. Right?"

He gave a non-committal shrug, waving away the distinction, so I didn't press and turned to Bethany.

"How about you girls?" I asked. "Any talent training going on in your special wing?"

Mon parted her lips as though she were about to speak, then clamped her mouth shut and exchanged a look with Bethany. The two quickly turned away from each other as if embarrassed, which made me wonder if there might be a little something going on between them. Owen must have gotten the same idea because he leaned in with a smug leer. Bethany looked up, overcoming whatever embarrassment had gripped her.

"Oh, grow up!" She threw the statement at Owen, and he caught it with a smooth chuckle and raised hands. "What Mon and I do or don't do is our own business and none of yours."

It was nice to see the fire back in Bethany. She'd been awfully quiet the past few weeks, her natural enthusiasm giving way to bouts of brooding. She'd had her head down in that sketchbook since day one, but always came up for air and to exchange friendly banter with the group. Those times were few and far between nowadays, and I was glad to see her engage.

"Nothing you boys would be interested in," she said in response to my question. "But Chad's right. Second semester can't get here soon enough."

That was something we all easily agreed upon, and nods flowed around the table. It had been quite the first few months at Attwater and a huge adjustment for most of us—especially given we couldn't exactly talk about magic with anyone outside of school.

"So have they got you working with a software graphics package yet? Rendering images or working with wire-frame models?" I tried to keep Bethany engaged.

"No, we're still just talking techniques," she mumbled and drifted out of the conversation.

When the warning whistle sounded, the table let out a collective groan, and we all pushed to our feet for afternoon class—all except Chad.

"Back to the grind." I tried to wave him to the door, but he didn't budge.

"Leave me, save yourselves." Chad rubbed his stomach as he leaned back against the cool stone pillar and eyed his ketchup-smeared plate. "Too many fries. There's no way I'm going to stay awake in class."

He closed his eyes and pulled his hat down as if actually intending to take a nap.

"Come on, cowboy." I kicked his boot. "It's environmental science for you next, right ? It'll be fun. Tell him, Bethany."

"What? Oh right." Aroused from her brooding, Bethany rose to the challenge. "We all agreed that school comes first. So up and at 'em, cowboy."

"Ugh, fine." Chad pushed off the column with a groan. "But they should just hold classes here to make life simpler."

As he lumbered to his feet and pushed away from the stone, the vents rattled with an airy exhalation as though the building had let out a disappointed sigh. Odd as it sounded, I'd take that over the rumbling quakes any time.

We all headed toward the security door that led to our classes. There were actually three more entrances spread around the outer ring, but we'd grown accustomed to using the one nearest the commons. Plus, this one didn't get the crowd from the atrium side trying to pour through at the last minute. Chad hung back with head down and brows furrowed as if mulling over a problem.

"What gives?" I dropped back to walk with him.

"This might sound weird." He reached out and ran a calloused hand over the smooth stones of the wall as we stopped at the door. "Do any of you feel like the school is...well, acting strange?"

He was asking about more than the lighting issues and shaking that we'd all come to expect. Since day one, Chad had marveled at the school's construction and brought good-natured jibes down on himself by talking about the school like it was a person. But underneath the banter, I couldn't shake the feeling that he'd formed a kind of connection with the building. On several occasions, he managed lead us back from a distant wing thanks to his innate "feel" for the place. Even the dim corridor lights favored Chad, bathing our ruminating friend in a golden glow while the rest of us walked in shadow. Before I could frame a response, Owen chimed in.

"Just around you, Cowboy." Owen raised an eyebrow at where Chad's hand rested lightly on stones polished smooth by generations of students. "But then, you fondle the old girl like she's a cheap whore."

Bethany and Mon each swiped through and hurried inside, shaking their heads and clearly not wanting to get into the middle of things. Chad's jaw dropped open, and he pulled his hand back from stroking the stonework, an unconscious habit we'd all noticed. Owen chuckled as Chad tried to stammer out a response.

Owen leaned in with hand to ear as if to hear the witty reply that never came, shrugged, and waved his own badge over the sensor. Instead of turning green, the light went red, and the keypad issued a harsh buzz.

"I'd go on to say something about getting your rocks off…" Owen's grin was pure evil as he swiped the badge again. "But it's too easy."

The denial buzz again marked his failed attempt. On Owen's third try, the light finally turned green. Owen yanked the handle, but the door jammed.

"Oh, come on!"

"I think you pissed her off," Chad said.

I started to laugh, but realized he was serious. Owen tugged hard, then put a foot up on the frame and really put his back into it. The door suddenly let loose and smacked him in the face. Owen grabbed his nose, and the door swung shut, the lock clicking.

"Maybe you should…apologize," I ventured.

We'd seen a lot weirder things than living castles. Chad had always been fascinated with the architecture. If anyone was going to bond with the inanimate, it was our big-hearted cowboy. His interest made me wonder if weather was truly the man's calling.

"For crying out loud." Owen rubbed his nose, then checked his fingers to ensure he wasn't bleeding. "Okay, I'm sorry. I was just having some fun. You know me."

"Sadly, yes." Chad grinned, clearly enjoying Owen's squirming, but waved at the access panel, inviting him to try again.

Eyes narrowed, Owen gave it another shot. The light blinked green, and the expected metallic snick sounded. He gave the handle a tentative pull, and the door swung smoothly open.

"Well, thanks." For once, Owen's voice didn't drip sarcasm.

We found the girls waiting on the other side. A few stragglers wandered the halls, but most students had already gone to class. Several of those left, Bethany, and Mon gaped at a normally unused classroom down the hall to our right. Orange and white light flashed through the partially open door as if something burned or sparked within.

"That doesn't look good at all." I headed for the doorway, and the others followed.

An electric sizzling and the distinct smell of ozone hit us as we drew near. Arcing and sparking for sure, much like the stick welding we'd been practicing that used consumable electrodes. But this was Attwater, so maybe there was just a small lightning storm in the room.

A bright flash lit up the back of the room where a familiar figure wearing overalls hefted his toolkit in one hand and shielded his eyes against the brilliant sparking with the other. I only got a glimpse before the door slammed in my face. The handle turned under my grip, but the door refused to budge.

"Mr. Gonzales is in there," I said as my friends crowded around. "He's way in the back working on what has to be a massive short circuit. We've got to get in and make sure he doesn't get electrocuted."

I threw my shoulder against the door. The wood shuddered but didn't give. Chad slammed a meaty fist against the surface.

"Mr. Gonzales!" Chad pounded again. "You okay?"

"A little earth magic ought to open this puppy right up." Owen pushed between us with hands outstretched.

Power gathered at his fingers. But when he released the spell, the magic literally bounced off the door. The backlash threw Owen back three paces, and he crashed into Bethany, who managed to keep him on his feet.

"Geez!" Owen blew on his hands.

"The old girl's keeping us out." Chad patted the door. "Must be for our own good."

"Yeah, but if Mr. G's in trouble, we need to get in there." I said. "We can't just stand around and—"

The door swung open, and the maintenance manager nearly crashed into me as he shot from the room.

"Ah, pardon me."

"You okay, Mr. G?" I asked. "Looked like a nasty electrical short in there."

"No, no. Everything's fine…Jason, right?" He blinked at the others, then caught me looking at his tool kit.

Three battery capture canisters poked from the bag, tops still glowing and curling smoke from recent use. He adjusted his grip and swung the bag behind his leg. "But I do have to get going. It's all good now."

"More gremlins?" I kept my voice low and looked around for eavesdroppers. Except for my friends, the other students had drifted away.

"Annoying little buggers, but we're getting it under control," He made as if to leave. "If you'll excuse me, I have to deal with these."

"Oh, sure." I stepped aside. "See you Friday? Last rounds before holiday break."

He started at my words, but gave a slow nod. "Yes, of course."

Mr. Gonzales headed off down the hall toward the supply lockers where we sometimes met on Friday mornings.

"Seems a little confused." Owen poked his head into the room before entering, and the rest of us followed him in. "Looks normal in here."

The old classroom hadn't seen use in a long time. A handful of desks had been pushed off to the sides, and the chairs were long gone. As with other rooms, a dais stood near the front and lockers lined the back. The hanging Edison bulbs reminded me of our common core classroom, giving the place a similar early-modernism-classic-dungeon vibe.

"If everything's under control here"— Bethany traded a look with Mon— "being late is *not* appreciated by our lovely instructors."

"Guys, check this out." Owen waved us over to an alcove behind the lockers.

As with so many other areas of the school, plumbing, electrical cables, and vents ran up the back wall. But Owen found several charred spots at eye level on the thickest cable run and one on the adjacent plumbing.

"I knew that was sparking," I said, but the gremlin in the coffee maker hadn't caused that kind of effect.

"It's more than that." Bethany pushed past me and examined the scorch marks. "There's a pattern in these. See the lines?"

Chad found a switch and turned on more lights. Sure enough, the burns were irregular starbursts, but a clear geometric patter lay underneath—a pair of nested diamonds lightly etched under the soot. Compact squiggles inscribed near the edges of each symbol looked like archaic letters or hieroglyphs.

"I've seen this before," Bethany said. "On a cable outside the storage room where I…keep my art supplies."

"Maybe this is where Mr. G. drew gremlins out," I said. "Might be something left by his traps when the snakes aren't out in the open like at the coffee machine."

"Maybe." She looked skeptical. "How many has he captured so far?"

"Wish I knew." I scratched my head. "More importantly, where the hell are they coming from? The official word is that the building's system problems are caused by outside influences. I'm starting to wonder if that's accurate or if these things are to blame. Mr. G. seems confident he's got it under control."

The final whistle blew, and we had no choice but to head to class. Bethany and Mon hurried toward the inner chambers, Chad followed but turned off at his room, and Owen and I headed in the other direction.

15. Welding Class

C ONCENTRATING IN CLASS proved difficult. I'd have to ask the dean on Wednesday what he made of the gremlins. Maybe our next project could be to design filters for the utility systems to exclude or catch the little monsters. Otherwise, Attwater needed to hire more help. These things were like rats. Every time I saw Mr. G. lately he was busy carting off at least one smoking trap. And the people involved with the initial investigation after Bethany's drawing escaped must have returned to their day jobs because I hadn't seen a single person helping out in months. One man just couldn't care for such a massive building.

Hell, maybe the snake gremlins were finding their way back, repeat offenders from a catch and release program. It was time to press for answers on the Friday rounds. Mr. G. needed to at least let me help him out.

Although my academic classes dragged like anchors as we approached the holiday break, welding 101 turned ever more interesting—thanks in no small part to Gina's coaching. I found myself looking forward to her smile and dimples more each day.

That afternoon's lecture focused on the principles, proper storage, and use of inert gases. Gina helped with the demonstrations. After the class broke off to assignments at our individual work areas, she headed over to inspect my progress. I flipped up my visor, powered down the welder, and stepped back.

"Now that's a good weld." I nodded as I blinked away magenta after images thanks to taking the visor off too quickly.

"Certainly better than that first try when you couldn't go two inches without getting the electrode stuck." Gina leaned over to inspect the joined plate metal slabs and bit her lower lip. "Work on uniformity. You want the weld to be the same width along its entire length. See these bubbles and ripples—now, don't frown at me. These just mean you stalled out a bit. Easy to do. It's hard to see past that brilliant nova of light. Give yourself time to develop a feel for the proper speed. A lot depends on the material and how fast the welding rod gets used up. There's some artistry involved. You'll get there. How about trying the flip side?"

"Sure." I tried not to let my disappointment show; I'd been really proud of that weld.

After several more passes, I got marginally better. Ripples still marked my jerky movements, but at least there were no wide puddles. Gina smiled at my progress, continuing to dole out encouragement and tips on adjusting my power settings as we changed up electrode sizes.

"Why are you so nice to me?" I asked as we finished for the day. "Am I *that* much worse than the others?"

"Hell, no." Her laugh was light and sunshine. "Everyone is a noob in the beginning. Don't you like my company?"

"I…well, that is…" Stupid, I know, but between her batting eyelids and impish grin, my brain decided to go on strike.

"That's adorable." She giggled at my confusion. "Dean Gladstone asked me to keep an eye on you. He's quite taken with your work on his clock."

"Gladstone told you about that?"

"The dean grabs a student or two each year to work on special projects. He's particularly fond of those of us with mechanical abilities that mirror his own interests. Even after you're done working with him, you'll enjoy more access to the dean than other students."

"You've worked with him too." That would explain how she'd happened to get into a conversation with Gladstone about me.

"Got it in one. I still swing by and chat every couple of weeks. The dean told me about the clock, and asked me to make sure you were getting the basics down. These techniques are building blocks for future tinker work." She waved at the gear, then caught my scowl. "Not that I mind."

Gina looked down at her feet in that pretty way she had when embarrassed, and my flash of annoyance at being coddled vanished. I wondered if she felt the same attraction I did—like a magnet always trying to drag my feet a step closer. Talking to women had never been my forte, and I fumbled around for something to say—most of which came out as inarticulate "ums" and "ahs."

"Working with the dean is a blast," I finally blurted out. "No idea what's next. He said he'll find another project, but everything in his office is a damned clock."

"He'll definitely have more for you, and I promise it'll be interesting. You know"—she lowered her voice, and leaned in close— "he doesn't just build and fix clocks. Sure, the man's a perfectionist who could make anything from a pocket watch to

Big Ben if he wanted to. But it's more than that. The dean works with the *concept* of clocks, not just their mechanics."

"Okay." What was I to make of that? Clocks were only used for one reason in general, to keep track of— "Are you saying his magic has something to do with time?"

"Yep." She nodded vigorously. "Nobody really knows the extent of it, but there's plenty of rumors. Like that Gladstone can slow things down, stretch moments out. Given what he accomplishes, the notion seems plausible."

"Or he just has wicked time management skills." The quip gave me time to process. *Damn!*

"Very funny. I've never seen it firsthand, but it's fun to imagine. What if he really does have that power?"

"He'd be in H. G. Wells land." I thought back to the *Time Machine* story we'd read in school.

"I know, right? Go visit the dinosaurs or the distant future."

"Yeah, that didn't work out so well for David. Was he the main character?" It had been years since I read the book or saw the movie.

"Hopefully no flesh-eating sub-humans running underground factories," she agreed.

"Gina, you seem to be in the know about Attwater. What's with maintenance here? How can one guy take care of the place?"

"Mike Gonzales is a sharp cookie," she snapped, mistaking my meaning. "They pull in help when needed, but I wouldn't worry. That man's a gem. He was a student here himself, and a damned fine one."

"Don't get me wrong; I like the guy and even make rounds with him before class on Fridays. But he's clearly overworked, especially hunting down the gremlins that are running around."

"Really? Gremlins?" Her annoyance vanished as she tapped her chin in thought. "I knew they'd discovered something after the open house, but never heard any details. I don't know Mike's exact discipline, but he's another of Gladstone's favorites. Maybe the dean helps him…you know, get it all done in time." She clapped her hands. "Enough chitchat. We need to wrap this up. I've got places to be, and you need to take care of this gear."

"So where do you want to work after graduation?" I asked as we stowed the equipment.

"I figure a transportation center like a train depot or shipyard, although ship work is hard to come by nowadays. Underwater welding is my absolute dream job, but would mean a whole new level of training that Attwater doesn't offer. I've been dive certified forever, but never handled a torch underwater. A dream for the future I guess. What about you?"

She tucked a dark curl behind her right ear and waited. I envied her ready answer and that she had an even bigger dream. School and working my projects hadn't left much time for career planning. Though I definitely didn't share her aspiration to wield burning tools while wearing a wetsuit.

"I like building machines that can be programmed for independent operation. They're automata, but everyone calls them robots, which I guess isn't that far off. But right now, my magic still trips things up." I held up the coiled welding lead. "I doubt this trade will land me in a robotic research facility."

"Probably not." She had a cute way of biting her lower lip in thought. "But what about the auto industry or other large-scale production plants? Those segments use tons of robotics. Probably not fully autonomous because most are tethered to a production line, but still might be a good opportunity."

"Yeah, I'll give that some thought, and see what guidance says when I get further down the road. Everything hinges on integrating my tinker ability better. The dean's helping me figure it out, but thinks my magic might not be well suited to animating machines. He's already suggested that I might want to stick to repairs."

"If anybody can help get that sorted, Dean Gladstone's your man. Last year, I was in a similar boat. I mean, how do you use salamanders to weld?"

"Magic fire creatures?" I guessed.

"Yep, I've always seen those molten little lizards in the fire. The dean helped me communicate with them and now they guide the molten metal as I work. Working in a foundry would make me wicked powerful because there're just piles of salamanders around smelting operations. But we'll see what placement recommends closer to graduation next summer."

"Cool!" I could relate. She clearly loved working with fire lizards, but it wasn't the kind of skill you could practice in your garage—unless it was fireproof. The thought had another question popping into my head. "Does Mr. Gonzales have a maintenance locker for his tools and equipment? I make rounds with him once a week, but we usually just meet out in the commons or by the supply lockers. I'm curious if he has a main workshop."

In my mind's eye "the workshop" would be where the magic happened—pun intended.

"Oh, sure," Gina said. "Somewhere in the inner ring where all the building utilities converge. I've never been there, but the dean mentioned it a couple of times. I'm sure he'd be happy to show it off if you just ask."

"Think I will." I nodded and shoved the welder firmly onto its shelf. "I'm curious to see what happens to the gremlins he's captured. My guess is they go back to his shop for disposal."

"Seems like we'd hear about it if there are that many around." She raised a questioning eyebrow and gathered up her books.

"Yeah, it's been kept pretty quiet. I just happened to be there when one popped out of the coffee machine. Nasty thing tried to bite me."

"Weird. Gremlins usually just attack machinery. Maybe your tinker blood is just too tasty. Either way, gremlins aren't covered much in defensive lectures. I get the feeling they're a kind of domestic menace. I'm not even sure they're part of the demon hierarchy. And speaking of the big bad uglies, my night class is heading out to hunt a low class lurker that's causing problems at a power substation. You'll get to go on neat little jaunts next year. Gives us first-hand training. But I have to get my butt in gear and pick up dinner for Mom before coming back to class. Catch you later, okay?"

"Sure thing, and thanks."

The next couple of days slid by smoothly. I found myself at the dean's office early Wednesday, anxiously awaiting whatever project he might have lined up for us to work on next. After sitting outside his door for a half an hour, I slipped back out to see the receptionist.

"Dean's not answering his door," I said as Miranda Glovefire, the office manager, strolled in carrying a steaming cup of coffee. "We have a weekly independent study session scheduled."

She consulted her computer and looked up with a frown from beneath wavy copper hair that came down to her shoulders. "I'm sorry, dear. The dean's in a video conference discussing his upcoming trip to the Bashar School. It should be just about over. You're welcome to wait."

Dean Gladstone swept in a few minutes later, looking distracted. He was dressed in a suit similar to the old-fashioned three-piece he'd worn that very first day in the courtroom. The outfit so thoroughly changed him from eccentric inventor to dapper professional that I hardly recognized him at first.

"Jason, I apologize for not getting word to you cancelling today's session." He waved me into his office as he bustled through the door and leaned his cane against the workbench. "We'll have to postpone until after holiday break. There's a situation brewing at our sister school that's demanding my attention."

"No problem, sir." I headed for my usual coffee, but stopped short because the side table by the window stood empty. "Do they have gremlin issues too?"

"Gremlins?" He cocked an eye at me. "I doubt it. Solitary creatures and nothing to get too worked up about."

He yanked open drawers along the workbench in search of something, but his dismissive statement made me wonder.

"Dean, you do know that Mr. Gonzales has been finding gremlins all over Attwater?"

"Is that so?" He continued to open drawers until he found a gem-studded pen that he tucked into his bag before continuing the scavenger hunt.

"Sure is. The first one was way back during orientation."

"Well, no one's ever taken care of Attwater better than Mike Gonzales. One of my best students back in the day. I have full confidence he's handling the situation appropriately." He paused in his rummaging and tapped a long finger against the corner of his mouth. "Say, why not make that your next project while I'm gone?" He pulled out the pen, wrote a note, and handed it to me. "Find this book in the inner library and give it a good read through. If memory serves, it describes the various types of gremlins and how to deal with them, a fascinating compilation of how different cultures historically handle the nuisance.

"Beef yourself up and tell Mr. Gonzales that your next project is to help him ensure Attwater stays gremlin-free. We'll call that phase two of your credit work, a self-study module. After the holidays, you can fill me in on what you learned and what measures you two have put in place. Then we'll decided if a third phase of study is needed to finish up the course."

I took the slip of paper and stuffed it in my pocket.

"You'll need these to access the library wing." He circled the desk, pulled two thin laminated cards from the top drawer, and handed them over. "I'll make sure you're on record as having temporary access to the inner ring and library, but don't go nosing around the other rooms. Many of those teaching advanced classes are protective and don't tolerate their lessons being interrupted."

"Sounds like fun." I'd been wanting to help Mr. G. out anyway. "Is there anything in particular you think I'll need to do with my tinker abilities?"

"I doubt your magic will be necessary on this one. But any experience dealing with creatures you might encounter on the job is appropriate course material. If our maintenance manager actually suspects gremlins, it'll give you a chance to use the techniques in that book on a relatively benign threat. Though annoying, gremlins are a red-headed step-child of the lesser demon classes and not terribly dangerous."

"Sounds like a plan," I said. "Good luck with the clock."

"Lin is going to love it. Thanks again for your help. That snake came out perfect."

16. The Library

"**I'M GOING WITH YOU**," Bethany declared when I told the gang about the gremlin book at the library. "They haven't given me full access, but your pass might get us both in. I've been trying to research that symbol we found under the burn marks, but so far, the books in the outer annex are useless. The main stacks hold more promise if you can get us in."

Bethany met me outside the locked door to the advanced wing at the five-o'clock rumble, a recent manifestation of the school's woes. As the building settled down from the mini-quake, we swiped through without issue—thanks to the fact neither of us had recently insulted the building.

"Second year practical labs are down to the left." Bethany played tour guide as we worked our way deeper. "Rooms are scattered across at least two floors, but I don't know about the basement."

"What's that way?" I pointed down two corridors that headed off to the right, seeming as though they should cut across the outer ring classrooms. The place was a warren.

"That's where they hold practical lessons. Mon and I are down the first one. Just more classrooms like the ones you've already seen. Not so sure about the other. Very few students get invited to that wing. Let's take the stairs down a level. I've only ever been into the outer library."

The library entrance was basically a tunnel. Ventilation systems labored overhead, and the air grew warm as we approached. The arched entrance consisted of glass panes and wood doors that stood wide open, despite the keypad with swipe access mounted on the wall to the left.

"Dehumidification system," I said, noting the dry air.

"Climate control is good for the books," she agreed. "All this stuff out front is your basic trade manuals, certification standards, specifications, building codes, things of that nature. I've already been through a lot of these and haven't found anything terribly useful. Over on the right wall is a small section on magic, but let's check the catalog and look up your book."

I pulled out the scrap of paper from the dean. "No author, but the title is *Magical Menaces*."

Bethany grabbed the slip and fired up an odd looking computer with a rounded monitor that looked like an old-style black and white television set. But the screen sprang to life with vivid colors. While she keyed in a search, I looked around. The room wasn't much different from any other public library I'd visited.

Neatly bound technical manuals lined the waist-high wooden shelves in the center of the room. Bits of machinery and art were on display along the smooth tops, reminding me of a museum. Tall shelves three deep stood silent sentinel around the perimeter of the room. An empty main desk sat to the left of the doors, so the librarian was likely off on rounds. A few students sat scattered at low tables, hunched over their reading material with notebooks and pens at the ready.

High-wattage white lights replaced the crawling Edison bulbs that were everywhere else, making it easily the brightest space I'd encountered at Attwater. Those heavy V-shaped fixtures hung from the ceiling like a fleet of battleships. The clean lines of the ceiling had me trying to figure out what was off until I realized this was the first room I'd come across that lacked exposed pipes and wires.

"Got it," Bethany announced, pulling my attention back to the task at hand. "Just like I suspected, it's in the vaulted room down a half level in the back. You have the dean's library pass?"

I held up the little red and white laminated card.

"The notes say these books can't be checked out." She consulted the screen with a sigh. "We'll just have to settle in for some heavy reading. We still have a few hours until curfew."

Vaulted stacks was a good term for the area. The big circular door glinted in the bright lights, looking much like a vault entrance, although it lacked the ship's-wheel handle I would have expected.

Instead of using a proximity sensor, the dean's card fit into a slot. Once activated, the burnished door rolled off to the side like a giant wheel. Inside, a small reading area mirrored the main library, but sprawled under dimmer lighting. The stacks were tight, narrow affairs with metal hand-wheels on each end. A quick test showed that each long row of shelves could be cranked off to the side to access to the next one over. The system allowed for three times more shelf space than a fixed arrangement could accommodate. I just wouldn't want to be between the stacks if someone decided to crank them closed.

More motion-activated lights clicked on as we moved deeper. The book turned out to be a large volume, but not terribly old. What it lacked in age, it more than made up for in sheer poundage. The massive tome was a good four inches thick with onion-thin pages—thousands of pages crowded with small font and tons of diagrams. I sighed at the daunting task of reading even a fraction in one sitting.

"You look through that," Bethany said as she spun on her heel. "There are a couple others I want to grab."

I hefted my volume over to the seating area and plopped down, wishing for a cup of coffee and protein bar. I'd grown way too used to snacking after classes. I flipped through various magical issues and solutions dealing with system maintenance, troubleshooting, and alignment. Supernatural attacks on equipment were more commonplace than we ever suspected.

When I finally found mention of gremlins, it was not the easy straightforward description I'd hoped for, but more of a history lesson. No quick answers here, so I sat back and got comfortable.

Bethany returned with a slim, hard-bound volume and a big landscape-formatted binder. She sat at the far end of the table and dug in.

"Looking for that symbol and a few things related to my talent," she said in response to my raised eyebrow.

We kept at it a couple of hours, me poring through the massive text and Bethany alternating between scribbling notes and scurrying back into the stacks for more volumes. I glared down at my massive tomb, jealous of the thin books she'd selected.

"Argh! This just doesn't make sense." I slammed the book shut, making Bethany jump.

"Nothing on gremlins?" she asked.

"There's plenty, too much in fact." I pushed the book across the table in disgust. "None of these look like what we're dealing with here. This thing has accounts from all over the world, and gremlins are always small scaly creatures. Sometimes they have wings, sometimes not, and one account documents a cute furry critter. But nothing talks about the smoky snake that came out of the coffee machine.

"There's also a ton of info about scaring them off and identifying damage, but no talk of capturing gremlins. And certainly nothing about traps like Mr. G. uses. I'm missing something."

"Show me."

I circled around the table and flipped to the closest match I'd found. "These are like long lizards with blocky heads and stubby legs. But not a lot of similarities to the snake."

She read through the sections, flipping back and forth to the pages I'd marked with a handful of small colorful stickies. The term "gremlin" had gained notoriety during World War II as the universal scapegoats to blame for anything and everything that went wrong with aircraft during the war. But this text traced the species much further back. Written and oral records within the mystical communities spoke of the destructive vermin that reveled in causing mechanical problems, especially ones that led to injury or death. *Not so benign after all, then.*

I glanced down at the books scattered around Bethany, much older texts than the monstrous volume I'd been reading. From history to summoning and binding, they all dealt with demonology and demon classification. If I didn't know any better, I'd say Bethany was obsessed with the opponent we'd someday face. She'd made copious notes and even traced out a few symbols. None of the later matched what had been left behind when the gremlins—or whatever they were—got trapped.

"What's this all about?" I pointed to her notes.

"Nothing important. Dead ends like you ran into." She jammed the loose pages back into her binder and tapped the bottom of my open book. "But take a look at these footnotes. There's a much older book called *Oculus Demontros* referenced in several places."

"Really?" I hadn't had the patience to drill down into the layers of cryptically formatted footnotes, and she wasn't on a page I'd flagged. "That's not even a section about gremlins."

"Sometimes you have to use the index." Bethany flipped to the end of the book, picked another term from the tightly-packed listing, and turned to a page on demon hierarchies. "Let's go to the card catalog."

Bethany carried the big book over to an antiquated terminal matching the one we'd used in the main room and looked up *Oculus Demontros*.

"Wow, really old." She whistled. "Roman-numerals-only kind of old. Give me a minute to figure out the year of publication."

"Fifteen-twenty-seven." I'd always had a knack for Roman numerals. "Is it actually here, or off in a museum someplace?"

"Says it's in the stacks." She scrolled down further. "Translations in several languages, including English."

It took a solid fifteen minutes to find the volumes in question. The set sat along the top shelf that I had to find a stepladder to reach. A dark crimson binding enclosed the densely-packed pages of the English version, which was the size of a standard bible. There was a weight to the book, making it feel every bit as old as it looked. The thick pages proved surprisingly supple. I stepped back and let Bethany do her thing.

Even with her mad research skills, it took her almost twenty minutes to find a page that, plain as day, held the symbol with interlocked diamonds we'd found on the electrical conduit. I'd thought she'd been looking for gremlins, not the sigil.

"Geez, this is ridiculous," Bethany complained as her finger moved down the text alongside the diagram. "Looks like Middle English, Early-Modern, or maybe a combination. Might as well be a foreign language…Ah, here we go." She cleared her throat and read a section aloud. "Al be that the carecter of twofold diamaunts beth impressen on a sely wight skin, ich height hem nyght kynde demon."

"Um…okay." My brain hurt trying to reason out the paragraph, but the gist was there underneath the back and forth prose. "That symbol deals with demons!"

"Yup, the 'night kind' when two diamonds are inscribed on the skin." Bethany nodded and flipped back several pages. "Low-level shadow demons if I'm reading this right. No mention of gremlins at all."

"The dean needs to see these. If Attwater faces a demon threat instead of simple gremlins, he'll want to take action." I whipped out my phone and snapped pictures of the symbol, its description, and a few key pages from the original text Dean Gladstone recommended.

What the heck had been unleashed on the school? My opinion of Mr. Gonzales soared even higher. If we were reading this right, the man wasn't just defending Attwater from run-of-the-mill nuisances, he'd taken point on fighting off a demon incursion.

My mind raced. Although classes hadn't yet touched much on the demon menace that had grown so strong in recent years, these books painted a picture of what we might be up against.

Even if Mr. G. had things fully under control—something that the continued tremors and power issues would argue against—just knowing what to look for should make it easier to mop up any remaining snakes in the system.

"This could help get the school back to normal fast!" The prospect of helping Mr. G in a substantial way had me fired up.

I grinned like a maniac as we filed the books back into their proper slots in the stacks. On our way out, I realized Bethany didn't share my enthusiasm. In fact, she looked positively morose. The outer library was empty except for a smiling woman in a knit sweater sitting behind the desk. She gave us a friendly wave.

"Okay, what gives?" I stepped in front of Bethany and almost got run over for my trouble thanks to how she studied the floor and seemed to be mentally elsewhere.

"What?" She stopped short just in time.

"We dug up a lot of useful information back there but you're in another world."

Her face shattered as she looked up with tears in her brown eyes and shook her sketchbook in my face. "I make monsters, Jason. They're real!"

"What, your drawings?" I couldn't understand her desolate nod. "Sure, just like my robots or the dean's clocks. Those are just our magical talents."

It felt funny to say that, considering a few short months ago I wouldn't have believed it myself. But a lot had happened since then.

"It's more than just magic." She sighed and swallowed hard. "I think it's demonology, dark magic. What I do, the characters I create, they're twisted. Those texts say the talent is rare, but dates all the way back to some early cave drawings animated by ancient tribes to kill their enemies."

"Maybe that was just for protection." I needed to stop Bethany from spiraling down. No wonder she'd been so withdrawn lately; she thought she was evil. "How you use your power means more than any fixed notion of good or evil. I've got to believe that. You've never drawn a picture to hurt someone, have you?"

"Well, no…"

"There you go then." I put my hand on her shoulder and gave a reassuring squeeze.

"But they've studied creatures like mine, and they're closely related to the demons we'll fight."

"I just wouldn't read too much into it," I said. "Especially in a day and age where we learn to control our magic in a school we travel to through portals. Musty old books aren't necessarily our guides anymore. Heck, Dean Gladstone wouldn't have recruited someone who creates the demons Attwater's sworn to destroy."

"We're called scriptomancers," she said. "Some make living drawings, others can actually bring their words to life. It's dark, Jason, dark magic."

"From where I stand, Bethany Daniels is a sweet person. I don't think your magic is evil." I winced at her sullen expression. "Look, you have friends here. Don't let things like this eat you up inside. Talk to me or the gang. Even if it's just to complain or rant. Life's tough, and we all need a sympathetic ear once in a while. Promise me you won't bottle things like this up?"

She looked down at her notes and nodded. "I will."

"Good! By the way, thanks for the help. Things don't add up yet, but at least I have a theory to float past the dean." I tapped my phone as we walked. "He needs to see ye olde sigil that doth be manifesting within yon hallowed halls."

If nothing else, my butchered impression of old-style English pulled a smile from her.

17. Dean

S LEEPING THAT NIGHT proved difficult because my stupid brain kept trying to connect the dots. I had to be missing something obvious in those gremlin descriptions. Maybe the battery traps were developed after the book's publication date. That would explain their omission but not why that first gremlin at school looked so different from the illustrations and descriptions.

Dean Gladstone would certainly have a reason for the discrepancies, and I dragged my bleary butt to his office before class. Unfortunately, he was out. I waited until the morning whistle announced first period and forced me to postpone our discussion until the lunch break.

Paying attention in class was more difficult than usual.

"What did the dean say?" Bethany whispered as everyone took a seat in common core.

"He wasn't in. The receptionist said he got pulled away for another emergency video-conference. But I'll catch him at lunch. Do you want to come?"

"I can't." She got that dejected look again, but I didn't think it was due to a moral dilemma this time. "We have a practical exam right after lunch, and I need to prepare. I'll join up with everyone in the commons after classes. You can fill me in then. Okay?"

"Deal."

"Settle down and give me your attention. I have a holiday treat for you," Ms. Eisner said by way of introduction. "A little tradition I like to share this time of year, regardless of what holiday you observe or however else you spend your week off. I have a small charm for you that will spread good cheer." She picked through an assortment of items arrayed on a rolling table at the front of the room. "Does anyone care to guess what element such a spell might be based on?"

"Water, for winter ice," Lars called out from the back, where he'd been relegated weeks ago to supposedly keep him from interrupting.

"No, it's got to be spirit," countered Pete. Our timid classmate had found his voice recently, and his comment drew a scowl from my childhood bully.

"Good guess, Lars." Ms. Eisner never gave up trying. "But spirit aligns well for a job like this. This spell is best focused through fond memories, but for starting out we'll use an external focus. I have everything from candy canes to dreidels and poinsettias to use. So, on your feet. Come grab an object that resonates, and then we will begin."

When everyone had an article in hand back at their seats, the teacher held up her sprig of holly and proceeded to weave a subtle bit of magic. She explained as she went along and had us follow each step with our own focus. I'd snagged one of the mini candy canes.

"It's important to understand this is not mind control. Do not experiment or try to make this spell more than what it is. This is a natural enhancing of the joy already residing in people. I like to think of it as spreading the holiday spirit in the way a jolly tune or pleasant smile can bring good feelings. For your homework, you may try this outside the school on at least three people, but not more than five. The effects will be subtle and vary, so keep notes. After holiday break we will compare our experiences in a roundtable discussion."

She finished tying off the spell, but I must have missed something. Although I'd been following along, the energy that had started to build quickly faded. Judging by the jingling power dancing on Ms. Eisner's fingers, my spell had fizzled out. Several others around the room had similar issues. Owen and Bethany of course looked to have nailed it first try, as had a couple others.

"Not to worry," Ms. Eisner said in response to my frown. "We have today and the first half of tomorrow's class to practice. I'm confident everyone will have a working grasp of the charm. We'll finish tomorrow with a review session for your written exam. I dare say, objective evaluations will not be nearly as enjoyable. So let's have a little fun casting good cheer on each other. It's important to know what the spell feels like firsthand. This is how you cast."

By the end of the class, we had two dozen pretty darn happy people. Even Bethany smiled and seemed to no longer dread her afternoon classes. We again promised to touch base at the end of the day. Unfortunately, the artificial good cheer didn't hold up well to mechanical system vibration analysis lectures. *Surprise.*

The administration wing bustled with activity during lunch, but again, no one answered when I knocked on the dean's door. I hunted up Margaret, this month's receptionist, and found the pinch-faced woman who'd checked me in that first day busily making copies.

"Sorry, you just missed him." She didn't sound sorry. "The dean left early for his visit to the Bashar School. He returns a week from next Wednesday. Should I put you on the calendar?"

"No thanks." I couldn't believe I'd missed him again.

I thanked her and turned in time to catch a glimpse of someone ducking into the dean's office. Maybe he'd forgotten something. I hurried down the hall, found the door ajar, and peeked in. Someone bustled around the desk by the window, clearing space amidst the dean's trinkets and stacks of paper and turning the organized chaos into a fair acre of open desktop. But the middle-aged black woman with tightly cropped hair was certainly not Mr. Gladstone.

This had to be Ms. Robles setting herself up as acting dean, although I'd figured she'd use her own office. Instead, she'd moved right in, setting out pens and books as if meaning to stay much longer than a week. Then again, this was where students were used to finding the Dean of Students. Even if school was only in session a couple of days to either side of holiday break, I guess moving in made sense.

I raised my fist to knock, but froze when a second person stepped into sight to talk to Ms. Robles. Even from behind, I couldn't mistake the trim athletic woman with blond hair cascading down from her severe ponytail. She whispered urgently to the temporary dean, gesturing to a stack of reports precariously balanced on the corner of the desk. Ms. Schlaza was back.

18. Twain

"SCHLAZA'S BACK?" Bethany gaped from the other side of the table.

"And whispering in the temporary dean's ear," Owen said. "Gotta wonder what that means."

"It means that I'm not getting any help from the front office." I'd stood outside the door for a full minute trying to decide whether or not to go in and speak with Ms. Robles.

In the end, I hadn't. Before her sabbatical I'd never seen Schlaza in the administration wing, let alone the dean's office.

"But she's a teacher." Bethany had always defended the woman's draconian tactics, and the rest of us tacitly agreed that might be because Schlaza acted an awful lot like our friend's mother.

"Sure, a teacher who mysteriously disappeared right after the school started having problems." Owen raised an eyebrow full of implication. "And now she reappears when the dean's called off on some emergency."

"A planned trip," Bethany corrected.

"Yes, one that suddenly had its timeline accelerated," Owen said.

Jim Stein

"We've got to focus on Attwater." Chad had both hands on the stone pillar. "There's more gremlins or whatever they are in the systems. She's still hurting and needs them gone."

Owen snorted, but wisely didn't comment. On more than one occasion, the building had reacted to his derisive comments about Chad's growing link with Attwater. He'd learned to keep the snide comments to himself or risk the building's wrath, which usually manifested as simple pranks like locked doors, condensation unexpectedly dumping on his head, those sorts of things.

Sometimes it felt like my friends needed professional help. Bethany seemed marginally happier since our discussion after the library run, but now Chad was depressed. Our resident cowboy constantly obsessed over the building's trauma and had withdrawn into himself. He desperately wanted to help Attwater recover, but none of us knew how.

"You're right about that, Chad." My comment earned a sigh of approval from the overhead vents. "But if Schlaza's interfering with Ms. Robles, I'd rather just talk to Mr. Gonzales. The man has firsthand knowledge about what's been cropping up inside these walls. We'll put our heads together and try to figure out why the book descriptions are different than what came out of the coffee machine. Tomorrow's a half-day, but I'll be spending all afternoon with Mr. G. The dean has me working in maintenance for the next phase of my independent study."

"Make sure you find out how he's disposing of them," Bethany said. "They're probably like rats. Any he throws outside or dumps nearby might just circle back to be caught again. We might only be dealing with a few that keep coming back."

"If there's anything we can do to help, I want to know," Chad said. "Hell, if I could cast that Christmas cheer spell on Attwater itself, I would."

"Yeah, I don't think that works on inanimate objects." Owen hurried on as the pipes rattled ominously. "Not that there's anything wrong with that, but the spell releases dopamine and serotonin, maybe even endorphins. A building just doesn't have the physiology to work with—no offense!" That last bit was called up into the rafters. "I'm looking forward to busting a little holiday cheer on a few local grinches next week."

"Only you could make spreading good will sound like a dirty prank." Bethany shook her head, but couldn't help grinning.

Owen was a rogue and a loner. Early on, I'd been annoyed by his habitual rule breaking and penchant for mischief. But I'd come to see him as a healthy balance to Bethany's gloom, Chad's clean-cut virtue, and my own—well, there wasn't anything out of whack with me, except maybe a mild obsession for getting my robots to run correctly.

The funny thing was how damned affable the man could be. Owen grew on you, and his intentions never came across as malicious.

"Weaponized good cheer." I played into the thought process. "Maybe we can direct some of that at the ice queen. I hope to hell she doesn't take over core classes again. Mary's doing a great job. We don't need our progress derailed right before finals."

"Let us know what you discover, Jason." Chad pushed away from his column with visible effort. "Being away for over a week sucks. I'll be worried sick about the school."

We exchanged numbers so I could text with any pertinent data working with Mr. G. uncovered. Night school students soon began to filter in, a sure sign we needed to get moving.

"Anyone need Mon's number?" Bethany asked, but no one jumped on the offer. "Well, I have it just in case."

"Where's she at today?" I was still trying to figure out if the secretive girl was part of our group or not.

"I'm sure she headed straight home," Bethany said. "Mon had a wickedly rough practical session."

"Rough cosmetology." Owen smirked. "Like an eyeshadow disaster or something?"

"No, it's just—" Bethany bit off her hot response and took a deep breath. "Yes, Owen, something like that. Makeup can be a real bitch."

Owen gave a knowing smile, which confused me until I saw Gina threading her way through the tables and heading our way. She crossed the commons just as the building gave one of its short, wet-dog shudders.

"That must be the sign for all the little first term students to head home," Gina said with a playful glint in her eye.

I smiled because the implication was that we wouldn't be first term students much longer. After holidays, finals, and the semester break, then we'd be lofty second-term students.

"Gina-machina, how's it sparking?" Owen gave her a friendly slap on the shoulder, but his hand lingered too long.

No, no, no! I did not need charming Owen zeroing in on Gina. How the heck did they even know each other? I'd talked about her to the group often enough, but everyone was usually gone by the time she came through for evening classes.

"Walker, you make it too easy." Owen took pity on me and explained. "Gina helps with emergency repairs for the auto shop when we have a truly messed up frame."

"That I do." She cocked her head and pantomimed a regal nod of acknowledgement. "And I am not sneaking in at night to chop the frame of that beater project of yours. So you can stop asking."

"Peace." Owen held up both hands in surrender.

My jaw ached, and I caught myself grinding my teeth at their witty banter, which I was *sooo* not enjoying.

"Is your maintenance bonanza still on for tomorrow?" Gina gave me a dazzling smile.

"Sure is." A satisfied flutter rose in my stomach at the way she turned her back on Owen. "Why? You care to join me in getting to the bottom of the whole gremlin caper?"

I could do witty banter too.

"No…thanks?" Her hesitation made it sound more like a question. "But maybe you could steer Mr. Gonzales to the lower-level hallway. Mr. Martin is trying to set up for the graduation ceremony outside the heartstone chamber, but the wiring is on the fritz, lights are a mess, and the junction panels keep sparking."

"What's a heartstone?" Chad was suddenly all ears.

"Basically, the figurative heart and soul of the school," Gina said. "It's traditional to award certifications outside the chamber. Even off-season graduations are held down there in hopes of bestowing good luck in the students' coming careers."

"Like kissing the blarney stone," I said.

"A little bit." Gina's tinkling laugh warmed me. "Of course we can't go into the chamber, no one can. There isn't really a door, just a commemorative plaque. I get the feeling the chamber is more myth than fact, but it's cozy down there close to the center of this grand building. There's an open space that's perfect for ceremonies. At the moment, bad wiring is shooting out sparks that would set our new grads on fire. Mr.

Martin has been sending in trouble reports for a week, but I guess maintenance is stretched too thin. Either that or Mr. Gonzales can't work out a solution. Anyway, maybe you could get him down there and get things straightened out. Graduation is a week after break."

"I'll see what I can do." I resisted asking again for her to come along.

"You're the best." She gave me an awkward half-hug that was more of a slap on the back. "Well, I need to get to class, and curfew's coming up fast. If I don't see you all tomorrow, have a merry Christmas…or Chanukah…or holiday." She looked at the floor as if worried she'd offended someone.

As she walked away, I realized that Gina herself would be graduating after next semester. My heart sunk at the thought. I might not be her type, but a guy could dream. Maybe after the holidays it was finally time to ask her out.

* * *

Friday promised to be short and easy. Afternoon classes were cancelled to let everyone get a jump on the holidays, and I'd have free rein with Mr. Gonzales all afternoon. I looked forward to starting the morning practicing Ms. Eisner's holiday cheer spell, and our mechanical systems instructor had promised a movie on hydroelectric power, which would be an easy, popcorn-munching couple of hours for me and Owen. On paper the schedule looked to be shaping up to be the perfect day before break.

We'd mostly gotten the hang of Ms. Eisner's cheer spell on Thursday, but more practice wouldn't hurt. The whole class was looking forward to another giddy rush before heading off on holiday. I grinned at the thought as I pushed into the classroom.

But all thoughts of good cheer ran screaming. The ice queen stood by the podium, relegating Mary Eisner to a nook by her cartful of holiday knickknacks. Frowns and hard-set jaws made the room anything but cheerful as my classmates mentally prepared for two hours of whatever torture Ms. Schlaza had in store.

I took my seat between Owen and Bethany, and the three of us exchanged worried looks. The quiet murmuring cut off as Ms. Schlaza raked the room with that icy gaze, her normally piercing blue eyes flat with disinterest as though she just wanted to get the class over with.

"To paraphrase the infamous words of Mark Twain"—Ms. Schlaza paused for effect and drew herself up tall— "Rumors of my demise have been greatly exaggerated."

She let out what I could only assume was a laugh, three precise barks with her lips curved into an approximation of a smile.

"Ms. Schlaza made a joke?" Owen whispered. "What's next, a plague of locusts?"

"Today we will focus on your end of semester exams. Passing is critical to continue your studies."

Here we go. I cringed, remembering the mind-numbing repetition and verbal abuse the woman heaped on us in those initial days. No doubt we'd be lining up again for militant drills and browbeating. The collective groan that rose from the class signaled that the others knew what was coming too. We'd survived Schlaza's lessons before, but I sent up a silent prayer for her to not be on my schedule next semester.

"I'm going to share a few easy tips and tricks, to ensure each and every one of you passes your exam." Her smile was back, but didn't reach those flat blue eyes. "First and foremost, read all test instructions thoroughly. The tests are designed to trip you up and seem harder than they truly are." Her voice was light and conversational as if she discussed the weather over a cup of tea.

"Now she's being helpful?" Bethany hissed, as confused as I was.

"At least we know why she left on sabbatical." Owen smiled at our confusion. "She went off to have a lobotomy."

"We're supposed to practice the good cheer charm," Lars called from the back, interrupting her explanation of important keywords that would be used in exam questions.

Lars had been one of the few struggling to get his spell to work. He must be desperate to get somebody into the holiday spirit. Either that, or the bully in him had risen to goad a kinder, gentler Ms. Schlaza. And the queen under the ice responded. Our teacher's jaw clenched at the interruption, and fire flashed behind her eyes.

"That is…" Lars looked about nervously, belatedly raising his hand. "We're supposed to get the first half of the period to practice the spell because we have an assignment over holiday break."

"That is true." Ms. Eisner's voice quavered, and she continued as if speaking to herself. "I promised more time."

Schlaza's gaze swung to pin Ms. Eisner, who went distinctly pale and gave an apologetic shrug. The class held its breath, but Ms. Schlaza's features softened, her angry glare slipping back to disinterest as though she barely registered the other woman.

"But of course." Schlaza's tinkling laugh was a parody of Eisner's nervous one as she flipped her ponytail around to tug on the end. "By all means, have your practice session. We'll resume exam review at the top of the hour."

"Are you sure?"

I didn't blame Ms. Eisner for being cautious; it could be a trap. But the ice queen just gave a gracious nod, yielded the floor, and tugged hard on her braid. An odd dark patch stood out underneath the leather wrap binding Schlaza's ponytail. She either had a tattoo at the base of her neck or dark roots that meant bleached hair and the whole Nordic blonde look was a sham.

"Did you see that?" Bethany's breath came hard and shallow.

"Yeah, it's like she had a personality adjustment." I said, agreeing with Owen's lobotomy comment.

Mary Eisner called for those still needing a focus to come up and select their item of choice, then launched into a recap of the spell's mechanics—all the while shooting nervous glances back at Ms. Schlaza, who leaned with one foot planted against the wall as she twirled the end of her ponytail.

"No, I mean the markings on the back of her neck. It's the sigil!"

"Are you sure?" I tried to build an image of what I'd just seen, but it was just a dark patch. Bethany had a better angle.

"Positive, just like the marks we found under those burns on the electrical cables."

What the hell?

The morning class flew by, giving us limited opportunity to discuss Bethany's claim. Ms. Schlaza stepped up at the top of the hour and gave what amounted to a ridiculously thorough review session for our exam questions. Amazingly she skipped right past "useful advice" and seemed to simply feed us actual test questions.

Once the class got over their initial shock and a kind of freakish delight underpinning Schlaza's words, notebooks sprang open and everyone scribbled frantically. The whole thing hardly felt ethical, but this was the first class the woman had "taught" that left her students wanting more.

In our next class, Owen and I enjoyed stunning cinematic footage of dams and turbines with an engagingly informative voice over. But my mind kept straying back to the moment Ms. Schlaza flipped her ponytail out of the way. All I recalled was a dark flash of…something. I just couldn't be certain.

What if Bethany was right? Ms. Schlaza had changed for the better during her time off. Whatever she'd been up to had certainly helped the woman's militant anger issues. Ethics…not so much. Still, if she didn't take her inner demons out on us the rest of the semester, so much the better. Right?

When the lunch whistle blew, you would have thought the building was on fire. Everyone jumped to their feet and the room exploded into a cacophony of students discussing holiday plans. The halls flooded with people racing toward the exit, and emptied faster than during the open house disaster.

Mr. Gonzales intercepted Owen and me before we hit the doors separating rings. I would have liked to talk with the gang about what Ms. Schlaza's change of heart might mean, but instead settled for asking Owen to say happy holidays for me and promising I'd text if anything important came up.

19. Holiday Headache

M Y AFTERNOON WITH Mr. Gonzales was not what I expected. Instead of simply having me follow him on his normal rounds, he had mapped out an orientation. The man had serious objectives in mind and even provided a qualification guide to certify me as a maintenance assistant over the coming week.

"So I've been wondering about the gremlins you've caught." I finally broached the topic after an hour of following gas pipes in search of the main regulator marked on our schematic. "The dean had me read a book called *Magical Menaces*. All its gremlin descriptions talk about scaly little creatures."

"What did you tell Gladstone?" He narrowed his eyes as if worried I'd told the dean he couldn't handle his job.

"Just that we had a gremlin in the coffee machine and that you've been finding more." The hurt look in his eyes made me feel like I'd ratted him out, so I hurried on. "Dean Gladstone said you were his best student back in the day and that you'd be all over the problem. I guess he figured working for you was the best way for me to learn how to deal with stuff like this."

That seemed to mollify the man. He laid a hand over the pipe we'd been tracing, in the same affectionate way Chad caressed his stone pillar.

"Well, gremlins come in many shapes and sizes. I'm sure your book would agree. Other texts might show the type we've got here. In fact, some of the ones I've found are more like you describe. You're right though, that snake we caught in the commons is new. Hopefully Dean Gladstone can tell me more about it."

Strange—the dean had acted surprised about the gremlins and certainly would have mentioned if he had one for study. Then again, maybe examining the snake had been delegated to another teacher.

"But where do they come from? How many are left? What do you do with the ones you catch?" The questions just poured out of their own accord.

"Jason, we'll get there." He chuckled at my eagerness, apparently fully forgiving any faux pas I'd made in talking to the dean about his job. "I don't think many are left."

I pointed to the trap poking out of his tool bag. "The book talks about warding with salt and spells, but doesn't mention traps. It's more about making them unwelcome than catching them."

"Yes, well, these are new." Mr. Gonzales tucked the device down into his bag. "Based on Faraday cage principles to contain spiritual essence. Cutting edge stuff. You might find the method mentioned in a magical trade journal, but I doubt it's made it to textbooks yet. I got these from a friend over at the Bashar School. Maintenance guys have to stick together. It's the only way to keep these old buildings humming along."

"So the building's issues have all been due to gremlins from the start?" I asked.

"Yep. I don't know exactly what they're doing in there, but part of it's due to their direct interference. Certainly the lighting is. A lot of the tremors are the building's own defenses kicking in and trying to handle the problem. But we're close. I expect to have this all wrapped up during the holiday break."

The two-o'clock rumble hit as if emphasizing his words.

"That's a relief." As was hearing the gremlins were the root cause of the problem, so it had never been Bethany's drawing. "Some of us were worried that something else had gotten into the works and caused problems."

"Something else?" His head snapped up.

"Funny coincidence. One of my friend's drawings went missing the day of the open house. She was worried that it had gotten itself into trouble. Saying it out loud sounds silly."

A lightbulb went on over Mr. G's head. "Ah, young Ms. Daniels and her ever-present sketch book."

Of course, he'd met my friends, but I was surprised he knew Bethany's last name. We all expected teachers to memorize names. Sometimes it never occurred to us that library, cleaning, and maintenance staff were around as many or more hours than the instructors. Still, Mr. Gonzales seemed more interested than angry, so I didn't think he was walking back on the cause of Attwater's woes.

"Yeah, Bethany was pretty broken up about it and took steps to make sure it never happens again. But no harm done, right?"

"None. Her drawings certainly didn't hurt Attwater."

"I'd like to see what you do with the gremlins. Do you banish them or something? What keeps them from coming back?"

"Let's just say that I put them where they belong. I'll show you soon, but for now we have more systems to trace. I want to get through this module today." He laughed at my disappointment and slapped me on the shoulder. "Tell you what, I'll show you how the traps work and where the pests go next week. In fact, why not invite Ms. Daniels so she can see for herself that her little pets aren't a problem for me. Let's make it the Wednesday after Christmas."

"Thanks. Bethany would like that. I think it'll really put her mind at ease."

"Perfect! I'll make sure the access ports stay open," he said as I turned back to the schematic.

One thing was for sure, Mr. Gonzales was in good shape. By the end of the day, my feet were killing me as we pawed through an obscure corner of the lower level where the tangle of equipment turned impossibly dense. Mr. G. laughed at my confusion as I hunted for the last steam manifold.

"You'll eventually get a feel for these things, Jason. No one's an expert their first time out. After a few months on the job, you'll know every nook and cranny of your facility. Believe me, once you 'own' the place it won't be confusing at all."

"If you say so." I'd almost forgotten about Gina's request and mentally kicked myself. "While we're down here, the welding shop says there are problems in hallway H. Can we check that out so they can finish setting up for graduation?"

"Ah, yes, the heartstone ceremony." He sighed as if about to decline, then nodded and headed down the darkened corridor. "This way."

"What *is* a heartstone anyway?" I hurried to follow.

"It's the thing that makes this building Attwater." Passion built with his words as he elaborated. "Old machines and buildings—very old, mind you—can develop a personality or imprint from all the people who interact with them."

"We noticed that." I thought back to Chad's rapport. "I have a friend who swears he can sense the building's moods, and I'm starting to believe him."

"Truly? That's interesting; I'd like to meet that young man. As the cumulative experiences that flow through the doors settle in the structure, a kind of consciousness grows. Though not precisely alive, places like Attwater ascend to be more than simple architectural structures."

"And the heartstone?" I prompted.

"That is a matter of some debate. The theory is that a chamber deep within the foundation becomes the focus for that evolving consciousness. Like a pearl, over the decades and centuries, a core will grow. Few have ever seen one, so take this with a grain of salt. It's half mysticism, half folklore, and maybe half wishful thinking." He chuckled at the bad math. "But some swear there's a gem embodying the building's spirit. That's why graduations are superstitiously held down here where there happens to be a nice open area. No family or friends, just an intimate ceremony in hopes that the good will of the school will follow each student into the world. Nostalgic thinking if you ask me, but traditions matter, I guess. Ah, here we are."

One side of the main corridor opened into a long, low-ceilinged room. The wedge-shaped area funneled toward an archway, which undoubtedly led to the heartstone chamber. Or it would if there were actually a door set in the arched alcove at the far end instead of a stone wall. A brass plaque rested on a granite pedestal within the recess.

Dozens of folding chairs were scattered across the floor. Someone had started to set up for the ceremony. But they would have been driven out in a hurry by the popping sparks raining down from several electrical junction boxes set high on the walls. The overhead bulbs had blown out, leaving the area bathed in ghastly flat contrast from emergency lights near the ceiling.

Mr. Gonzales pulled on a pair of thick rubber gloves, selected an insulated wrench and screwdriver, and stepped into the alcove. I followed, squinting against the little explosions and wishing for my tinted welding goggles. My eyes streamed despite not looking directly at the source of the sparks. Mr. G held one hand in front of his face as bits of molten metal rained down. Sweat popped out on his forehead despite the cool, damp air.

He got within two feet of the first box, but the junction popped and sizzled, driving him back with a new flare of sparks. It took a second to realize he'd gone into full retreat. Maybe my recent welding had made me more confident. I could have flipped the cover open to at least get a look at the problem. But without insulating gloves, caution was the better part of valor. I followed his example and fell back. Mr. G. stripped off the gloves and braked out a curse full of hard guttural words we'd never learned in high school Spanish.

"Close," he said after catching his breath. "I'll get down here over the weekend and straighten this out."

As we backed away from the entrance, I could have sworn the plaque at the end of the room glowed with sullen red light. I blinked, and the light was gone, likely an afterimage from the bright arcing.

"That's not the heart, right?" I was sure he'd said it would be a pearl or gem.

"No, just a dedication," he said. "Heartstone chambers aren't known for easy access. If there was going to be a door that would be the spot. Way before I ever showed up here, the staff decided this place had indeed developed a heartstone and commemorated the miracle with that plaque. Read it when you get the chance. It details a few key points in Attwater's history and construction. Never discount the strength of symbols in magic. If nothing else, that hunk of metal provides a focus for honoring the school."

"Shouldn't we at least cut the power?" I didn't like the idea of leaving such violent shorts. Something could easily catch fire. Although, on second thought, it wouldn't be the stone floors, walls, or ceiling. But still…

"This loop is tricky to isolate, but I'll see what I can do to watch for fires."

"You okay?" I reached out as he stumbled.

"Just tired." He waved me back. "It's been a long week. I'll be fine. Let's stow this gear and your workbooks. Go home, enjoy your holiday, and I'll see you and Ms. Daniels on Wednesday."

Leaving for the night felt surreal as I wandered the deserted halls heading for the upper level. Everyone was gone, including the faculty. Even the commons stood deserted. With night classes cancelled I wouldn't get to see Gina's smiling face either, which made me glum.

The building shook and shivered as if it too mourned the empty halls, and I couldn't shake the feeling that Attwater wanted me to stay. I snorted out a laugh at the very Chad-like thought.

"Don't worry." I passed the atrium on my way to the exit. "Your cowboy will be back before you know it."

Yep, as bad as Chad.

Back home, I sent out a sappy text wishing everyone a safe and happy holiday. I told the gang that Mr. Gonzales had invited us back on Wednesday. He'd been keen to meet Bethany and had perked up when I mentioned Chad's connection with Attwater, so I figured the man wouldn't mind a little extra company. Plus Chad would be going insane away from his architecturally-challenged friend and would be itching to read that heartstone dedication plaque—if we could get close enough. Owen...well, Owen put on a brave front, but I felt sorry for the guy. With no family, for all I knew he would spend Christmas at the bar, assuming he celebrated.

After the texting fest, boredom quickly set in. I was about to go to the garage and fire up an experiment when a horrible thought crossed my mind. Forget about the gremlins, the heartstone, and the mysterious reappearance of Ms. Schlaza. More sinister problems were afoot. I hadn't shopped for gifts yet.

After a night of emergency consumerism, I spent Saturday programming four new Warts. I figured they could patrol the halls for gremlins before classes started up, which should help Mr. G. clear the building once and for all. My latest Herb waited patiently in the corner, basic programming intact, but I hadn't activated him in weeks. The holiday break presented the perfect opportunity to move my experiments to the utility room the dean had offered up as a workshop. My workshop— I liked the sound of that.

The Warts could run overnight as an automated staff with cameras recording. Their simple instructions required little decision making, so it would be safe. Then it would just be a matter of fast forwarding through their video to spot any unwanted activity. The evolving plan was likely to have me spending even more hours on independent study. But I'd take that deal in a minute if it meant putting my creations to good use.

I ran Wart Thirteen down the test ramp, following a length of PVC pipe, and watched through the dean's spectrum goggles. With each course adjustment the energy feedback within my construct tipped into what I considered the yellow range, but quickly dropped back to a muted glow that was safely in the green.

Even following the twists and turns at the end of the short course didn't push the feedback energies to critical. By the end of the night. I was confident none of the Warts would go offline or explode. A few more trials before Wednesday would verify cruising the building for hours wouldn't have a cumulative effect, but I was pretty sure my design was solid. *Where have these goggles been all my life?*

I fingered the mini candy cane in my pocket, my focus for Ms. Eisner's spell. In the morning, I'd have to pick a few likely candidates.

* * *

"Bethany, we've got hot cocoa and fresh-made gingerbread! Come down and help trim the tree."

Bethany smiled as her mother's voice drifted up the stairs. The holiday spirit spell certainly worked. The woman hadn't criticized her all weekend or tried to push her out of Attwater to get a real job instead of wasting time on a dubious certification program. Mom hadn't even complained about women at work wasting money on gifts or sending their bratty children to college—not that Bethany expected to get any Christmas gifts. Refreshing the cheer spell each morning might just make this the best Christmas ever.

"Be right down," Bethany called through the bedroom door.

Ms. Eisner hadn't said anything about casting the spell on the same person more than once. Hopefully there wouldn't be a hangover effect when the magic faded. After three peaceful days Bethany wouldn't be able to take the backlash if things swung the other way. For now, everything was going great.

Jason's text inviting her and the others back to school was just icing on the cake. Better yet, he'd sent a private message to let her know that Mr. Gonzales didn't think Mortimer had anything to do with Attwater's troubles. *Huge relief.* The poor guy was still recuperating, and a niggling suspicion had her wondering if her drawing had tangled with one of the gremlins. If that was the case, he'd been defending rather than attacking the school. Going back during the break offered a chance to check on him and touch up his wounds again if needed.

She added a few more pencil strokes to the massive canvas propped on the easel in the corner, placing spiny quills along the reptilian back. She'd been working on the project for weeks, away from Attwater's prying eyes, and took care not to breathe life into the dragon-dinosaur hybrid. Between its defensive and offensive abilities, Hilda would have approved of the dream-inspired creature, not that she intended to ever show it to that psycho-bitch.

The recurring dream—or more accurately, the nightmare—always faded quickly. Bethany never caught much context, but an image of the dragon stayed with her. Drawing out what she remembered eased the knot of fear that too often accompanied waking.

He needed a name. She racked her brain for a decent one from television, but refused to go the Barney route—maybe something simple like Dinacus. Bethany shrugged. There'd be time to work on that later.

20. Attwater Divided

THE GANG AGREED to gathered Wednesday morning at—you guessed it—our finest lunch table. I arrived earlier to move projects and tools into my newly christened workshop on the second floor. I waited for the others with lucky Wart Thirteen poised prominently in the center of the table. Call me crazy, but I'd decided to own the bad luck my creations encountered.

The crew must have met up at the atrium because they came down the dim hall together, worry painted on their faces. I'd had a similar reaction. The building shook and pipes clanged overhead like it was the end of the fricking world.

"What the hell happened?" Chad yelled when he spotted me.

Wart danced back and forth across the tabletop, keeping balance thanks to a gyroscope that kept decision making to a minimum and didn't risk the little guy's destruction.

"No idea," I said as the tremors subsided. "It was like this when I arrived. They come and go, but it's way worse than anything we've seen before."

Dust and debris blanketed the commons, testifying to the increased severity. Chad rushed over and basically hugged his favorite column.

"She's really hurting," Chad said after a long minute, then smiled. "But she missed me."

"Oh my god, get a room." Owen rolled his eyes, then squawked and jumped as a big chunk of plaster shattered on the floor where he'd been standing. "Too slow!"

"Taunting the building is not going to help," Bethany said. "But what the heck, Jason?"

"It'll stop in a minute," I assured her. "I've been here for an hour. This is more than just the morning light show and rumbles. Intensity is up an order of magnitude."

"More gremlins?" Chad asked.

"Must be." I pulled Wart over in front of me as the others sat. "One way or another, we're going to find out today. Mr. Gonzales promised to show me what he does with the ones he catches. Maybe that'll give us a clue."

The quake subsided, making discussion easier, and I filled them in on recent happenings.

"What's with the robot-man...man?" Owen poked a finger in Wart Thirteen's face, which would show up on his button camera feed as a huge beige sausage.

"Surveillance to see what's going on at night. With things getting so much worse, these critters must be coming in when no one's around."

"Eyes on the ground are no good if they explode," Owen said.

"I've got that covered." I held up the dean's special goggles. "My new bots can monitor without having to make a bunch of decisions, so no exploding Warts."

"That sounds all kind of disturbing. But let's get on with it and make things better." Owen jumped to his feet, keeping a wary eye on the ceiling. When nothing fell, he gave a courtly bow and wave. "Lead on, mon warty capitan."

The hallways were a mess. As with the commons, miscellaneous debris and piles of stone dust littered the floors. Even worse, the violent shaking must have ruptured the utility lines because spurious gouts of steam and dripping water came from the systems tucked up against the ceiling.

"You boys are going to have a hell of a time cleaning all this up before Monday," Owen said as we swiped through to the inner ring.

"Forget clean up." Chad looked pale, and a sheen of sweat coated his face. "Top priority is helping Mr. Gonzales with the gremlins. I think Attwater's dying."

"Try thinking happy thoughts," I suggested. "Maybe that will help calm the building."

Chad nodded, but looked like he was about to throw up. Hopefully the exercise would calm our friend too. The bond he'd developed was turning into a liability and giving sick-building syndrome a whole new meaning.

We stood around the distribution panels where Mr. G. and I had started my lesson. After fifteen minutes he still hadn't shown up. Despite Chad's happy thoughts, a steady vibration built in the stones around us.

"Could that be him working down there?" Bethany waived her sketchbook at an open door at the far end of the hall.

In contrast to the faltering yellow lights illuminating the hallway, a steady white glow shone from the room.

"Only one way to find out," I said.

The others trailed me down the hall. I'd set my little robot to follow mode, and he rolled along obediently a few steps behind. Preprogramming would let me easily shift him over to night patrol when we left for the day. Ad-hoc mode allowed on-the-fly programming, but I didn't plan to layer on untested instructions and risk damaging Wart.

As we neared the door, the light spilling from the room jumped and shifted as though someone walked between the source and doorway. A female voice drifted from inside, muffled and indistinct but certainly not belonging to Mr. Gonzales. We gathered around the door and peered inside.

"Just hold still!" Ms. Schlaza's back was to us, and she wrestled a five-foot-long shadowy form that wriggled and tried to escape her gasp.

Her long hair slapped left and right as she struggled with the gremlin that looked much like that very first one, but on steroids. Metal glinted in her left hand as she raised one of the battery capture devices. The gremlin snake thrashed violently as it shrank, and Schlaza strained as if holding it in place took every ounce of effort.

Bethany and I exchanged a confused look. Now Ms. Schlaza was one of the good guys? I almost stepped into the room to see if I could help, but something was off. The woman's hands were too wide apart. The gremlin sort of floated in front of her as it continued to shrink out of sight. The ice queen relaxed and lowered her arms with a nod.

"Now that wasn't so bad. Was it?" Ms. Schlaza tossed the trap aside and stepped back to reveal a short woman with dark skin and hair.

The other woman faced away from us, the smoky outline of the last foot of the gremlin snake's tail thrashing against her shoulders. I couldn't pull my eyes away as the gremlin disappeared into the base of the shorter woman's neck, leaving a glowing red sigil on her cocoa skin. The mark quickly faded to black, matching the one we'd seen on the electric cables.

"It was...uncomfortable." The dark-haired woman turned.

We all pulled back from the door frame, but not before catching the woman's profile. The elegant nose and round cheeks could only belong to one person, Ms. Robles, our temporary dean.

"*WTF.*" Bethany mouthed the acronym at me, eyebrows knitted together, then turned and did the same across to where Owen and Chad stood on the far side of the doorway.

"This is bad." I turned my back on the others to muffle my whispered words. "If she's stealing the captured gremlins and—"

"What is that?" Ms. Schlaza shrieked from inside.

I looked back, worried she'd caught sight of one of the others, only to find Wart standing smack in the middle of the doorway. He rolled contentedly back and forth, making tiny adjustments to keep his station as I shifted uncertainly. True to his programming, he'd slipped around to his follow position when I'd turned to speak to Bethany.

A scrape sounded from inside. We had to go!

Making a snap decision, I waved Chad and Owen down the hall, thumping my chest with a fist and mouthing "heartstone plaque." We couldn't afford to be identified.

I pulled Bethany into a run in the opposite direction. Wart followed. The women had certainly seen the robot, but I doubted either knew what my homegrown projects looked like.

As we made the end of the hall, a glance back showed Schlaza just emerging from the room. Something dark and dangerous spilled out with her. Its smoky outline made me think it was the gremlin at first, but this was bigger—much bigger. It walked on all fours like some kind of mutant shadow dog with one glowing red eye level with the woman's shoulder. We skidded around the corner. I was pretty sure she hadn't spotted us.

"To the stairs!" I raced ahead and opened the doors as quietly as I could manage.

We plunged down the spiraling stairs with Wart thumping along behind. I'd already told the others about the ceremony area, but it might take the guys a while to find their way down from the atrium side of the building.

A breathy howl echoed from the stairwell above as we spilled into the lower level. The thing had our scent. Another spectral wail drove us onward. We wound our way toward the center of the building, putting distance between us and our pursuer.

Sparks flashed from the alcove ahead, marking the graduation area and testifying to the fact Mr. G. hadn't been able to cut the power for repairs. We couldn't afford to get cornered, and I pushed on past with Bethany in tow, figuring we'd run into the others and come up with plan B. But the zip-flash of electricity illuminated two figures crouched at the back of the room. Owen and Chad had beat us.

"How the hell did you get here so fast?" I asked as we ducked under a shower of sparks.

Chad straightened from examining the commemorative plaque, and Owen just shrugged.

"Auto shops are on the ground floor." Owen jerked a thumb off to his right. "I've been working my way through the lower levels for the past month, just trying to figure out where everything is. So when you mentioned the graduation area, I knew exactly where to head."

"Got it, but we can't stay." I looked back over my shoulder. "Schlaza released some kind of shadow animal. It's hot on our trail."

"Correction." Bethany's voice quavered. "It's found us."

Sure enough, the hound padded silently around the corner, its single eye blazing and shadowy mouth gaping wide to expose smoky teeth. It might not have gleaming white fangs, but after seeing the snake slither into Ms. Robles, I had no interest in finding out what a bite from our friendly demon hound would do.

By staying quiet, it had fooled me into thinking we'd lost it, which meant it was smart. The room was wide. Fanning out and rushing by to either side might confuse it enough for us to get out of the dead-end trap. But we'd have to time it so no one got a face full of molten sparks. The beast cringed back from those bright flashes, keeping to the center of the room as it stalked closer. Before I could tell the others what I was thinking, Bethany and Owen took the situation into their own hands.

"Eat fire, Fido!" Owen launched a ball of flame straight at the thing's head.

Bethany's spell came right on its heels, but lower and to the left to take out a muscular front leg. Sometimes it paid to be friends with the best students in common core. I'd never been able to cast fire that quickly.

Owen's spell smashed into the demon's face with a muffled whoosh and simply…disappeared. Bethany's struck its front right shoulder and did the same. Smoky tendrils swallowed the blazing orange balls. The dog's outline glowed from within for a second, dark wisps standing out along its back like raised hackles. Then both fireballs zoomed on to smash into the wall by the alcove's entrance. Matching scorch marks blossomed on the stonework as the spells spent their energy and winked out.

"Shit!" Owen looked down at his hands. "They passed right through the damned thing."

"Time to run." I waved Owen and Chad off to the right and got ready to go left. "End run tight to the walls. It can't get us all."

Not much of a pep talk, but there was no time to come up with something better. The only problem was, Chad didn't budge. Instead he laid a hand on the dedication plaque, which had turned the sullen red of overheated iron. Magic gathered around him—lots of it—a building static charge. The junction boxes crackled frantically, cascades of sparks flaring to either side of the chamber. But instead of arching to the floor, the glowing particles swirled upward, smoke and sparks coalescing into a flat disc like a storm cloud that spread across the ceiling of the chamber.

The plaque flared with energy, and Chad cried out as he raised his fist and struck down with fingers splayed wide. Lightning exploded from the swirling cloud, a sizzling bolt that slammed into the thing hunting us. The demon dog's red eye narrowed as it whipped toward Chad with a rasping snarl. The dog took a slow, menacing step forward. A second bolt blazed down, and the creature exploded.

Oily black smoke blew out in all directions, washing over us with the scent of burnt rubber and rotten meat. I choked, tried not to inhale, but ended up with hands on knees, coughing. Thankfully, the foul smoked dissipated fast.

"That was different." Chad groaned and slid to the floor as the glow faded from the plaque.

"I think cowboy tapped an artery," Owen said. "That's more than just *predicting* the weather."

"Give me a hand." I crouched down and shook Chad's shoulder before trying to hoist him up.

The cowboy gave me a goofy, exhausted smile and a thumbs up. I grabbed him under the left shoulder and Owen took his right. We wrestled Chad to his feet.

"You okay?" I asked.

"Yeah, just wiped out." He nodded and was able to stand on his own, but looked decidedly loopy.

"We need the library," Bethany said, and we all must have given her the same look because she threw up her hands in exasperation. "Our teacher is controlling shadow demons, and one's inside the acting principal—inside her! The library is the only place to research demonic possession. There might be a way to save them."

"Save them?" Owen's jaw hung open. "Schlaza's trying to kill us!"

To be fair, she might have only sent the dog to corner or maim us. But we had seen one of the smoky creatures go right into Ms. Robles, which was all kinds of bad. If the school didn't magically dampen cell phone signals, we could call for help. Of course, the staff phone numbers probably rang to the front office, and civilian authorities would be useless. Hell, we didn't even know where our school was—probably another reason phones and their GPS signals were disabled once we crossed through each morning.

With everyone gone on break, Mr. Gonzales was the only help we had a chance of reaching. Even better, he had experience catching these things, at least the small ones.

"Library first, then we find Mr. Gonzales," I said to curtail further argument.

Bethany nodded, Owen sputtered, and Chad just swayed on his feet as if drunk. I led the others back to the hall, ducking under a weak spray of sparks and checking that the coast was clear. The junction boxes only sparked occasionally now, as if Chad had drawn off their energy to power his spell.

"All clear." Owen took lead and waved for us to follow.

Only problem was, he went the wrong way. Well, that and Chad managed about three steps before stumbling. I caught him before he fell and glared at Owen.

"Plan B," I said. "Bethany and I will do some hasty research. Take Chad up to the commons until the aftereffects of that spell wear off. Teachers avoid the commons like the plague, but keep an eye out for Schlaza. We'll meet you there in an hour. If Chad's better, we can all go find Mr. G."

21. The Nerve Center

SOON BETHANY AND I were pouring through yet another stack of books. We'd started with three from her prior visit and added two more. The deeper we dug the more confusing things became.

"They don't do it." Bethany shook her head in frustration. "It just isn't normal for shadow demons to possess people. Kill them, sure, but they don't take people over like in the movies. Even mimic demons don't; those are just crafty shape shifters."

"So we're dealing with another species. Something no one's encountered before." It was the only thing that made sense.

"Maybe, but it *has* to be linked to this sigil." She slapped her palm down on the book with the only exact match for the symbol we'd found around Attwater. "And the damned thing just doesn't show up, not in ceremonies, or summoning, or warding. Our hour's almost up, and I'm sick of all these dead ends."

"Sick and tired." My eyes were crossing, but something in the sentiment struck a chord. Could it be that simple? "There have got to be texts on magical maladies, curses, and things like that. If possessions have happened before…"

"…we might find answers in medical journals," she finished my statement, rushed to the computer, and searched the catalog.

Ten minutes later, she had a dusty old tome open to a truly disturbing drawing. Mages in long red robes were casting people into a pit of burning logs. The victims had been stripped naked, and each sported the intricate design we'd been searching for somewhere on their body. An hourglass dangled from a rope belt at the waist of each red-robed individual, the ones doing the killing.

"Not much of a cure." I squinted at the flowing calligraphy beneath the image, trying to make out the words. But my high school hadn't offered Gaelic. Fortunately, there were typed notes in—you guessed it—really old English. "Does that say black death?"

"It looks like they had a lot of euphemisms, but no solutions once someone was possessed. Anon shaltow make purgen firbrenning and mitte faith." Bethany's brow knitted after reading the last line of the main text. "Quickly make pure with fire and faith, I think."

She ran a finger down through the translated footnotes and flipped to the back of the book where a meticulously drawn sigil above cramped text looked real enough to pick up. "This language is more contemporary. The monks in those red cloaks blame something called the Shadow Master for bringing the scourge to the mainland. They burned the infected and eventually cast the Shadow Master back to whatever hell it came from."

As much as I disliked Ms. Schlaza, tossing our teacher into a burning pit just didn't seem like the right answer. A stunt like that would probably go on our permanent records. I was about to ask Bethany to double check the index, when soft footsteps sounded in the main room.

"Schlaza's found us," I hissed, and we both dove for cover as the door rolled open.

We crouched between the stacks, dust tickling my nose and making me want to sneeze. Stupid brain. The dust hadn't bothered me while we read. The books scattered across the table drew our stalker's attention and the footsteps veered away. From our hiding spot, I could just make out the table legs. Instead of the ice queen's toned calves and high heels, khakis pants ending in steel-toed loafers walked around the table as their owner pawed through our reading material.

"Jason, are you in here?" The familiar male voice was not Ms. Schlaza's.

Instead of answering, I listened hard for someone else, but heard only the steady breathing of the man by our reading nook. Bethany grimaced and shrugged. It wasn't as if we could sneak out anyway.

"Down here, Mr. Gonzales." I strolled out of the stacks as casually as I could manage, trying not to look guilty.

"Ah, there you are." Mr. G. wore his perpetual smile, eyes twinkling as he caught sight of Bethany slipping out behind me. Wart followed dutifully close on her heels. "And Ms. Daniels. So nice to see you." He waved at our books. "Given our last discussion, I thought I might find you studying up. This was the first place I looked when you weren't in the commons. Not exactly light reading though."

"No, but check this out." I showed him the texts discussing demons and flashed the original sigil info we'd found. "I think we've got more than simple gremlins on our hands. These seem like shadow demons. We just dealt with a big dog-shaped one so there's definitely more than the small snakes around."

"A canine shadow?" His eyes narrowed as he studied my face. "When did you run across that?"

"Just this morning." I hurried on in the face of his skepticism. "Don't worry. We took care of it. Fireballs didn't faze it, but Chad pulled up a couple of lightning bolts that did the trick."

Bethany helped describe how we'd been cornered on the basement level, and the brief battle that ensued. We downplayed the encounter, neither of us wanting to be sent away due to some misguided notion that the situation was too dangerous for new students. I also didn't want to come across as accusing him of misjudging the threat facing Attwater. Nonetheless, the conclusion still held. Even if that first coffee-loving snake was a gremlin, there were definitely demons in the mix now.

"This symbol has popped up in several spots around school." I traced a finger over the drawing in our reading and described what we'd found.

We didn't mention Ms. Schlaza or possession. With a lack of solid proof, I found myself second-guessing what we'd seen. Maybe our initial impression was right and the women had actually been fighting off the shadows. It had looked that way when I first peeked into the classroom. The dog demon might have simply decided to chase Wart. Maybe Schlaza hadn't commanded him at all. I just wasn't ready to lay out accusations.

"And the robot?" Mr. Gonzales kept his voice carefully neutral as we ran out of things to say.

"A hobby." I shrugged, having given up fighting for people to call my machines automata. "My robots have cameras, so I'd planned to ask if they could patrol the halls overnight and watch for gremlin activity. But now…" Now, the situation had changed.

He nodded as I trailed off, and the three stared down at the books. Mr. G. looked as if he might reject the story as a wild tale. Who could blame the man? He practically lived in Attwater. That the demons had managed to stay hidden from him showed they were a wily bunch and certainly would cast doubt on our account. But a sudden resolve settled over his features.

"If what you say is true—" he waved away whatever expression crossed my face and laid a hand on the nearest book. "Not that I don't believe you. But if all this is true, we're going to have to change tactics." He scratched his chin and peered down at Wart as if considering options. "Show me these sigils."

We snapped a few more pictures of our research, including the ghastly, red-robed ceremony, put the books away, and hurried from the library. Bethany and I led him to the classroom where we'd first found the symbol after he'd captured two of the creatures. Wart trundled along in our wake. I kept an eye out for Ms. Schlaza and Ms. Robles. Thankfully, Attwater was huge, and we didn't cross paths. Maybe they'd retreated to the administrative wing.

"How about that." Mr. G. wiped soot off the burnt conduit to get a better look at the faint markings. "I caught a pair of gremlins right here, didn't I?"

"Yes, sir. We think it's a kind of magical signature they leave behind when entering or exiting a system." Or person, but I didn't say that out loud. If the books were accurate, these things didn't leave humans.

"Is it possible there's just a couple of them that keep coming back?" Bethany asked.

"Don't think so." He turned away from the symbols and stuck the dirty rag in his pocket. "I have a special way of dealing with these gremlins—or whatever they are. Would you like to see?"

"Yes," Bethany and I said in unison.

If it was as simple matter of improper disposal, we could figure out a better method or even leave them in the traps to get ahead of the infestation.

"Follow me." Mr. Gonzales led us into the hall.

His workshop turned out to be on the level between the classrooms and basement, in a section of the ring that would be just about over the graduation chamber where we'd fought the dog. Two workbenches took up an entire wall. The cavernous equipment room acted as a hub for the building's systems with archaic analog gauges and meters to the right of the door. Electric, gas, and water lines were joined by steam and bright yellow piping that would be fuel or hydraulic fluid. The aroma of hot metal, grease, and sawdust made me feel right at home.

Twisted sections of pipe and wire, the half-formed art of the caretaker's craft, decorated the bench tops. A line of ten or so of the battery traps sat in clips on the wall near a rolling stool.

"Looks like you're loaded for bear." I pointed to the devices.

Even if he downplayed the trouble, Mr. G. clearly took the infestation seriously. Compared to my new cubby upstairs, this place practically had me salivating. To have this much room to run experiments and dial in my designs would be heaven. Some day!

A green glow from the far end of the room, where a shimmering curtain of energy hung on the wall just beyond the traps, caught my eye.

"What's this?" I walked over to the big patch of energy that clung to the wall like a pulsing oil stain.

"*That* is my secret weapon," Mr. Gonzales said as he came over and shooed me back. "Not too close. It's a one-way portal."

"So you banish your catch?" I looked from the line of traps to the magical doorway, boggled by the level of effort the man went to in keeping our school safe.

Such herculean measures seemed like something the dean himself might undertake. We hadn't learned diddly about advanced magic, but maintaining a gateway to wherever he dumped the gremlins had to take immense power and skill. Suddenly the idea of positioning working class folks to protect the world from evil made a lot more sense. A blue-collar front line of defense would be largely overlooked by the civilian authorities and hopefully the enemy. Mr. G. made me proud to imagine my future self as part of that invisible army.

"This is how it works." He popped a trap out of its clips, waved a hand over the doorway, and chanted something in a guttural language. The green curtain bulged inward as he held up the device.

"Don't you need to catch one first?" I asked.

"Just watch." His confident smile should have put me at ease, but the power pulsing in the doorway felt off, stained.

The bulging barrier swelled, and a dark shape pushed through. I thought it was one of the snake gremlins, but as soon as the bulbous head with its one red eye poked into the room, it stretched like mist and was drawn into the trap Mr. G. held. With an electric pop, the tail disappeared, and the electrodes atop the device sizzled and released a wisp of smoke.

"I don't get it." Bethany came over to stand by me and Wart. "I thought you said it was a one-way portal."

"I did indeed." He waved the trap and smiled as if telling the richest joke in the world. "These make the difference."

Bragging wasn't the man's usual style. But, then again, those traps must be pretty strong if they could pull banished creatures back through the portal.

"Knock, knock." The lilting words came on the heels light tapping as the door swung open. Ms. Robles looked around the room to ensure she wasn't interrupting, then stepped inside with Ms. Schlaza in tow. "You wanted to see us, Ma—Michael?"

She changed his name midstream with a look in my direction. I'd been bracing for some kind of supernatural encounter if we ran across this pair in the corridors, but they looked so…normal. Both wore a pleasant smile as they crossed the room and headed for Mr. G. Ms. Schlaza even gave me a very un-ice-queenly wink as she passed. That should have been my first clue.

"Ladies, so good of you to come!" The maintenance manager beamed and spread his arms wide in welcome. "Your timing is impeccable. I was just demonstrating how we fix Attwater."

After the wink, Ms. Schlaza's lips stretched into a ghastly smile and her eyes glowed crimson like those of the gremlins and demon dog. A few steps from Mr. G., Ms. Robles bent down as if she'd dropped something. Wisps of smoke rose from her back and neck.

"You can't trust them!" I yelled.

"What's gotten into you, Jason?" Mr. Gonzales looked hurt. "Your teachers deserve more respect. These women are friends."

My mind reeled as a shadowy outline rose around the ice queen. Any lingering doubt vanished. Both of them were possessed. We needed to get out of there.

But using the trap must have destabilized something, because another bulge formed on the green surface behind the man. A second dark shadow pushed into the room, followed by a third.

"They're being controlled. Look behind you!" I couldn't get to Mr. Gonzales, so pulled Bethany back until we bumped into the benches.

The first shadow creature stepped into the room on four thick legs, a beefy, barrel-chested dog like the one Chad had defeated. The other was basically a writhing mass of tentacles that drifted two feet above the floor.

"I think someone's had too much caffeine." Mr. G. gave me a toothy grin and didn't even notice the creatures move up to flank him.

"What is your wish, Master?" Ms. Robles knelt with head bowed at the man's feet.

Crap!

Bethany and I took two steps toward the open door, but with a flick of her wrist, Schlaza sent out a wave of magic. The door slammed shut.

"Don't leave just yet." Mr. Gonzales laid a hand on the dog's head and petted the dark creature as it nuzzled up close. "I have so much more to show you both."

He stretched tall, much taller than the Latino man's five-eight frame should have allowed. His features twisted, becoming sharp and angular. Crimson gold shown from his eyes like glowing gems, and he laughed. The quiet sound held despair instead of mirth, violence in place of levity, and a cold lump formed in the pit of my stomach.

"Jason?" Bethany backed toward the door. "I think we've found the Shadow Master."

"It is so refreshing to deal with informed individuals." He motioned Robles to her feet. "Ah, ah, ah."

The last was directed at me with a wagging finger as I sent out a questing air flow—one of my better spells—to turn the door handle. The door swung open, but the tentacled abomination swept across the room to block any escape.

"I think you will both make fine additions to the cause," the thing that had been Mr. Gonzales said conversationally as he strode over, plucked an empty trap from the line, and brought it up to the portal.

Another snake pushed through and was sucked into the smoking trap. I finally understood.

"You aren't catching creatures and sending them away. You've been releasing them into Attwater all along! But why?"

I kicked myself for not seeing it sooner, for assuming Mr. G. had been hauling things away when in fact he'd been smuggling shadow creatures in.

"All will become clear once you are a bit more…compliant, shall we say?" He brandished the traps, clearly intending to infect us the same way Schlaza had infected the acting dean. His accent was gone, and his voice took on a gravelly echo. "Your tinker talents must be brought to the surface, and with training will aid my plans well.

"As for *your* talents, girl." Those glowing eyes looked hungry as they turned on my friend. "Such a remarkable gift. My servants would see you put down like a dog. But scriptomancers are as rare as tinkers. Your creations are strong, but nosy like you. Imagine my surprise at discovering another creature hunting my own through the electrical lines. My shadows drove it away at great cost." He nodded at the look of horror on the girl. "Yes, incorporating your talent will enable bolder moves as the humans fall."

Bethany locked her sketchbook in a death grip, but the emotion that radiated from her in fierce waves bore little resemblance to fear—she was furious. Nothing mattered more than her drawings, and this guy just admitted his demons almost killed Mortimer. She sucked in a big breath and opened her book with shaking hands to a cute unicorn sketch done in colored pencil. Its patchwork hide was incomplete and it didn't yet have a hind end—a work in progress.

"If you like my drawings so much—" she caressed the picture with fingertips, eyes full of regret as her magic flared. "Then you can have them!"

Bethany flung her hand forward and the partially drawn unicorn flew from the page. The two-dimensional sketch grew and twisted into 3D as rainbow sparks flew from its truncated midsection, and thundering front hoofs drove toward the man's face. Cute was no longer a term I could justify as fire flashed in its eyes, and the equine mouth opened impossibly wide to expose t-rex teeth.

Mr. Gonzales cursed as it slammed into his upraised arm and bit down. He slapped out with a burst of energy, and the shadow dog snapped the drawing from the air. The unicorn kicked and bit, tearing chunks of smoking material from the dog's muzzle and neck, but soon grew still.

Bethany gasped in pain, but riffled through her pages and launched another drawing, and another. Three new forms flew at the group by the portal, a couple of sea creatures and a melty-looking humanoid that might have been made of clay, with hooks for hands.

"Go, go, go!" Bethany pushed me toward the door as the portal swelled and new dark forms poured into the room.

The black bulk of the tentacle monster blocked our retreat. I tried to skid to a halt, but Bethany shouldered me forward as a wire-framed rhino beetle the size of a toddler and a vampire bat streaked past. Tentacles lashed out, but couldn't hit the bat, while the beetle bulldozed the demon out of our way.

"That's not going to stop them." I'd always had a quick grasp of the obvious.

I headed left as we spilled into the hall, intending to grab our friends at the commons and get the hell out of the school.

"No, this way." She grabbed my arm and pulled me in the opposite direction, further into the maze of interior corridors.

At the first intersection, Bethany turned one last time. A veritable wave of shadow demons crashed down the hall toward us, led by the tentacle blob, which looked to be missing several appendages from its scrap with beetle and bat. Schlaza and Robles stalked along, waist deep and perfectly at home among the aberrations. We ducked low as a fireball left our teacher's hand.

Bethany flipped through her pages, releasing everything she had. Pencil, charcoal, and ink sketches leapt from the pages at her command, half-formed doodles that were no more than stick figures sailing alongside detailed renderings to intercept our pursuers. Her hand flew until nothing remained except blank pages. She sagged as the meager line of defenders crashed against the demon horde, buying us time.

"Good job, but not time to rest." I hauled her upright and got us moving.

Pain creased her features as one by one her creations winked out of existence. We needed a place to hide and come up with a plan. If we could sneak out of the building unseen, I might be able to get a call off to Dean Gladstone. Surely the emergency after-hours number would relay a call. But ducking into a random classroom until the coast was clear didn't seem like a good idea. Our pursuers still had eyes on us so hiding would only get us trapped.

Wart rolled along on our heels. I risked telling him to do more than just follow and to let me know if the demons got too close. Hopefully, Owen and Chad had gone to ground or left the building. I didn't like the fact that Mr. Gonzales said he had looked for me in the commons first.

"Make a right up ahead. There's an alcove about fifty yards down." Bethany still pointed the way despite the fact I damn near carried her.

"You better have a good hiding place."

22. Octopus

A S BETHANY STOPPED alongside a recessed metal door, Wart's alarm blared out the "*awooga*" tones of a submarine dive warning.

The footsteps clicking down the hall didn't exactly sound threatening, but the ragged line of shadow demons flanking Ms. Schlaza turned my blood cold. Dozens of monstrous shapes flowed along in silence. Dark hair bobbed under the flickering lights further back among the monsters. Ms. Robles couldn't quite keep up with the other woman's long strides.

With our luck Mr. Gonz—the Shadow Master—would be bringing up the rear. Yes, thinking of him that way didn't tear at my gut so badly. The friendly Mr. Fix-it I'd known was gone—if he'd ever really existed.

"Silence alarm," I told my bot, then looked from Bethany to the door. "Not a chance of sneaking in there unseen, so unless that room has a back door…"

I let the implied question hang in the air, feeling the noose tighten. We'd have to keep running, get out of sight, and pick another hidey-hole. Bethany shook her head and went to the door anyway.

"We've got to run," I said as she pulled a key from her pocket and unlocked the heavy door.

"I *want* them to follow." Sweat gleamed on her face from the exertion and psychological beating she'd taken losing her drawings.

A kind of mad light gleamed in her eyes as if she had a wicked secret. I looked at the door and dark room beyond. A utility room if I didn't miss my guess. The door was heavy duty, so maybe she figured we could wait them out. But I had a suspicion that a simple barrier wouldn't stop the demons. Hell, Schlaza could probably just blast it off the hinges to get at us. So why did I let myself be pulled inside? Maybe it was friendship or simply trust.

Wart swerved around me and disappeared into the darkness amid a strange flapping sound as if leaves fluttered in his wake. Bethany pulled the door shut and dragged me to the back of the dark room. For a fleeting moment, I thought maybe there was another way out and that she planned to somehow trap our pursuers in the tiny room. We huddled in the dark, waiting for the click-slap of high heeled shoes to pass by. But of course they stopped outside.

After a breathless moment the door swung open to reveal the ice queen herself. Bethany hadn't even locked it! Flickering light spilled in from the corridor. The narrow room was maybe fifteen feet deep and lined with metal shelves. Flyers or inventory sheets taped to the shelves fluttered again as a breeze rushed in from the hall.

"Do you want to come out or must we do this the hard way?" Schlaza was cautious despite her magic being vastly superior.

Neither of us moved. To be honest, I couldn't think of anything to say. Something manly and brave from the movies might be good. But "go ahead, make my day" and "I'll be back" were the only lines that popped into my head, and neither fit our dire circumstances. Then I thought of the Staypuff marshmallow man and wished I had an unlicensed nuclear accelerator strapped to my back. *God, I'm such a geek.*

Devil woman Schlaza sighed at our silence. But instead of entering, she stepped aside. Darkness filled the doorway, darkness with tentacles. The creature floated toward us with maybe ten more demons crowding in behind it.

We'd already seen that these things were immune to fire, and I suspected water would have little effect. No one in our class could throw lightning like Chad, let alone Attwater-powered bolts. Air and spirit might sweep them back if I could generate enough energy. I concentrated on a spell we used to create little whirlwinds and did my best to visualize a class F5 tornado.

I felt Bethany ready magic beside me, a small flicker of power that tasted of her talent instead of an elemental spell. What was she up to? Maybe she'd sketched another character as we huddled in the dark, but the demons had already destroyed a dozen of her creations. One hastily drawn figure wouldn't do much good.

"Tina," Bethany called into the darkness. "Time to be tenacious."

Two twisting shapes stretched toward us from the tentacle demon, each looking much like a snake gremlin. When a glowing red eye opened on the bulbous end of each grasping arm, I knew those things would burrow into us and take over. I thrust my hands out to release my whirlwind, but blinked in confusion.

The tangled ball had grown more arms. The tentacles with the glowing eyes retreated and fought with the ones alongside them. The tentacle demon turned on itself, its own arms tangling the ones intent on possessing us. But instead of being dark shadow, these new arms gleamed steely blue in the scant light. White suckers the size of silver dollars lined the underside of each.

"Time for a bit of illumination." Bethany slapped at a glint of metal on the wall, a light switch.

At a glance, the room looked like one giant crime board from a campy detective show, but without colorful yarn pinned up to connect clues. Every shelf edge, every surface, was lined with Bethany's pictures, her own private art exhibit. This had to be where she spent all those extra hours outside class. I dropped my hands, but held my spell at the ready.

A bulging, pebbly form the size of a garbage bag flowed along the top shelf. Intelligent brown eyes looked out from two prominent ridges that formed a mouthless face on what could only be an octopus. A large blank canvas panel taped over the door looked to have been the drawing's home. The octopus, Tina presumably, appeared more substantial than Bethany's other creatures. Densely drawn in colored pencil, it was only slightly translucent, and I wondered if the vibrant markings meant she'd somehow made it poisonous.

Octopus legs twined around shadowy tentacles then withdrew with a jerk. Hooked talons along the row of suckers ripped at the shadowy substance of the lead demon. The two snake tentacles that had threatened us dropped to the floor and puffed out of existence. Tina's skirt flared as she methodically dismembered the tentacle demon. The dying creature keened and thrashed, breaking the eerie silence of the attack.

One of the canine shapes latched its jaws around an octopus arm, which in turn twisted like a python to encircle the demon.

Colorful arms scythed through the crowd of attackers, dealing spectacular damage, but more demons filled the doorway.

I felt Bethany's power building beside me, and quite frankly got scared. In addition to the hanging sheets, sketchpads were piled in short stacks along the bottom shelf.

Ms. Schlaza must have realized what Bethany was up to because her eyes went wide. She pushed her way through the demons, and gathered power into a spell of her own.

"My monsters are real." Bethany half-sang, half-sobbed out the words in a small, trembling voice, maybe thinking of the old "Monsters" song by Shinedown.

Bethany's magic washed over me, and the room exploded into chaos. Every drawing came to life. Reptiles, insects, disembodied heads, and more all broke free of their canvas and executed that peculiar twist into three dimensions. And boy were they angry.

Dozens of her drawings tore into the demon pack, dismembering the ones crowding the room in short order. Some went for Schlaza, but the woman beat them back with flashes of green energy.

The horde of shadows outside tried to pour through the door to replace those that fell, but the animated drawings went on the offensive. Schlaza managed to protect herself, but couldn't stop my friend's living art from streaming into the hall where they clashed with the demons. Demons and drawing alike were torn apart just outside, and Bethany's sharp intake of breath spoke of her pain.

The fighting was fierce and pitched, but the stacks of sketchpads along the lower shelf vibrated and danced as their contents fought to escape. A wave of fresh drawing flew out to join the battle, easily doubling the number of defenders. Ms. Schlaza managed to swat two from the air as the masses whizzed by, turned angry red eyes on us, and gathered her magic.

I let my whirlwind fly. The spell tugged at my clothes as it spun toward our assailant, gathering speed and ripping blank pages from the shelves so that a white tornado of paper smashed into our former teacher.

"Finally, a halfway decent attempt, Mr. Walker." With a chop of her hand and flash of power, my spell winked out of existence. She stepped over the loose pages that drifted to the floor. "But the master has so much more planned for—"

Her words turned into a strangled cry as Tina wrapped a tentacle as thick as my arm around Schlaza's neck and slammed the woman against the shelves. Another deft twist spun Schlaza so her back was to us. A second octopus arm whipped out, slapping against the sigil at the base of her neck.

Schlaza screamed and thrashed, but two more legs slithered across the narrow space to pin her arms and legs. Her eyes glowed crimson with hate, and her glare promised a world of pain for Bethany. Tina tugged with the tentacle now affixed to the back of Schlaza's neck, yanking another scream from the woman—and something else.

The tentacle pulled away. A blob of darkness bridged the gap between suction cups and skin. Wickedly curved hooks extending from each suction cup pierced the blackness, stretching and pulling a yard-long shadow out of the teacher. The shadow snake's bulbous head came out last, its single eye burning angry red. Like removing the candle from a jack-o-lantern, the woman's crimson eyes faded to the icy blue that had chilled me on so many occasions.

"What?" Schlaza looked shell-shocked but recovered quickly as Bethany's pet eased its hold. "Destroy that abomination!"

Another spell leapt to Schlaza's fingertips, and I could only hope the abomination she referred to was the snake and not Tina. But in one swift maneuver, the octopus drew the demon under its skirt. The snake went still with a loud crack. More crunching drew the shadow in as a wicked brown beak flashed at the base of the tentacles. Tina ate the snake demon in three swift bites.

"Well! That was certainly unpleasant." Ms. Schlaza eyed Tina warily and straightened her skirt.

"You and Ms. Robles were possessed by shadow demons." I grasped for the most pertinent facts to bring her up to speed as screeches and screams drifted in from the hall. "Mr. Gonzales too. He's been bringing demons in to take over Attwater."

"No need to prattle on, Mr. Walker." She quickly regained her aloof bearing, which made me feel like I was back in class giving wrong answers. "Regrettably, I remember everything even if I was unable to act. Thank the stars for you, Ms. Daniels. Your little army is giving these demons a run for their money."

Yep, I was still a second class student. The building chose that moment to heave violently, nearly throwing us off our feet. Just as we regained our balance, a fireball burst against the open door. The scorching shockwave slammed me against the shelves. Pain blossomed as my hip caught the metal edge, and the stench of burnt hair filled my nostrils.

Bethany was on the floor panting in pain. A patch of hair along her temple smoked and felt crispy as I patted away the singed ends and helped her to her feet. She looked terrible, but I didn't think due to the spell.

"Drawings don't like fire," she gasped, hands on knees.

"For goodness sakes!" Ms. Schlaza looked exasperated as she waved a hand in front of Bethany, leaving a wall of subtle spirit energy with a simple casting. "Protect yourself, child, or you might as well be out there getting beat up alongside your creations."

When the woman drew her hand away, Bethany sagged with relief, then straightened and marveled as the shield followed her movements. "So much better. I still feel them, but it's bearable."

"The spirit energy takes the brunt of the snap back when your constructs…die, for lack of a better term. Cast your own when you get the chance and customize how much you want to experience, never leave yourself fully open or you'll be of little use in a fight. And speaking of fights." She scooped up a red pencil and blank sheet of paper and scribbled out a series of digits that looked like a phone number with two area codes. "I'll handle Robles and our self-appointed Shadow Master. You two get to the outer ring and call Dean Gladstone. Tell him what's going on and to get his ass here now."

I made a grab for the page, but she pushed it into Bethany's hand. *Yeah, getting snubbed by this woman never gets old.*

"But there's no cell service," I complained.

"Yes, there is." Ms. Schlaza pointed to the extra prefix. "This code disables the suppression spell, but you need to get up to the next level or closer to an exterior wall."

Bethany staggered, but regret instead of pain filled her eyes as another burst of light illuminated the dark hallway. Schlaza ducked halfway through the door, pulled her arm back, and threw a bit of magic down toward the fight. I didn't see what kind, but the spell bounced off the stone walls with a metallic ricochet as though she'd launched a triangle from music class into the fray…or maybe a throwing star.

"I'll get to Robles, if your creature will help." She raised an eyebrow at the octopus, who was now too big to easily sit on the upper shelf and gripped the ceiling and walls with suckered legs.

"Help Ms. Schlaza, Tina." Bethany shooed the undulating beast toward the doorway. "Help them all."

Schlaza followed Tina out, fired off another spell, and turned back to us. "Get out of here and make that call!"

23. Heartstone

BETHANY AND I scrambled through the door and headed away from the fray. I risked a glance back to see Ms. Schlaza fighting her way through drawings and demons locked in battle. Tina flowed along the ceiling like a billowing storm cloud, her free tentacles whipping out to flay ragged black strips from demons wherever one of my friend's creations looked overmatched.

Ms. Robles screeched like a banshee when she saw us running away. I figured she wanted to take Bethany out, which would have disabled the animated drawings. But when the angry woman tried to surge forward, Ms. Schlaza and Tina blocked her path. Farther down the hall, a man strode toward the fight—Mr. Gonzales. An eerie cry went up from the demon horde as they welcomed their master.

A right turn had us sprinting for the stairs and put us out of sight of the standoff. But Attwater shuddered, forcing us to slow because the lights blacked out for a good five seconds. Flashes of energy illuminated the darkness behind as we felt our way down the shifting hall.

Just past the next intersection, the lights flickered to life, and a door on the left slammed open. A foul smelling creature stumbled into our path, arms and curses flying.

"Damn it to hell!" Owen slapped at the dark stains splashed across his front and didn't even notice us gaping.

"You should have known that wouldn't work." A second person emerged from the room—the men's room—and headed down the hall. "We have to keep moving. This way."

"Chad! Owen!" My call brought them up short, although the latter barely looked up as he continued to wipe at his shirt with a wad of paper towels.

"Oh, hey guys." Chad had recovered his strength, but looked worried as he cast furtive glances over his shoulder in the direction opposite the fighting. "Hurry, this way."

I couldn't tell if the cowboy was running away from or toward something, but we followed him to the stairs. Chad had managed to stay pristine, while Owen looked as though he'd been crawling through a sewer. In fact, he smelled like it too.

"Bethany's drawings are fighting a ton of shadow demons back there." I jerked a thumb over my shoulder as we hurried along. "Ms. Schlaza is back on our side and helping."

"Back on our side?" Owen spat out the question, grimaced, and hawked up a foul-looking wad.

I gave a ten-second summary of what we'd discovered in the library and our encounter with the Shadow Master and his demons.

"No wonder Attwater's going ballistic!" Chad said when I'd finished. "She needs us downstairs."

"We've got to go up and call the dean," I said as we approached the stairwell door, which mysteriously opened of its own accord.

"Good luck with that. The building's been herding us along. If we stop or try to go somewhere else, there's always a gentle reminder to keep moving." Owen gave up trying to clean his clothes, tossed away the dirty paper towels, and followed Chad into the stairwell.

"He's right. The school needs us." Chad pointed down the twisting staircase, then toward the ascending steps. "And she's not going to take no for an answer."

The door had jammed against the stairs going up, which should have been impossible. I was certain the heavy slab of wood didn't usually overlap the steps to either side. But the door seemed wider than usual and the landing had twisted so that the railings were too close.

I shrugged and tugged on the door, but it refused to budge—at all. *No problem.* I grabbed the iron rail, intending to climb up the few feet needed to swing myself onto the stairs beyond the blockage. But the metal was so slick that I couldn't hold on, slipped, and nearly cracked my head. I expected to find my palms slathered in grease or something, but they came away clean.

"Really?" I gaped at my friends.

"Yep." Chad's frown managed to hold admiration. "She drove us out of the commons like the sky was falling. If we head the wrong way the lights go out or doors get stuck. And if we stop to hide—"

"Toilets explode!" Owen's voice definitely held a sentiment different than the cowboy's warm regard, and he managed to include the building in the glare he shot Chad. "Always me, never him. So it's good to see someone else take grief for a change."

"We need to get to where we can call." Bethany still winced every few seconds, so the fighting wasn't over, even with the ice queen in our corner.

I looked up through the central gap the stairs spiraled around and could see all the way to the upper floors. That just might be enough to get a few bars. I pulled out my phone and punched in the too-long number Ms. Schlaza had written down. A series of odd beeps was followed by silence. I was about to hang up when it started ringing.

"Bingo! Oh, sorry." A woman had answered. "This is Jason Walker, a first year student. There's a problem at the school."

I described the situation as succinctly as possible, emphasizing the fact that our recently possessed teacher was battling our possessed temporary dean and that she needed Dean Gladstone's help immediately.

"Okay, help's on the way," I said despite the fact that the others probably caught both sides of the brief conversation. "I guess we can go down if it's important. Either that or we wait for the dean and the cavalry."

The landing shuddered and tilted, dumping us all onto the steps leading down.

"Can't wait." Chad gave an apologetic smile and took the steps two at a time, forcing us to follow.

My Wart series wasn't designed for stairs, but Wart Thirteen again managed to clunk down behind us. I'd have to carry him back up later, but he weighed in at less than five pounds so tucking him under my arm wouldn't be a problem.

Attwater's lower halls shook constantly, as if resonating with the violence of the battle taking place above. Something more than conveniently opening doors and blocked corridors guided Chad. He moved with purpose, drawn along by the unseen power of his connection with the school, leading us unerringly back to the area where he'd vanquished the first demon dog. That's where the force guiding him faltered.

"Dead end." Chad ran a hand over the dedication plaque at the back of the graduation chamber, looking confused. "But it wants us to continue."

"Secret passage?" Bethany asked.

"Must be." I tested a few stones around the archway. "Look for a lever or button. That's what they'd find in the movies."

Except this was real life. The four of us poked and prodded for a good five minutes, but came up empty. We even went so far as to set a chair leg on fire and then snuff it out. But the drifting smoke just made me sneeze instead of revealing any telltale draft from a hidden entrance. Chad grew agitated and insisted time was short, though he admitted to not knowing why.

"Back to the hall then." Owen pulled Chad away from the plaque. "Triangulating from a different spot might help."

As we headed down the hall, Chad kept his right arm stretched out to point in the direction of the pull he felt. Halfway down the hall it became obvious that our destination was well behind the plaque alcove.

"Now the pull is waffling," Chad said. "Like it can't decide on going back or continuing on."

"Recalculating," Owen said in a passable impression of a car's GPS. "Maybe it wants us to head outside."

A pipe overhead gurgled, making Owen jump. Our brash friend had become pretty gun shy of the building's antics, but instead of belching nasty substances at him, the sound settled into a sigh.

"Huh, she agrees." Chad scratched his chin. "But how?"

"Through the garages, my friend." Owen's smug smile blossomed under Attwater's approval. "How do you think we get cars and bikes in to work on?"

Two more turns and a straight-away brought us to the auto shop, a vast bay filled with vehicles from ancient to modern in various stages of repair. Some looked like they were being stripped down for parts or simply to see what made them tick. Owen led the way across the bay to three metal roller doors big enough to bring a semi through.

"Hmmm, this might be tricky." Owen studied the keypad on the wall and raised his hand uncertainly. "I'm not sure if my code will—"

A clunk sounded from the big gearbox at the top of the door, followed by metallic ratcheting like a rollercoaster chugging up an incline, and the door slowly rose.

"Good job." I slapped Owen on the back and stepped out into warm sunshine.

The school surrounded open grassy gardens in a horseshoe with two wings sweeping out from the main building. I craned my neck to take in the high stone walls. The four-story structure was more impressive from ground level than the bit I'd seen from the dean's office window. And speaking of windows, there looked to be plenty of high-arched panes decorating the stonework despite the fact our classrooms lacked them.

A cobblestone drive circled in front of the garage entrance before joining a road that meandered out across the rolling hills. A neatly trimmed hedgerow provided a decorative border for a short distance, but except for a sidewalk running along the base of the building and a few trees, there was little else in the way of landscaping. The warm air seemed at odds with the snow-covered mountains off in the distance. Maybe magic kept the area in perpetual spring, or simple elevation differences accounted for the snowy peaks.

"Oh, yes!" Chad headed down the right-hand sidewalk and we all followed.

At ground level there were few entrances. An industrial metal door sat off to the side of the big rollers we'd come through, and I spotted two more archways further down the expanse ahead. Presumably there would be two matching entrances on the other wing.

But Chad stopped right at the corner where wing met main building. He stepped up and ran a finger down the mortar between interlocking stones, and damned if the wall didn't open up like he'd pulled down a jagged zipper.

We ducked into a narrow passage that slanted steeply downward. Mismatched stone and brick made up walls, ceiling, and floor as if the building materials had been mixed up in a big vat and poured around the passage. As Chad moved deeper, grating sounds rose from the darkness ahead, the tunnel forming itself to allow us passage.

"A little light?" Chad asked.

Bethany threw a golden ball up to the ceiling, and the light paced us as we crept forward. After maybe thirty yards the floor leveled off and took a sharp right turn. The air grew thick, and I resisted the urge to spit because my mouth tasted as though I'd bitten into moldy cheese.

"Dead end ahead." Chad signaled a halt outside a doorway that was little more than a narrow arch.

Light poured from the other side, and we jostled for position to peer into the chamber beyond. Just like the tunnel, various materials framed a circular room about half the size of the commons area. Like the commons, the room sported plenty of pipes and wires, but instead of following well-planned tracks, these came through walls, ceiling, and floor at random spots.

A glowing stalagmite shaped like an inverted tear stood in the center and illuminated the room with a sickly green glow. Three squat mounds, each about four feet tall, were arrayed equidistant around that central feature.

"The heartstone." Chad's reverent whisper echoed, and the central stone pulsed, its light shifting from green to yellow.

But those ugly smaller stones sucked up the golden light. The next beat of the heartstone edged closer to green and was notably weaker. Shadows danced around the room, and panic rose in my chest at the thought of demons, but they were simply cast by the three stone mounds surrounding the heartstone. In contrast to the elegant lines of the heartstone, the mounds were black heaps of slag.

"They're like puddles left over from a botched weld." I thought back to my early attempts under Gina's watchful eye. "What are they?"

"Nothing good," Owen said.

"They're killing the heartstone." Chad's eyes glistened as he stroked the wall with a calloused hand.

Steam sputtered from a crack in a pipe elbow sticking from the floor at the foot of the nearest black mound. But the white puff quickly darkened. Black vapor coalesced into a fat blob the size of a toddler with stubby legs and one red eye in the center of its featureless face.

24. Final Mission

T HE NEWLY FORMED demon stretched as if waking and stomped over to touch the heartstone. The surface of the golden stone dimmed to dark green under the creature's hand. I fumbled in my pocket for the dean's goggles and slipped them on.

Dark energy swirled around the demon's stubby fingers, trying to bore into the heartstone. It withdrew its hand after a moment, and a glob of the energy pulled out into a thin thread as it headed back to the nearest dark mound. The foul spell it affixed to the stone stretched like molten cheese, oily black corruption compared to the radiance of the heartstone.

That splendor buried deep inside the stone dimmed as the toddler demon climbed the dark mound, laid across the top, and…melted. The shadow oozed and merged with the existing dark pillar, the glowing red eye turning liquid and flowing like molten veins through the new layer to make the mound just a bit larger.

The thread of magic still connected the heartstone to the mound. In fact, there were dozens of threads stretching from each of the three dark mounds to the heartstone, syphoning off its energy. I could tell because the threads swelled with each heartbeat throb of power and light. I didn't know where that energy was supposed to go, but it certainly wasn't meant to feed the Shadow Master's fused piles of demons. A transparent blue sphere, a shield, surrounded the entire arrangement as a sparking deterrent to interference.

"This is bad." I passed the goggles to Chad for a second opinion. "Take a look."

Chad sucked in a sharp breath as he studied the scene, then handed the goggles to Owen. After everyone got a chance to assess the situation, we huddled up to discuss options.

"We need to cut those tethers," Bethany said.

"I've seen the energy surrounding those mounds before." I thought back to my experiments with the dean. "That kind of shield won't be easy to unlock."

"We've got to try." Chad cast a look back at the stone. "She's fading. I doubt we have half an hour, especially if those things keep coming."

"Those things" were the demons lending their lives to the mounds. During our discussion, two more had emerged and melted onto the other mounds. One sprayed forth on a jet of mist from the water main, and the other sparked into being from a burnt section of exposed wire.

"Who's up to trying?" My own skills were pretty lame, but judging by Chad's worried expression and the fading heartstone, we needed to do something fast.

"I've got nothing," Chad said. "Throwing those lightning bolts sucked me dry."

"I'm game, but we'll need a way to deal with the demons when we get through." Bethany rummaged around in her pockets and came up with three pencil stubs. "No paper, but I can speed sketch something on the wall."

"Right. Good thinking." I'd never seen the girl without her trusty sketchpad. The fact that she could draw on anything somehow made her talent even more impressive.

"I see where this is going." Owen pushed off the wall, cracked his knuckles, and strode into the chamber.

I held my breath, but the mounds didn't spring to life and tear the cocky bastard limb from limb. So, that was a good start. Another good sign was that the fire spell he directed at the complex knot of energy at the shield's nexus didn't trigger any booby-traps. Unfortunately, his questing magic also had no effect, and Owen soon dropped it in favor of another spell.

He spent a full five minutes cycling through the different elements to no avail. As his frustration grew, he dropped any pretext of subtlety and tried a few full strength spells that looked combat worthy. Through the goggles I watched each attempt splash harmlessly against the shield as if his magic refused to interact with the shimmering blue energy.

"They just haven't taught us this stuff yet," Owen concluded as he joined us back at the entrance. "I thought a spell wedged between the seams where that shield is tied off might crack the seal, but there's just no leverage. We'd need to blast it open. Only problem is elemental magic rolls right off."

"There might be a way." I looked down at poor, clueless Wart Thirteen as he balanced on his heel wheels, his only concern making sure he followed me. "My magic interacts with shields."

"No offense, Walker, but I've seen you in common core," Owen said.

"Not elemental spells. My tinker talent can touch shields." I cut off the offensive no-offense sentiment and gave a sad little nod toward Wart. "At least, it can when it goes wrong."

"Jason?" Bethany knew exactly what it was like to lose a creation. Hell, she'd lost tons of them in the past hour.

"It'll be okay," I said. "Let me make a few adjustments."

Wart's microprocessor was pretty rudimentary, so I couldn't just run him up to the shield and have him compute the exact value of pi. I wouldn't be making a habit of blowing up my work, but the logical portion of my mind filed the idea away as a handy self-destruct mechanism.

For now, I'd simply send the little guy to touch the heartstone, with an error condition to try from a different angle if something got in his way and a stop condition of reaching the stone. Even with the retry delay set to the minimum of one second, it would take a little time for the looping commands to result in an overload.

While I gave Wart what would be his final set of instructions, Bethany put a few finishing touches on the massive spider she'd drawn on the wall. I suspected the hairy tarantula would give the demons more to worry about than wicked fangs and spider silk. And with eight shiny black eyes, Silky—as she dubbed her drawing—probably had damned near a three-sixty field of view.

"Everyone ready?" At their nods, I slipped on the dean's goggles and sent in Wart.

Bethany stood poised with both hands on Silky, ready to send her into the fray. A whirlwind spell danced on Owen's fingers. Even Chad had managed to call up crackling energy, though it wouldn't be anywhere near as powerful as the spell Attwater had funneled through the cowboy.

The shield sparked when Wart bumped into it, his tinker driving force interacting with the protective spell more than Owen's magic. He swung ten degrees left and tried again, then rolled right. By his fifth attempt, a subtle glow rose around his torso. By the tenth, he glimmered from head to toe—well, wheel—with energy. My tinker magic just didn't like being used improperly. The power grew exponentially in a kind of feedback loop.

"Almost there!" I felt stupid for yelling, but thirty seconds in, Wart was barely visible through a white-hot glare of power and my head buzzed with the imminent release of— "Crap!"

I doubled over as Wart blew apart and a knife of pain twisted under my ribs. The goggles filtered out the flaming bits, letting me see the sphere of gold-white tinker energy that expanded with the destruction. The shield darkened and fractured where the energies collided, cracks letting the golden glow of the heartstone shine through. But power flowed from the undamaged areas, the fractures shrank, and the shield stabilized. We'd failed.

I passed the goggles around while I caught my breath. It felt like a rib had cracked, but that pain was nothing compared to the aching hole left in my heart. I'd miss Wart Thirteen. *It almost worked.*

"Need a bigger bang." Owen broke the numbed silence. "Where can we get some C-4?"

"Poor little guy." Bethany laid a hand on my forearm, and I wasn't certain if she was talking about Wart or me.

Since I stood a head taller than she did, Bethany likely meant my robot. He'd just been too small to get the job done, but it had been a close thing. With just a little more power we might…

"We need Herb," I whispered, not truly wanting to let the thought escape.

"It might be legal in your state, but smoking a joint isn't going to help," Owen said, then raised his eyebrows as though reconsidering.

"Not herb," I said, dropping the H. "Herb, my full scale automaton. Herb Three is here in my new workshop. Warts are just small testing prototypes. Herb is more sophisticated and bigger." Which in this case translated to more powerful. "Five minutes there and five back. Do we have time?" I looked to Chad and the weakly pumping heartstone.

Things within the magic shield had gone from bad to worse. Two new demons were in the process of melting over their respective slag heaps while others formed at the three sections of damaged utility lines. Peeking through the goggles, I saw that energy was now being actively pulled from the heartstone between beats. Worse than that, the surface of the three mounds had grown translucent and a massive dark shape stirred within each like an embryo ready to hatch.

"Don't think so…maybe." Chad grabbed the goggles and took in the scene. "Hurry!"

"Keep the tunnel open!" I called to the others as I tore back along the passage.

25. Tinker Time

FOOTSTEPS POUNDED BEHIND me as I entered the building proper and dashed toward my workshop. A glance back showed Bethany hot on my heels.

"Stay with the others," I panted. "You'll have to release Silky."

"Not until you get back and bring down that shield, I don't." She caught up when I slowed to pull open the door to the back stairs. "Somebody needs to watch your back."

"Fine." I took the steps two at a time, feeling guilty, but we were out of time.

I needn't have worried. Bethany kept pace, dancing up the stairs with agile ease. My shop wasn't far from the landing, and it only took a minute to coax Herb to life and check his batteries. Fully charged.

Where Wart had clonked down the stairs on inappropriate wheels, Herb's articulated legs nearly outdid my own on the way back. Steps posed a real problem for most robots, and I took a great deal of pride in the fact my creations could negotiate them so well. Of course, most robots didn't have magic programming that gave them the balance of their creator.

We crossed through the auto shop and shot outside. Cool afternoon shadows stretched from the floors above. Gloom painted the courtyard as we hurried along the stone wall of the foundation. Relief replaced panic as my eyes adjusted, and a darker patch resolved: the tunnel entrance. I rushed forward, grabbed the edge of the rough opening, and ushered Bethany through.

The roar of an explosion behind us slammed a Mack truck into my back, driving me to the ground. My palms and knees slid on the sidewalk, skin grating away in a hot wash of pain. I sat up, blinking and trying to figure out what happened.

A smoking crater in the gravel just past the sidewalk would have been where Herb had been following. I cast about frantically. White legs with black joints stuck out from a leafy shrub. Herb was still in one piece, but his movements were jerky and erratic as he tried to right himself.

My robot's knees were broken, the lower extremities dangling uselessly. It wasn't like he felt pain, so nothing came back along the bond. But his logic kept telling him to get up, and the feedback energies were already building. A quick mental command to be still kept him from going critical—prematurely.

"Very thoughtful of you to open an access for me." Mr. Gonzales stood near the entrance flanked by a pair of dog demons. Dark energy curled around his hands, and he held up a warning finger when I reached for a fire spell. "Do not test me, Jason. Tinker abilities aside, we both know your magic is too weak to do you any good."

He scratched at his chin, which had grown distinctly pointy under cheekbones sharp enough to cut. His complexion had darkened, and black veins throbbed just beneath the skin. But those smoldering midnight eyes were what held my attention.

"It's remarkable that you've managed to open an access to the heartstone chamber. That makes my task ever so much easier." He sounded amused. "I suppose I should thank you. I'll be able to witness the birth of my new servants firsthand."

"You don't want to do this, Mr. G." I had to believe he was still in there.

"Appealing to my underlying 'humanity' is futile." He motioned the dogs forward. "I am the bringer of darkness, the herald of the end times."

I circled toward Herb, holding my ground despite the menacing shadow demons, desperate to keep his attention as a dark blob moved down the side of the building.

"The dean will stop you."

"Please, Gladstone won't even realize I've infiltrated his precious school until it is much too late." He let out an all-too-human snort of derision. "You and the other practitioners here will be my agents. After Attwater's fall, we will bring down the rest of this land's pitiful defenses."

"Someone truly powerful wouldn't have sneaked around like a cowardly saboteur for months." I needed to keep him talking.

"So naïve. That was the only way for my minions to access the heartstone and harness its power. Once the schools fall, even the monks at the edge of the world will be unable to—"

The demon dog to his left yipped as it vanished, and the one on his right managed a growl and spun before being hoisted into the air.

"No!" The Shadow Master looked up and released a blast of energy that missed the next thick blue tentacle that dropped to encircle him.

Tina clung to the wall above. Two flailing arms each held a demon dog that she pulled into her skirt where her wicked beak finished the pair. Apparently demons were good for a growing octopus. She'd easily doubled in size, and I couldn't help thinking there was no longer a canvas big enough for Bethany's drawing.

A second tentacle looped around the struggling Shadow Master as Tina flowed off the stonework and settled over her prize. As with Ms. Schlaza, suction cups slapped at the back of Mr. Gonzales's neck, clearly trying to extract the demon possessing him. But Tina soon abandoned the attempt and focused on containing her prey as the man fought back and energy flashed between the ropy coils.

I spun and yanked Herb out of the bushes. He only weighed twenty pounds, but carrying him was awkward. I ended up looping one arm under his broken legs and grasping the rim of his body canister. Skirting Tina and Gonzales, I darted into the passage and nearly ran into Bethany.

"Tina won't be able to hold him for long." She threw out a mage light and led the way to the chamber.

The heartstone beat in weak, sporadic pulses now, its light fading fast. Owen and Chad helped me get Herb through the door. We leaned him up against the shield near where Wart had died. I waved them back and reached into my creation with magic.

Herb had an access panel on his torso, where commands and settings could be manually manipulated, but I hadn't used that since discovering my tinker power. As I activated his systems, Herb burbled and chirped along our shared bond, acknowledging my directives with stoic resignation.

"Brave little trooper." I sighed at the foolishness of talking out loud and finished my work.

Compared to my Wart series, Herb boasted complex subsystems to handle decision making, locomotion and balance, image and auditory processing, and much more. I brought them all online, and stumbled back as the feedback built.

The four of us huddled at the entrance, bathed in the green light from the demon mounds. Attwater's heartstone grew dark, the last of her light swirling away along dozens of leaching threads even as Herb's frame glowed with power. A high-pitched keen along my bond drove an icepick though my right temple, and still the energy built. I only hoped we were in time and that the explosion wouldn't destroy the heartstone.

As if sensing their danger, the form inside each demon pillar twisted and clawed at the encasing material. Two red eyes glared from each and cracks ran up the outside of the nearest mound.

The headache had my eyes watering, but worse was yet to come. Losing my first two Herbs had been painful enough, and those hadn't been on purpose or nearly as energetic as what we were attempting here. I'd learned from experience; this was going to hurt.

Stupid!

I mentally kicked myself, remembering the protection spell Schlaza had shown us, the one to help dampen backlash when Bethany's drawings expired. I hastily erected the best barrier I could muster. The icepick slid from my temple and settled for pricking my forehead. I sighed. *Better.*

"Tina!" Bethany dropped to her knees with a gasp, face in her hands. "He's coming."

Then the world exploded.

Hard stone pressed into my back as I blinked away magenta images burned on my retina. I didn't remember falling, just the roar of energy and blinding light as my bond with Herb disintegrated. The hastily made shield probably saved me from blacking out. Even with the protection, a gaping hole with molten edges dripped fire beneath my ribs in place of the twisting dagger a failed experiment usually left behind.

But I'd been hit by more than just magic backlash. Chad and Owen pushed shakily to their feet, then helped Bethany and me stand. The chamber reeked of sulfur and rotten garbage, a sour, foul smell that had us all covering our noses as we stepped inside.

Absolutely nothing remained of Herb, but he'd taken the blue shield with him. The two nearest slag mounds were shattered as if an axe had chopped them off halfway up. Noxious red liquid pooled around each, and for a horrifying moment, I imagined the creatures inside had hatched.

But beyond each decimated mound lay a twisted, broken form—both clearly dead. These were no wispy shadow demons. Each was solid with an iridescent-black hide of glistening scales. Thick legs with curved claws stood out at odd angles from sinuous bodies that had been folded back upon themselves. A fanged reptilian head jutted out beneath what might have been a snapped wing on one.

"She's alive!" Chad had his arms wrapped protectively around the teardrop heart, cooing and coaxing as a weak but steady beat returned.

Chad slapped at the air when a streamer of light left the stone and zipped past him. On the opposite side of the stone from where Herb exploded, the third mound stood intact, still tethered to the heartstone by one last thread of power. Another swallow of energy coursed from stone to mound, illuminating the latter from within. Though its surface was scarred and cracked, the creature within still moved. The tip of a claw punctured the shell with a quiet snick.

"That can't be good." Owen looked from egg to stone.

"Oh, it's quite the opposite, I assure you." The Shadow Master strode through the entrance.

It was difficult to think of the tall lanky form hobbling through the doorway as our mild head of maintenance. The man's body had stretched again, and he stood at least a foot taller than before. His pant legs and shirt sleeves hung in ragged strips at knees and elbows, those over-long appendages giving a ghoulish appearance. He may have bested Tina, but fighting the octopus had taken a toll. Aside from the ruined clothing, a band of white suction marks circled his neck and rips in his mottled skin oozed dark blood.

"Stay back!" I warned, knowing the magic that sprang to my fingers wasn't much of a deterrent.

A series of crackling pops drew everyone's attention as a network of cracks extended from the talon piercing the smoky material of the remaining mound. A clawed hand twice the size of my own smashed through, and the shell shattered. Viscous red liquid splashed to the stone floor, and a midnight-black dragon stepped forth on four thick legs. The creature was the size of a pony, with a long barbed tail and wings folded tight to its sleek body.

"No!" Chad yelled as amber power pulsed from the stone, infusing our friend as it had in the graduation chamber.

With a chopping motion, Chad's glowing hand cut through the remaining cord binding the stone to the newly hatched dragon, severing the connection. The monster whirled and hissed, mouth open to expose rows of needle teeth and a blood-red interior.

A beanbag chair dropped from above, landing on the dragon's back. Eight furry legs stamped along the dark hide as Silky sank hers fangs into the back of the dragon's neck. Bethany must have released her drawing after the explosion.

"Destroy the stone!" The Shadow Master yelled.

The dragon reared up with wings spread wide, and gleaming obsidian talons slashed down at Chad and the heartstone.

26. Déjà vu

"**O**H, IT'S QUITE the opposite, I assure you." Mr. Gonzales hobbled through the doorway, looking ragged and gaunt, as though the Shadow Master's control had stretched the man into a taller caricature of his former self.

I blinked at his torn clothes, then looked back at the dragon egg with that single talon sticking through the shell. The world tipped on its axis, and a wave of vertigo threatened to dump me on my butt.

I'd seen this before…hadn't I? The Shadow Master, the dragon. Wait…how did I know that was a dragon in there waiting to hatch?

The twisted bodies from the two shattered mounds *did* look like big lizards that had gone through a blender. I mentally shrugged. It made sense to think there was a baby dragon waiting to hatch from the third mound.

My tornado spell was the best defense I could muster, but the feeling of déjà vu made it hard to concentrate. I reached for my magic, knowing I needed to be careful to not hit Silky, so the spider could go after the dragon. I looked to the ceiling. Sure enough, the animated drawing scurried along upside down, heading for our little standoff. *What the hell?*

Loud crackling signaled the dragon's birth, though how I knew that, I couldn't begin to say. But when all eyes turned to the egg encased in demon bodies, the reptilian shape within went still. Dust motes hung motionless near the dark surface where a faint nimbus of power enveloped the egg like a second shell.

"I think we've had quite enough excitement for one day." Dean Gladstone popped into existence between us and the Shadow Master.

A small bronze amulet dangled from the dean's left hand—an hourglass. He raised his right, leveling a spell at the Shadow Master, who let out a very inhuman hiss. I braced for an epic battle as two burly, uniformed guards stepped from the tunnel. Power gathered in the hands of both men, not quite elemental but with similarities to earth and fire, so some special talent. The Shadow Master took in his attackers, swept the room with an angry glare, and vanished in a flash of green energy reminiscent of the portal back in his workshop.

"Where'd he go?" Bethany flung her head left and right, trying to look in all directions at ones.

"To a place we cannot follow, I fear." The dean gave a sad shake of his head.

"The portal in the workshop!" Maybe we could head him off.

"I've sent people to check on that already, but judging by his power, our uninvited guest would not have needed to escape through that device. We will need to craft better protections to keep him from returning."

"So, my message got through." On the phone, I'd given a quick description of how the demons were entering Attwater.

"I only wish I could have come sooner. Several of us were sealed in sensitive discussions well into the evening and couldn't be contacted. Then of course it took a while to locate you." He looked about the room, taking in the crater that had been Herb, Chad resting against the strengthening heartstone, and Silky dangling from a thread of webbing overhead. "You four have certainly been busy. Well done."

"So you're just letting the Shadow Master go?" Owen examined the egg, running a hand along its surface—or as close to the surface as he could get, because his palm stopped at the boundary of frozen dust swirls. "What about this thing?"

"That thing, Mr. Jones, is a dragon egg." Gladstone stepped over and laid his own hand on the invisible surface. "Sadly, it has been corrupted with demon energy. I've placed it in what you might call stasis so that time does not pass for the hatchling. Hopefully, we can reverse the damage and return him to his rightful parents." He turned sad eyes on the two destroyed eggs. "That our nemesis was able to steal three eggs is beyond worrisome. We will have to speak to the dragon community about their losses. Not that I doubt it, but why did you call Mike Gonzales Shadow Master?"

Wow, so dragons are real, and there's a community of them. That fact sank in slowly, and opened the door to other questions about fantasy races. How much was real, how much simple fiction? Lost in my ponderings, it took a second to realize that Owen deferred to me to answer the dean's question.

"Bethany and I did some research and found an old text linking the demon symbols we'd been finding around the school to an evil entity called the Shadow Master." I whipped out my phone and flipped through several pertinent photos of our findings. "It looks like he's been banished before, but we didn't have time to dig into exactly how or when, probably hundreds of years ago."

Since the dean's squad of fully trained demon hunters were scouring the halls, we took the time to fill him in on our horrendous day. When we came to the part about Ms. Schlaza and Ms. Robles being possessed and how Tina had pulled the demon from the former, he stopped us and turned to the two guards.

"Find these women and get them to the infirmary. I will come ensure the sigil each acquired is fully neutralized." He gave a quick description of our teachers and turned twinkling blue eyes on Bethany. "Your creations certainly saved the day, especially that adorable octopus." His eyes softened, but for some reason he smiled at her sad nod. "She's very loyal and didn't even want to let *me* into the tunnel."

"Wait, what?" Bethany wiped her eyes, her face scrunching in confusion. "Tina's alive?"

"Alive and, I would guess, quite cross with me for barging past. I fear she will require significant patching up, but I'm sure you can take care of her injuries."

"Oh, I didn't realize." Bethany scrambled to her feet, rushed to the door, and gathered up the pencils she'd discarded after hastily drawing Silky. "So many bonds snapped, I couldn't keep track. Guys, I have to go."

She hurried back up the tunnel, and I looked around at the broken bodies and debris. Had we really made a difference? The dean would be watchful now, so Attwater was probably safe from further attempts. But the Shadow Master was the real threat, and he'd escaped—easily. And the bastard had taken Mr. Gonzales with him.

I clung to the thought of them being separate, but the man had changed so much there at the end. It was entirely possible our mild-mannered maintenance man was gone for good. The thought made my heart ache as much as the loss of Wart and Herb; this was not a happy victory.

"Once my people are certain the school is clear of hostiles, we'll get this cleaned up," Dean Gladstone said.

"Anything we can do to help?" Chad kept his right hand on the stone, and Owen still gazed into the dragon egg as though mesmerized.

"You three deserve to take it easy for the rest of the week." He chuckled. "But to be certain the tunnel to this chamber remains open, I'll ask you to stay here while I check on those poor women." He nodded as we agreed, then settled his gaze on Chad. "You, Mr. Stillman, have accomplished something that few others have. A heartstone chamber voluntarily opening is quite unique, and your presence is clearly helping the spirit of our school recover from her ordeal.

"I will offer a word of caution. This may be your only such opportunity. I don't presume to speak for Attwater, but a repeat invitation to this chamber is unlikely. That being said, I need to be notified if this entrance opens again during your time with us. As we just observed, an open door can invite unwanted visitors."

"Sure thing, Dean." Chad gave a thumbs up.

"I'll return as soon as possible." He turned to leave, but paused. "Make certain Ms. Daniels gets some rest before school resumes. I don't want that young lady to burn out playing nursemaid."

27. Marching Home

D OZENS OF BETHANY'S creations survived. They came limping back to her as she worked on rebuilding Tina's lost arms and a ragged tear in the back of the octopus's head.

"I can't believe we won." Bethany eased an animated Gila monster with pebbly black and yellow hide back onto a blank page in her sketchpad. It landed with a resounding thump, tongue lolling over powerful jaws in clear adoration of its creator.

Our friend had run back to her fortress of solitude to retrieve supplies while the guys and I lounged about waiting for Gladstone. The growing pile of repopulated sketch books spoke to her frantic repair work, as did the smears of color and charcoal decorating her hands and face. This latest drawing still had a stump in place of one hind leg, but Bethany had rounded the jagged end off and swore it would regrow on its own—a lizard thing.

"I can't believe how kickass your magic is." Without her help, we'd probably all be demon slaves by now, but I could tell our friend was hurting. It wasn't just from the ragged holes left by her destroyed creations—heaven knew I still felt those myself. There'd been a feel to her little hideaway, to the desperate pencil strokes that went into her more nightmarish drawings as if she'd been trying to exorcise her own inner demons. "You've been at this for hours. Time to close down triage and call it a day. If you want, I'll meet you tomorrow to hunt up stragglers."

We'd certainly find more. During the hour I'd kept her company, at least ten of those eerie three-dimensional drawings had limped, oozed, and—in one case—flown in to find their creator. Most of them had needed at least a quick patch job, and Bethany's pencils were down to stubs.

"You're right." She closed her book, stood, and stretched. "Meet tomorrow in the commons at eight?"

"Sure thing, and don't forget your ID. Security's going hands on with personal screenings in addition to the normal wards that keep non-students out." I offered to carry a few of the newly populated sketchbooks as we headed down the hall. She gave me a haggard smile of thanks through red-rimmed eyes. "Hey, if you ever need to just…talk. You know I'm here, right? We're all here."

A bit of the weariness evaporated as she flashed those pearly whites and nodded. "I know."

* * *

"And what's the purpose of the loop seals in the steam system?" Dean Gladstone looked over the rim of his glasses, hand poised above the clipboard where he'd been recording answers during my grueling oral exam.

"Basically, they move condensate out of the pressurized lines to holding tanks or drains." I'd known that much even before my short-lived training with Mr. Gonzales.

Getting called in for an oral exam for my independent studies class right after holiday break had been a surprise, but the dean insisted he had to assess what I'd learned in order to give me full credit. I could have argued that battling demons on behalf of the school should have exempted me from exams altogether.

"I believe that is sufficient, Mr. Walker." The dean made a final note and set the clipboard down on the gleaming wood table to his right.

We sat across from each other in the two plush chairs in front of his desk. I'd passed on the coffee this morning, not wanting to worry about having to pee while answering questions, but the rich aroma of dark Colombian had my mouth watering.

"How'd I do?" I finally asked.

"No wrong answers. I have no choice but to give you an A." Dean Gladstone adjusted his glasses and steepled his fingers under that thin white moustache, green eyes studying me. "Let's talk about your adventures last week."

"Um…okay," I said cautiously.

"Oh, don't look so worried. I just need to make certain you don't 'talk out of school' as it were. To have Attwater successfully targeted and infiltrated despite our precautions is a major security breach. I'll be seeing all your friends today and asking for their cooperation."

Our cooperation, a.k.a. silence, consisted of speaking to no one except the dean and his designated people about the Shadow Master, the demon horde, and everything else that had transpired. The clean-up team had not only removed the dragon eggs and secured the green portal, they'd scoured the school and erased all signs of the sigil we'd discovered. The one book we'd found that referenced the shadow master and his archaic design sat in the dean's office, destined for the secret council that handled such things.

Although he didn't come right out and admit it, I got the distinct feeling those sealed discussions at the Bashar school had been to address a credible threat of increased demon activity. But they'd had no idea it would start with Attwater.

"Speaking of new challenges…" I grabbed at a convenient segue when the dean moved on to a canned pep talk for next semester. "What's that?"

I strolled over to what looked like a squat shiny rocket perched on his workbench. Standing on triple fins with a small radar dish poking from the top, the device had been a real distraction during my exam. Coils of copper wire held out from the hull by tiny stanchions were evenly distributed along the upper half. Gauges or windows were built into concentric arcs around the nose cone; it was hard to tell which because the glass was currently dark.

Out of habit, I held the dean's spectrum goggles up and studied the magic signature. There wasn't much to see, just a slight yellow glow around the fins.

"Try the rose-colored lenses," Dean Gladstone suggested.

It took me a second to figure out how to flip up the standard yellow lenses, which were the main ones I'd used to date, and another moment to find the little brass catch that released what were closer to ruby lenses. As soon as they snapped into place, swirls of energy leapt into my field of view, coursing along the copper wire and creating a kind of reference signal against the magic infusing the main body. If I didn't miss my guess, the contraption would act as a magical spectrometer. The device could be calibrated for and measure specific types of energy. I said as much to the dean.

"Impressive deduction." The dean waved away the goggles when I tried to return them. "Keep them for your experiments. I have another pair. My good friend at the Bashar school has been working on this for some time. There may be just enough unique magical signature left in the shattered dragon eggs to properly calibrate the device."

"A chance to hunt the Shadow Master."

"Exactly!"

Epilogue

G OING BACK TO classes and exams felt surreal given demons had waged war in these very halls during break. But the few days of instruction we had left rolled by, and the school settled into an excited buzz having nothing to do with a megalomaniac taking over.

As for the building, Attwater only shuddered occasionally during our first two days back. Chad walked around with a goofy grin, floating through those final days like a love-struck puppy on cloud nine. Direct contact with the heartstone had strengthened his bond with the school, and he assured us that the dean had finally purged the last few demons from our hallowed halls. Of course the official story still called it a gremlin infestation.

You'd think Ms. Schlaza's whole demon possession and subsequent saving by a certain group of students—who would forever remain nameless—would have softened the ice queen toward me, but you'd be wrong. The common core test left me exhausted, burned, bruised, and embarrassed. That last was due to the fact that students were called up for their assessment results starting with the highest grades and working down the list. I ended up being in the bottom five, but at least I passed.

After all, the class was about steady improvement, not perfect performance.

To be fair, Schlaza actually smiled as she handed back my assessment, and she did give Mary Eisner a more active role during our testing. So maybe the ice queen had grown a little from her experience.

I pulled solid Bs in the rest of my courses and aced Industrial Designs class. I'd even managed to slap together a prototype for a new model of small automata more advanced than my Wart series. There were still plenty of bugs to work out. By incorporating a couple of subsystems that Billy designed and keeping them segregated from the magic instruction set, I had high hopes that my Amos (Autonomous Magic Operating System) bots would be an order of magnitude more stable and capable than earlier series.

"Honestly, it's like you want your robots to get beat up by the cool bots." Owen just shook his head when I unveiled the concept for my new machines at our table in the commons.

The last day of school had a party atmosphere. Classrooms were open for students to casually talk to their instructors, and next semester schedules were available in the front office. Toward the end of the day, the gang gathered at our usual hang spot for one last meet up as newbies. There'd be a new batch of mid-year students starting in two weeks when classes resumed, and we'd step up a rung on the academic ladder.

I was still trying to work out a snappy comeback to Owen when Gina stepped into the commons and headed for our table. Her form-fitting white halter top showed off way more curves than the heavy leather tunic she always wore. And there was something hypnotic about the way her jeans hugged—

"Hey, gang." She twirled a lock of hair around her forefinger and glanced at me out of the corner of her eye, so that I only caught half her smile.

"Hey yourself, girl." Bethany's eyebrows rose high. "You're looking fine!"

Gina's smile widened, and a blush of pink tinged her dimples. "Not having to worry about burning holes in your clothes really opens up wardrobe options. It'll be back to leather vests and goggles when next semester starts."

"You look great." I found my voice and worked hard to look her in the eyes, but doing so made it difficult to think of something to say. "Um…I can't wait for intermediate welding."

"You did pretty good on your practical exam." Her lips pulled down in a pretty little frown. "Your brazing is still messy. Work on that because sweating pipes could end up being your bread and butter out there."

"You'll get me squared away in no time," I said.

"Afraid you're on your own. My last semester schedule is stuffed. No teaching aide stipends for me after the break."

Oh.

"That sucks." I cringed at Owen's knowing look and hoped Gina took my sentiment as commentary on the lost income. But damn I'd miss her…help. "Um…maybe the dean could wrangle you some extra hours in the day. You know, with his talent."

"You're crazy." Gina shook her head, dark curls flying.

"But you know what I'm saying, right?" I pressed, trying to get a bit more insight to the man's abilities. "I mean, do you think that's something the dean could do if he wanted?"

"Maybe. I don't know." She looked uncomfortable and changed the subject. "Anyway, I just wanted to tell you all to have a great break. Rest up because the ride gets wilder from here." Gina missed the smirks around the table as she gave me another sideways glance. "As for you, I've got my eye on you, Walker."

She made a peace sign and pointed it at her own eyes and then mine as she backed away. Her eyebrows climbed high when she backed into a table butt first, and those freckles stood out against her blush. I watched her thread clumsily through the sea of tables and students, trying to guess which classroom she might head to as she disappeared down the hall. Maybe back to the welding shop for a final check.

"What, pray tell, was that all about?" Bethany gave me a wicked grin.

After getting her drawings wrangled and patched up, Bethany's morose introspection had all but vanished. Though I'd rather have her brooding than leering at me with that expectant, spill-the-beans look. Hell, I'd never even asked Gina out, unfortunately. So there wasn't anything to tell. Plus I had bigger things to discuss.

"Time magic." I deliberately answered the wrong question. "Gina says Dean Gladstone does more than work on clocks, that he manipulates time."

"Yeah, so?" Bethany was clearly peeved that I'd ducked the romantic line of questioning.

"So, I needed to schedule another study session and got a good look at the dean's schedule in the front office. I flipped back a couple of weeks. That closed-door meeting he was in when I called about the demons went on for hours. There's no way he could have made it back to Attwater as fast as he did."

Owen leaned forward with interest. Even Chad sat up from his spot at the pillar.

"Maybe the schedule was wrong and they finished early." Bethany shrugged. "Why's it matter?"

"His admin assistant assured me it was a long, grueling session." I dropped my voice to a whisper. "It matters because if the dean can travel back in time, why not just go back and stop Mr. G. from getting possessed in the first place?"

"Paradox," Bethany said after a moment. "If he went back to before you called, then you'd never call and he couldn't go back. The whole space-time continuum might collapse. At the very least doing something like that would erase or fracture the entire timeline from the point of re-entry to present. Who knows what wide-ranging damage that could cause?"

"Maybe, but I don't think events in the heartstone chamber happened the way they happened," I said carefully.

"He's addled by finals," Owen declared.

"Didn't any of you have a déjà vu moment when the Shadow Master showed up?" My shoulders slumped at their blank expressions, but I forged on. "It's hard to describe, but for a minute there I was certain things didn't go well, the last dragon hatched, and the Shadow master destroyed the heartstone. But then things…changed, the dean showed up, and we won." I pulled out my phone and flipped to the textbook picture of possessed people being cast into a burning pit. "Remember these red-robed monks? Look, the dean had a little hourglass just like the ones they all wore. That can't be a coincidence. Plus he may have a way to track the Shadow Master. I think he might be able to save Mr. Gonzales."

"You saw him, Ed." Bethany laid a hand on my forearm. "The man was pretty far gone, and Tina couldn't help him like she did for Ms. Schlaza and Robles."

"But there's a chance." Mr. G. had been my friend. I had to believe he was still alive even if his body had been taken over and warped.

"Hell, I'm with tinker man." Owen grabbed my phone and zoomed in on the text. "If these guys passed down the secrets to controlling time, anything's possible."

"Did you miss the part about blowing up the universe and erasing people?" Chad just shook his head at Owen's enthusiasm.

Owen's interest surprised me. Some of us watched too much *Doctor Who* growing up, but the brash mechanic didn't strike me as ever having been the geeky nerd type. Between the school resources and whatever info Dean Gladstone had access to about this ancient order of monks, I just hoped they could track down and save Mr. G.

"Well, those were the crappiest finals ever!" Mon stalked around the corner and wedged herself between me and Bethany, putting an effective stop to further discussion of demon masters and time travel.

"But you passed, right?" Bethany asked.

"Yep, and I actually have an aesthetician class next term, so finally get to learn some cosmetology basics." Mon grinned, the first smile I'd seen all semester.

"So we all made the grade." I looked to Chad figuring he was most likely to know since he had a couple of classes with my high school nemesis. "Any idea if a certain homeboy wannabe got cut?"

"Sorry, dude. Lars squeaked by." Chad screwed up his face in thought. "I think maybe he's sleeping with Ms. Hilda."

That had Bethany choking on her soda, which delightfully spewed from her nose.

"Did anybody wash out?" Their blank expressions had me grumbling under my breath. "Damn! What happened to the whole look right, look left thing?"

Despite my disappointment, discussing classes and the future proved better than obsessing over demons on our last day. Soon everyone was comparing schedules and trading good-natured jibes about those future career fields to which we all aspired.

Second semester would give everyone a chance to dig into their chosen disciplines and start training in their specific magical talent. Core studies didn't go away, but I also got classes on magical repairs and mystic mending in addition to more mundane engineering studies. Bethany, Owen, and I would be together in a mysterious class called Practical Exploration, a title that told us virtually nothing about the curriculum.

Owen and Chad argued over possible electives we could fill our empty timeslots with, while Bethany laughed and kept reminding the guys that the actual list of options wouldn't be posted until we returned from break.

As strangely as the school year had started, a warm feeling of rightness settled in my chest. I hadn't really made any new friends since high school and had never been much of a joiner, which had always been okay. I considered myself a loner, a rogue wolf with my experiments and creations—okay, a rogue geek. But belonging had perks too. I couldn't wait to see what next semester brought.

~

Loved it, hated it, somewhere in between? Let people know!

I'd be eternally grateful if you'd share your opinion of *The Heartstone Chamber* or any other books on my Amazon author page.

https://amazon.com/author/steinjim

Your review need not be long, only takes a minute, and is so very helpful to new authors. — Jim

Excerpt from *The Silver Portal*

"**D**AMN!" I DARTED out into the gloom in time to see a small critter scuttling away on all fours. My keys jangled across the concrete, the colorful lanyard trailing behind the animal as it took a left and headed along the gutter.

"Is that a raccoon?" Billy shined his light along the side of his truck, but the thing was fast.

"Come on! The little thief stole my keys." I jogged out into the street, spotted the burglar, and took off in pursuit. "My school badge is on that too."

My mind raced, trying to think of the best way to deal with raccoons. I'd always assumed they just stole food, but apparently they also liked shiny objects. School had done a good job drilling in the danger of getting rabies from wild animals, so I didn't want to risk a bite. If Billy wasn't following along, an elemental spell from common core might pluck the keys back on a well-timed air blast. Maybe I could pull it off without being obvious, make it look like a lucky gust of wind.

Billy crashed into a metal trash can and lost his balance. He cursed, but came up grinning with the lid held like a shield.

"What?" He asked when I shook my head. "Need *something* to tame the beast, unless you plan to sweet talk it. Oh, he took the alley behind the schoolyard up ahead. We've got him cornered."

The alley in question actually ran behind the local daycare. But Billy was right, the broken concrete ended at a block wall with a pair of big green dumpsters nestled into an alcove. At least, I assumed they were green. It was hard to tell in the rapidly failing light, and the undersized bulb in the sole streetlamp near the drive entrance seemed to blanch at the thought of illuminating the area. Since trash trucks had to back in with their harsh reverse alarms bleeping the whole neighborhood awake at six in the morning, the approach was plenty wide with ample room to skirt around the dumpsters.

I let Billy take point. After all, he had the trashcan lid. As he passed I saw he'd also grabbed a length of wood and brandished it like a club, or like a flag. Tattered strips of cloth dangled from his weapon as if it were maybe the leg of a broken up chair.

I hung back, blocking the exit and hoping he'd flush the coon out so I could use a tiny whirlwind to snag the keychain. As I reached for the tingling bit of power and tried to clear my mind, I couldn't help feeling as if someone watched. My neck prickled, the hairs raising as imagined eyes bored into the back of my head. I turned slowly, casually, as if in no hurry at all, and found…Amos swaying from side to side as he made tiny adjustments to his position.

I'd totally forgotten the little guy was in follow mode when we dashed from the garage. Amos definitely wasn't rattling because I hadn't even noticed him. Magic might not be needed at all, assuming we could corner the animal before it got smart and took to the trees lining the property.

I dropped the elemental spell and mentally compiled a few simple commands that would send my robot to fetch the keys without overloading the delicate magic-machine balance and turning him into slag. Melodramatic? Not really—it had happened before.

"Here, kitty, kitty." My giant friend crouched behind his makeshift shield and crept between the dumpsters, holding the length of wood before him like a pike.

"It's not a cat," I reminded him as Amos and I fanned out to keep our quarry from bolting.

"Well it's definitely not a raccoon either." Billy's deep voice rose half an octave and took on a distinct quaver. "It's smooth instead of fluffy. And what's with those teeth?"

"What the hell are you talking about?" I angled the beam from my flashlight between the dumpsters adding it the light streaming down the length of his stick.

Two red reflections shone from the darkness at about knee level, feral eyes set in a pointy, furless face. The word possum jumped to mind, but it was too big, and the swaying lights caught a pair of hands held against its chest, curved claws running along the bare belly. It sat on its hindquarters, a snarl rising deep in its throat. Possums had truly nasty looking teeth, but they were little needles, not the tusks that scissored together near the point of the animal's snout as it chewed out its warning growl.

"Whatever you are, mutant beasty, you're giving back those keys." Billy raised the club and stepped forward.

Something about this didn't feel right. My eyes streamed as if with allergies, and the animal waivered in my vision. Heck, the whole scene blurred. I wiped at my face. Billy hoisted the stick high, but the trailing material got caught on the edge of the dumpster to his right. The open lid slammed shut with a hollow boom. My vision wavered again, and I blinked in confusion. The big square container…moved.

Billy tried to pull the club free, but long claws sprouted from the metal and hooked through the material. A thick stubby arm swung in from the far side of the shifting mass, slamming across his back and driving my friend headfirst into the other dumpster. Billy's head hit with a hollow boom, and he crumpled to the ground.

Order your copy of *The Silver Portal* on Amazon today! https://www.amazon.com/dp/B08RV7YTQT

About the author

Jim Stein hungers for stories that transport readers to extraordinary realms. Despite sailing five of the seven seas and visiting abroad, he's fundamentally a geeky homebody who enjoys reading, nature, and rescuing old pinball machines. Jim grew up on a steady diet of science fiction and fantasy plucked from bookstore and library shelves. After writing short stories in school, two degrees in computer science, and three decades in the Navy, Jim has returned to his first passion. His speculative fiction often pits protagonists with strong moral fiber against supernatural elements or quirky aliens. Jim lives in northwestern Pennsylvania with his wife Claudia, a grandcat with a perpetually runny nose, and the memory of Marley the Greatest of Danes.

Visit https://JimSteinBooks.com/subscribe to get a free ebook, join my reader community, and sign up for my infrequent newsletter.

Made in the USA
Middletown, DE
08 November 2023

42225117R00167